1 FOUR SCALLIES

Jonno sat on the edge of his couch. His living room was bitterly cold, but this was not the cause of the uncontrollable shaking of his body. His strength was sapped, and he had no mental drive to move his frame from its fixed position. His eye twitched. He looked down at his blood covered hands and encrusted shirt and felt nauseas as he tried to fathom the traumatic series of events. His hands that had earlier grasped a lifeless body, now reeked of dry blood. He inhaled, and then released slowly, trying to reset his mind and analyse the most horrific night of his life. He'd never seen a dead body before, and certainly not a mutilated one. Watching the life slip slowly away from a person was an experience he'd not envisioned, and he was ill prepared for the aftershock.

He repeatedly tossed the *Glock* 9mm pistol between his hands. The dry blood assisted the movement of the handle from palm to palm. He held the weapon up and pointed it at the TV. His hand shook and he struggled to aim at the screen. His head was filled with wrath and his heart demanded revenge. He pulled the trigger of the unloaded gun three times in quick succession.

Click. Click. Click.

It would be an eventful year before the horrors of this awful night occurred. A year that could mould Jonno into someone his mum could be proud of, or a year that could irreparably break him.

***

Jonno cranked his head back for an optimum view of the slow-moving silver bird—causing every neck vertebra to painfully click. *That can't be right for a twenty-three-year old*, he thought. He screwed up his face and squinted to focus in on the 747 as the evening winter sun reflected from its wings. Flashes of yellow and fiery bronze reflected from its metal wings and bounced off into the blue. A wedge-shaped squadron of geese effortlessly cut through the darkening sky, and Jonno temporarily lost his concentration, before returning to his study of the plane. Its vapour trails unpleasantly cut the perfectly formed feathering of cloud and the distant din of its engines produced a hum that broke the stillness.

I wonder where they're flying to. I suppose anywhere would be better than this shithole.

The sky darkened. A gust of icy wind whistled as it swept through the concrete corridors of the shopping precinct. It pierced Jonno's flimsy barrier, injecting ice into his bones. The bully in his mind poked its finger in his ribs, proclaiming, *'you're here, and you're staying here, so learn to live with it.'*

Thump!

'What the fuck are you looking at, Jonno, you bellend?' Birchy's punch to the kidneys sent the air blowing from Jonno's lungs.

'What the fuck did you do that for, you tosser?'

Birchy was a colossal beast. He stood at six-foot-four and had spent ten years of his twenty-four in the gym. He was tough and lacked fear—a council estate upbringing can do that to a person. It is a dangerous weapon, but equally, a vulnerable weakness. His jab to Jonno's torso was of a controlled level and intended not to injure. In Birchy's eyes, it was possibly an action of affection, but Jonno still believed it warranted an answer.

By A Thread

L J BODEN

DEDICATION

Dedicated to the 96, and to my wife, the one person who truly always has my back.

CHAPTERS

COPYRIGHT

First Printing, 2021

ISBN 9798499158906

'Any fuckin' need for that, ya gobshite?'

'Biggest night of the year, we're about to get on it and you're fuckin' bird watchin'!'

That explains it, then, thought Jonno. *Looking into the sky more than deserves a punch.* Jonno briefly considered explaining to his pugilistic aggressor that his attention had been directed at an aeroplane, and not an ornithological moment, but he knew it was a waste of energy. Birchy would be likely to call him a *dickhead aeroplane-spotter* or similar.

Birchy was right—this was the biggest night out of the year and the four lads had been bubbling with excitement as they waited for 28th November to arrive. Additionally, it was payday, so it was inevitable that they would hit it hard. A slightly immature attitude for a twenty-three year old to take, but Jonno's philosophy was, *I work all week in a job I don't like, my pay is shit, I've got no girlfriend, and I live in a dump called Birkenhead. Do I need any more reasons to get rat-arsed at the weekend?*

Maxine's Bar had been shut for nearly three months for a major refurbishment and the lads were champing at the bit to get back in their local and party with some familiar faces. They had money in their pockets, two cans of Kronenbourg in their bellies, and new designer shirts—that they couldn't really afford—on their backs. At least, Nav, Steve and Jonno did. Birchy was wearing a typical 'pyjama top' type shirt he always sported. Nav and Jonno had already had a chuckle at Birchy's shirt when they met up earlier. Birchy may have thought he looked good, but the other three didn't concur. *As long as he felt good, that's all that matters at the end of the day,* thought Jonno.

Nav and Jonno were tight. They'd been friends since primary school and treated each other like brothers, without the fighting. They were brought up on the same streets, played in the same amateur football team, worked together and once they were old enough, they spent their drunken nights out together. Growing up in Birkenhead wasn't easy. Violence, crime, and drugs fluttered its eyelashes at them as teenagers. Temptation drew them close with a curled finger, yet, as others fell by the wayside, they managed to stay on track. They'd been through a lot together, but Jonno always thought that Naz had suffered some real heartache in his life, that he'd been fortunate enough to avoid. Naz endured the death of his mum at an early age to throat cancer. He was barely ten-years-old and was forced to 'man-up' and get on with his life. Naz told Jonno that the lack of a woman in his early life had made him rubbish at relationships. He was in a constant battle with his ex-girlfriend and continuously got sucked into explosive arguments with her. All four of the lads faced the continual toil to find money—it had become the norm. Never was there a time when they weren't struggling to breathe. The toxicity of the town choked them. They had strength from their history, and protection from their unity. Nothing could change that—they were unbreakable.

Jonno and Naz had met Birchy and Steve when joining their amateur football team. They shared the same type of humour and zest for life, regardless of the woes that surrounded them. Most of their time together involved drinking and occasionally, a night out could last a week.

Birchy was a bricklayer by trade and worked with his dad, although they called themselves '*builders*', which, Birchy insisted, meant you could undertake any type of work. This could possibly explain why he received regular phone calls from disgruntled customers complaining of their recently fitted bathroom suite flooding their street and their kitchen tiles leaving the wall quicker than they'd been put up. Jonno believed that a brickie was a brickie and should steer clear of plumbing, much to the distress of Birchy. Birchy had served a little time under Her Majesty's pleasure for offences Jonno wasn't entirely sure about. He knew Birchy had served around nine months, but whenever he asked anyone what it was for, they would clam up and remain tight-lipped. It had happened before he'd come to know him, and he had convinced himself that it couldn't have been anything that bad, for him to have served such an insignificant amount of time. It looked like one of those things best left buried, so Jonno put his spade back in the shed and stopped digging.

Steve Brookes was the coolest man on the planet, or at least he thought he was. He could come across as quite pompous, but there was no real malice in the lad. He insisted that the lads called him Steve rather than Brooksy, otherwise he'd get upset. Of course, Birchy didn't abide by this rule, much to the outrage of Steve, and continued to call him Brooksy. To be fair, Birchy didn't adhere to many rules, in football, work, or life. Steve was one of those lads that you could easily hate but there was also a magnetism that made you always want to be with him. He had a casual, nonchalant nature, and when you were around him, it made you feel cool, too. He was a good-looking fella, often referred to by Birchy as a *catalogue bender.* Steve was super-confident with women, which was supported by a fantastic 'copping-off' record in *Maxine's.* He was also a great footballer and generally great at most sports. He was the type of person lots of people would like to be, including Jonno. He worked for the local council, in the planning department. He was some sort of architect or building surveyor or something. (Jonno couldn't quite remember because every time he'd ask him what he does, he would get bored and switch off before Steve completed his explanation.) He was quite serious with a girl up to about twelve months ago, but she dumped him, and he took it quite badly. He now roams the earth picking up women and dropping them where he finds them, gobbling them up like chocolates and throwing the wrappers on the floor for someone else to tidy up. *'Making up for lost time,'* he told Jonno. A one-man assignment, to teach the female realm that he was not to be messed with, and if you attempted to do so, you would end up seriously hurt. Jonno admired his confidence and his unbeatable track record with women, but he had hurt a lot of girls emotionally and that didn't sit right with him. Steve appeared comfortable with his cruel actions, and it was none of Jonno's business, so he let it lie.

Nav and Jonno are painters and decorators and are currently employed by Quality Master Decorators, which is owned by Nav's uncle. The job is okay, but Jonno always thought he was capable of bigger and greater things. *I should be thankful to have a job in the current climate,* he thought, given that his current geographical location isn't the mecca of promise and opportunity. It didn't stop him having dreams about going to college and studying to gain better qualifications and maybe head off in a different direction. He had nothing against painting, but it hardly challenges the intellect. The biggest quandary a painter faces is discovering the location of the nearest electric socket where they can plug in the kettle and radio. He was by no means an academic, or had aspirations above his station, but he did feel he could offer the world something more than magnolia walls and anaglyptic wallpaper. *Maybe I'm kidding myself. Maybe I'm being too greedy,* he thought. There are quite a few lads in the football team that are on the dole and look like they will never gain employment, although they do look happy with that situation. Jonno's dad would call them '*sponges,*' draining the life out of society and making Britain not-so-great. Maybe they are playing a more ingenious game. Is it really worth working all week on minimum wage to gain twenty quid extra than if you stayed on the dole? *Who is the idiot here? I never quite understood how people not only survived on the dole, but how they looked more financially comfortable than me*, he bemoaned, *They, always have satellite TV, they're always out on the ale, or drugged up, and some of them manage to run a car as well. I work forty hours a week and then pile in between ten and twenty hours overtime, too. I struggle to survive—which is why I cherish my nights out with the lads so much.* It's obvious most of them are on some sort of fiddle, Jonno was at a loss to know what it was. They can't all be selling drugs or claiming compensation after some nasty accident involving a broken leg and a local council paving flag.

Jonno daydreamed about working as an insurance investigator for a living. Camped outside somebody's house, eating doughnuts, and drinking lukewarm coffee, trying to catch a decent photo of a skiver water-skiing when he is telling the social he needs two walking sticks to get around. *Fucking hilarious! How can those freeloaders live like that?* Living a permanent lie, never knowing when they might slip up and forget that they are actually perfectly able bodied. Jonno was brought up to work hard and earn his own money. *I'd often wondered, if I'd have been born with a silver spoon in my mouth and daddy had bought me a Porsche for my 18th Birthday, would I be the same person today? I certainly wouldn't be getting winded by a right hook from Birchy with two cans of lager in my stomach.* His thinking was that you get given your ticket and it's up to you what you do with it. That's why his choice of job was persistently eating away at his psyche, questioning him about reaching the targets he'd subconsciously set himself. He could do better, but at the moment, it suited him, and any ambitions he might have had, are repressed by his lethargy and disinclination.

It was freezing. The icy wind cut through the lads shirts with ease, so they took a short cut through the shopping precinct on their way to *Maxine's*. They could have jumped a taxi and circumvented the walk to the bar in conditions that Sir Ranulph Fiennes may have thought twice about, but it was what they always did. It was their tradition, and no one wants to mess around with tradition. It was the same every week. They'd all meet up at Steve's house at the agreed time. The three of them would be ready to go, but Steve would answer the door in a towel, and they would drink his beer whilst waiting for him to iron his shirt to perfection like a military operation. He would then preen and mould his hair with a thirty-quid tube of gel he'd purchased at a fancy hairdresser, probably to impress the girl behind the counter.

They went through the usual five minutes of mocking each other's clothes and then spent twenty minutes talking about how the night was going to go, what state they would end up in and what lucky girl would be blessed enough to end up in their clutch.

Jonno took a Mohammad Ali stance, a boxer with grace and finesse, unlike the street fighter demeanour Birchy usually opted for. He pitched a sharp, orthodox right-handed jab to his arm and followed with an unconvincing threat to Birchy,

'Do that again, you nipple, and I will put you to sleep.'
Birchy carried on walking and didn't even look at Jonno. Jonno received an agreeable pat on the back from Naz with the encouraging words,

'Danny Johnson, you're tough man, taking on Birchy, and credit to you, sir, to show such bravery when faced with a psychotic fucker.'

This was it. This was the night they'd all been pining for and they were hell-bent on making sure it was a night that would go down in history. From previous experiences, the nights you looked forward to the most would usually end up being drab, but they couldn't help building it up as something magical. Jonno's stomach was doing somersaults. It felt like he might vomit at any given minute. If he did puke, at least he'd have Birchy's shirt to wipe his mouth on.

***

Jodie was frantically multitasking while her screaming *three-year-old* was determined to halt her progression. Streams of sweat produced stripes down her newly applied foundation and her fresh nail varnish was stripping off as she fixed her hair. The babysitter was twenty minutes late and the central heating was on tropical mode. Jodie stooped down to attend to the irritated toddler.

'Emily, c'mon babe. Stop crying sweetheart. Mummy's going out for a bit with her friend and Auntie Lin is going to look after you.'

The news that Lin was going to babysit sent the child into a frenzy!

'Only me Jode,' Lin shouted from the bottom of the stairs. 'Sounds like you're havin' fun.'

'Oh, this one's bein' a madam isn't she. Make yourself a brew Lin, I'll be down in a minute.'

Jodie popped her sobbing child into bed and got dressed while calming down her emotional infant. The child had worn herself out and was asleep within five minutes. Jodie was still trying to fix her hair to an acceptable standard as she came down the stairs.

'Has she settled down?' asked Lin.

'Yeah. I thought the terrible twos were bad. What do they call the threes? She's been nuts lately.'

'Aw, you go out and enjoy yourself Jode. Have a night off. Where are you off to?'

'We're goin' to *Maxine's* in town.'

'It's been done out hasn't it. Aw, you'll have a ball girl.'

Jodie managed to slip on her shoes and apply a covering of fresh lipstick as the taxi beeped its horn.

2 NEON IN THE GREY

The lads turned the final corner of the shopping precinct and onto the home straight where the pub was situated. Jonno caught sight of Steve checking himself out in Burton's shop window, with a lick of the fingers and a thumbing of his heavily gelled hair, followed by a glance down at his creaseless shirt. The second they turned the corner they could feel the thud of the bass drum prodding their chests, and the merry dance that was going on in Jonno's stomach reached fever pitch.

A pink neon light illuminated the gloomy winter sky—a blur at first, but then becoming sharper as they shortened the distance and their eyes adjusted to the brightness.

Maxine's Bar.

She was an oasis in a desert, a candle in the darkness. She was the minuscule grain of hope that they could muster in their miserable lives. It wasn't just a bar to them; it was an institution. It was the book of their adult life that beheld a hundred stories. Tales of laughter, woe, love, friendship, and massive gaps in their memories. For all the memories she had created, the beer had wiped out half of them.

As they approached the condensation covered doors to their utopia, the doormen gave them a nod and a friendly smile. There would never be a problem with them getting in. They were well-known, and the manager liked them because they were the beer-guzzlers that were helping him achieve his alcohol sales targets. One of the door supervisors directed them to the front door, adorned with a giant letter *M*—although it was barely visible in the steam and smoke.

As the doors opened and they entered, Jonno felt he was in a surreal world. He felt confused and disorientated for thirty seconds as his eyes, ears and brain tried to adjust to the new surroundings. He felt a sort of vertigo, as if he may pass out for a minute. He'd tried to take too much in, too quickly. The place was covered in mirrors and cheese plants. It no longer looked like a pub, but more of a 1980's solicitors' office. Jonno wasn't sure he liked it. The brand-new carpet soaked up their feet as if it were a marshmallow footpath and the cloud of cigarette smoke snatched at Jonno's breath. The darkness in the room sporadically abated as the ultra-violet light ignited white clothing and teeth and intermittent red lasers bounced off enthusiastic punters. There was little seating in the room besides a cove of blue, fake leather sofas encircled by yucca plants and glass tubes that housed floating bubbles. A gigantic, silver disco ball loomed over their heads—an orb-shaped alien spacecraft, deflecting red laser beams as though it were firing a futuristic ray gun. The sound system was so good that music filled the room from all directions, swirling energy around its walls.

Jonno glanced over to their usual spot, right in front of the DJ and to the side of the dancefloor. During the refurbishment, they had removed the step where they used to gallantly prevail, to expand the dancefloor. This was a big blow to them. That step was their look-out perch that gave them leverage to assess the wilderness and to evaluate any military style plans of action. Without that step, they were on the same level as everyone else.

There was already too much going on around Jonno for his brain to cope with. He was second in a line of four. Birchy, of course was first. The place was a cattle market, but Birchy charged through the throng, parting the multitude with influence and clumsiness. He didn't care who he upset on the way, pushing people aside and spilling drinks over the two-hour old carpet. It was Jonno, placed in second position, who was receiving the abuse for his abundant lack in manners and belligerent bar approach. Jonno smiled at people apologetically as they pulled their elbows out of their friends' mouths and picked up their empty glasses.

'Ya fuckin' knobhead,' said a bleached blonde, irate reveller.

Birchy was oblivious to the abuse and derogatory comments as he continued his expedition towards the bar with only one thing on his mind—getting served.
Jonno smiled at his aggressor and apologised,

'Sorry, girl. He's got no manners and is a bit simple.'

She sneered with acceptance and they continued their trek to the bar, mimicking jungle pioneers scything through heavy vegetation with a machete.

***

Nicky returned from the bar with a Martini for Jodie and a Black Russian for herself.

'It's heavin' in 'ere, isn't it Jode?'

'I know, ya can't even sit down and these friggin' heels are killin' me already.'

'Ah, ya can't wear heels like that and have comfort too love,' cackled Nicky.

The girls found a corner with a bit of space and stuck their handbags behind a plant. They sipped their drinks while dancing cautiously and took in the new surroundings.

'Eh, he's lookin' at you Jode.'

'Ya wha?'

'Him over there—with the shirt on.'

'Behave. He's probably got a lazy eye. Anyway, I'm not lookin' for a fella. I've had enough of men to last a lifetime.'

***

As the lads pushed their way through the horde, Jonno glanced to the dancefloor on his left and caught sight of two of the footie lads, Willo and Isaiah. They were dancing like hapless seabirds trying to rid their soaked bodies of effluent oil following an environmental disaster— quite disturbing to the average spectator. They were both heavily stimulated—cocaine and ecstasy would probably be the cause of their embarrassing, disjointed attempt at the art of dance.

Jonno had never seen the attraction of recreational drug-taking. It was something he was fearful of and he gave it his utmost respect. He'd seen what it could do and where it could take you. He'd been constantly educated that if you start with cannabis, it will lead to heroin. There were a few older lads from his school who had died from its evil draw, so he certainly didn't want to risk it for a knee-trembler with Beelzebub. It just didn't float his boat and looking at those two on the dancefloor making idiots of themselves endorsed his decision. *Beer was my drug*, he supposed, *and the demon brew had also made me look a divvy on the dancefloor once or twice.* They both looked over at Jonno and acknowledged their arrival with a whooping cry and a punch in the air.

The lads were all pristinely clean and straight cut, smelling of Paco Rabanne and Paul Smith, while those two gyrating lunatics were dripping in sweat, and the night had only just started. Isaiah looked over at Jonno whilst pumping his fists into the air and awaiting recognition. His name wasn't really Isaiah. The boys didn't know his real name. They called him that because he had one eye slightly higher than the other. Jonno pointed a solitary finger into the air and nodded his head several times at him, and, satisfied, he immediately turned around and back to his primal shapeshifting.

As they huddled behind Birchy, Jonno glanced over to the DJ box and caught sight of the local resident DJ, Pete Crystalline. Of course, that wasn't his real name, he doubted anybody believed it was. Pete was a genuinely nice man with a heart of gold, but he was a man trapped in time and living in a paranormal universe. Everyone around him had managed to clamber out of the 1980's excavation, but Pete had somehow been missed and was left alone at the bottom of the trench with no suitable access out of there. In all fairness, Pete was a good-looking bloke who had his fair share of attention from the ladies, although he was the wrong side of forty now. He was different to your average pub DJ and it didn't take a genius to work out why he was an oddity. The first clue was plain to see and hard to discount—his *Miami Vice* aesthetic. His shoulder-length dyed blonde perm rested on the padded shoulders of a white linen blazer with the sleeves rolled up. His Hawaiian shirt had the top three buttons unfastened to reveal a tanned and shaggy chest, decorated with a polished gold crucifix. His white-rimmed sunglasses hovered over a wispy moustache. Pete may have been one of the pioneers of metrosexuals——Jonno was convinced his bathroom cabinet would be full of skin cleansers and moisturisers for men. His white chinos were held up by a blue canvas belt and turned up at the hem to reveal a slightly weathered pair of espadrilles housing his sockless, bronzed feet. To add to the unusualness of his attire, he also played classic sing-alongs and did his best to thwart the more modern dance music. But the thing that made Pete really special, was his dedication to his wife. He could quite easily pull a stunner every night if it were not for his dedication to the sanctity of marriage. His DJ box was consistently surrounded by a group of young hopeful females who ached to feel the softness of his black satin sheets and drink *Taboo* from his plastic flutes. Their lures were fruitless, unless he managed to pocket a weekly prize without anyone finding out about it. Pete also gave the lads the time of day, which gained respect in their circles and had hitherto attracted them to the now, removed step.

'For fuck's sake, Birchy lad,' Jonno snapped, as the overgrown meathead pushed a pint into his chest and removed the frothy head from the glass to the nearest absorbent material, which unfortunately was Jonno's new shirt.

'Get it down ya, Jonno, and stop ya bitchin', ya fuckin' dickhead.'

This was Birchy's unique way of saying '*cheers.*'

As Jonno replenished his desiccated tongue with a welcome gulp of lager, he scanned the room with the eager eyes of a predator and brushed off the excess lager from his shirt. His head rotated, and his eyes skimmed the area with a submarine periscope motion perusing the ocean waves for a prospective adversary. The other three were doing the same thing, bouncing up and down and looking in all directions. All seemed fine. People were having a good time: singing, dancing, and chatting to each other about insignificant drivel that didn't concern the lads. No one had the time to look over at them, which gave Jonno a good feeling in his bones. They hadn't been there long enough to draw attraction to themselves. For that one defining moment, although it was only a second, everything seemed perfect for Jonno. No money worries, no girlfriend trouble, no work problems. Bees stung the boys for five days of the week, but they tasted a drop of honey at the weekend. That is what made it worthwhile. They had cocooned themselves in their own little bubble of life, where no one could injure or offend them. They were a stronghold that was impenetrable by outsiders and speculators.

***

'Hiya girls, what's your name then?'

'I'm Jodie, and she's Nicky.'

He wasn't the best looking fella in the world, Jodie thought to herself, but she'd had a few drinks and no one else was paying her any attention. It was nice that someone had the balls to come up and talk to her.

'Sound, my name's Jay and this is Graham.'

'What's Jay short for then?' enquired Jodie.

'Ah, that's a secret innit. I'll tell ya if I get to know ya better. If ya 'av a dance with me, I might tell ya later.'

'If ya want to dance with me, you'll have to ask the DJ to put some decent music on,' Jodie demanded.

'No problem, we can defo sort that out.'

***

Naz was muttering something in Jonno's ear but he was paying little attention, partly because he was still attempting to soak up his surroundings, and partly because he was still distracted by the damp lager patch on his shirt. Naz gripped his elbow in a more demanding attempt for him to hear his words. It was unclear if Jonno actually listened to Naz's remarks or he perceived the observations for himself. Either way, it was of epic proportions and had a heavy-duty chance of screwing the whole night up for the lads.

What Naz had seen would affect him more than the others, but it had the potential to drag them all into a whirlwind of darkness and mayhem. They knew this from past experiences, and still hadn't found a suitable way of tackling it. It was an untameable monster that refused to be overcome. Tucked up in the corner, across the dancefloor, Naz had spotted a ghost from his past. Through the flickering lights and dry ice, he had identified Jodie, his ex-girlfriend and mother to his child. She was dancing with her mate.

Jodie was in a tight white dress that complimented her figure, and her tanned legs were accentuated by four-inch high white heels. As the ultra-violet light encased her animated body, it made her underwear slightly visible. She'd had her hair restyled since the last time Jonno had seen her, a little bit shorter and a little straighter. He got lost for a moment or two looking at her and realising how beautiful she was. His opinion of her had always been tainted by the stories from Naz of how nasty she'd been to him. *Why did good things always come with a caveat?* pondered Jonno. *Beer tastes great but fucks up your liver. Chips are beautiful but make you fat. Why couldn't Jodie be beautiful inside and out?* Maybe Jodie was a good person, and Jonno only had the judgment of Naz. Jonno made a mental note to himself that he should judge people as 'he' sees them, and not be influenced by others. It wasn't easy though, as Naz was like a brother to him, and he had to stand by him, and Jonno was far too easily influenced by others. Naz had been hurt by Jodie so many times, but the love for his three-year-old daughter had him in a no-win situation. Jodie could—and had—treated him badly so many times but he was shackled by their disagreeable parental situation. She had the ability to control him, and he was defenceless to the *you're not seeing Emily* card. Naz thought she was bad to the bone, but he'd probably never considered how difficult bringing up a child as a single parent could be. The whole situation was going to end up in heartache one day. Unfortunately, it would probably be Naz's or Emily's heart, thought Jonno.

Naz's expression changed. He had transformed from his usual relaxed self to an irritated, defensive agitator. His skin became clammy and had reddened to a dark, dirty crimson and his body looked twitchy. Trouble sneakily crept upon the group.

3 MURDER IN MAXINE'S

"What's wrong with you two bellends?" Birchy interrogated.

"Fuck all, mate, just chillin'." Jonno made a pathetic effort to throw Birchy off the scent.

Birchy wasn't the brightest, but he wasn't thick, and saw right through it. They'd been in *Maxine's* an hour and sunk four drinks already and Birchy had finally latched on to the fact that Naz and Jonno weren't themselves. Steve hadn't noticed anything, but that was him all over. *He had probably caught sight of a tasty girl—or more likely, a mirror* thought Jonno. Birchy's attitude changed. He became a hunting spaniel on red alert with his radar honing-in on the situation: ears pricked, pupils dilated. His beady eyes scanned the room until he hit the jackpot. *Boom!* He saw her.

'Eh, lad, there's your ex-tart there.'

Steve swivelled around 180 degrees. He looked distraught when he saw her.

'Oh, that's it, then, isn't it? Fuckin' night over if that battle-axe is in here!'

'For fuck's sake, Steve, keep a lid on it, mate,' Jonno said, trying to pacify the situation. He knew it was a desperate attempt and a rather pitiable one, but he couldn't see the point in lighting Naz's fuse quicker than it was going to burn anyway. While Jonno was desperately trying to keep the three elements of fire separated, Birchy picked up a hand grenade and hurled it at Naz's protective bubble, which was sure to see fragments explode into the dry, smoky atmosphere.

'Who's that twat she's dancin' with?'

Bingo! Strap up ladies and gentlemen. This is going to be an uncomfortable ride.

The lads spotted that Jodie and her friend had company. Jonno wasn't surprised—she's a good looking girl and there was plenty of alcohol filled suitors in the room.

Her main aficionado was an ugly, hard-looking man of around twenty-five. He was short, maybe five-six, but bulldog-stocky in build. He had short wiry hair and a clammy complexion. He looked over at the lads, whilst gyrating around the vicinity of Jodie's backside and thrusting his hips to and fro in a *fucking-like* action. When he noticed the attention the lads were giving him, his unshaven lip curled to a snarl, highlighting a scar from a previous beating he'd taken. This gargoyle type creature was far too ugly for Jodie, thought Jonno, but he was there to wind Naz up and he was filling the role perfectly.

The other admirer had hooked up with Jodie's mate and would have to be assessed before flying in, gung-ho. He was taller than *The Gargoyle*, maybe six foot in stature and again, broad around the shoulders. He must've been a gym-nut. He had ginger hair and piercing blue eyes, with a long, thin nose that looked like it had been broken on more than one occasion.

Jonno drew his gaze from the potential aggressors to ask Birchy's advice and consider their options. It was too late. Naz had gone. Off with the thrust of a rocket, with the sole intention of causing damage and pandemonium. Birchy was close on his heels.

Naz wagged his finger in her face as he spoke to her in an uncontrollable rage.

'Who's got Emily while you're out getting leathered, ya fuckin' tramp?'

'What the fuck's it got to do with you, and who are you calling a tramp?'

Naz became more irritable and belligerent. Only Jodie could wind him up this way, pressing buttons that only she knew existed. When they came together, it was the equivalent of walking through a war-torn field littered with unexploded devices. One uncalculated decision could cause the mother of all explosions.

'What's it got to do with me? I'm her fuckin' dad, and if she lived with me, I wouldn't be out gettin' pissed!'

'Well she doesn't live with you, and she never will. You haven't got a clue about what I have to do. If you don't fuck off, you'll never see her again.'

Bang! A bullet in his head. That was the arsenal that beat him every time and which he could offer no defence to. Naz's shoulders sunk lower as his spirit deflated. He was broken. *If I could get hold of him and drag him away, this powder keg may just not detonate*, thought Jonno. He pushed passed a couple of girls dancing and tried to get hold of Naz's arm, but it was too late, *The Gargoyle* had decided to speak.

'You heard her, lad, fuck off. She doesn't want ya 'ere!'

As he spoke, a purple strobe light reflected off his yellowish, dog eyes and made him look terrifyingly evil. His breath reeked of stale garlic. He was rancid. Jodie had really done herself proud hooking up with this monster.

His words delivered an invitation to Naz, one he must react to, either offensively, or defensively. To retreat and laugh at this ugly beast would be the rational option, but common sense was sparce when your blood was fuelled with rage and alcohol. Sense sits in a locked drawer in the cupboard of a drunken fool's mind. Alcohol clouds our judgement, affects our perception of risk, and stirs our bravado with an invincible stick. It makes us hard; harder than what we are, and that can be extremely dangerous. As Naz addressed his rival, he wrapped his hand around *The Gargoyle's* neck.

'Shut the fuck up, you ugly cunt, before I crack ya.'

Birchy had taken position in front of *The Gargoyle's* mate and pressed his head against his adversary's to display his obvious height advantage.

'Wanna dance, ya ginger cunt?'

Birchy's opponent backed off to regain some personal space and was instantly permissive. However, *The Gargoyle* had more fire in his belly. He gripped Naz's hand, forcefully removed it from around his neck, and sent Naz scuttling backwards. Drinks went flying as he clumsily retreated. The doormen were quick to react. One of the bouncers approached Birchy, who was always going to be the main antagonist.

'What's goin' on, lad?'

'You better chuck these two knobheads out before I deck them,' enraged Birchy.

The bouncers didn't ask any questions and grabbed *The Gargoyle* and his ginger accomplice and frog-marched them out of the establishment, to the tune of cursing from the disgruntled pair and the sound of glasses hitting the floor. The ejected duo took position outside the window, *The Gargoyle* reigniting the dampening fire by running his index finger slowly across his neck from left to right. Birchy laughed at them and mimed a '*wanker*' fist. There was something more sinister than the usual type of threat. Watching the gargoyle threaten to slit their throats with warm air exhausting from his fetid mouth, made Jonno's skin crawl. It played heavy on his mind for a second until he heard the crack of Jodie's palm smash against the already reddened cheek of Naz's face.

'Fuck off, ya knobhead, and take yer wanker mates with ya!'

They didn't stick around to argue with her, partly because she was right about them being wankers, and partly because they'd caused enough commotion for the time being.

They made their way back to the bar to refuel and reassess the situation. DJ Pete browsed over at Jonno and shook his head in disapproval. He was a very placid, and timid man who didn't have a single aggressive bone in his body. Moreover, he was always sober, which made drunken anarchy look twice as bad. Upsetting Pete was the least of their worries and Steve sharply raised his chin to him, as if to say, '*so what?*'

They sank a few more pints, coupled with chasers, then moved onto a nightclub, but the mood was sour, the night ruined. Naz scarcely spoke all night and became very withdrawn as he struggled to contain his anger. Birchy was still wired from the confrontation and became more lairy as the night went on. Jonno could vaguely remember Birchy pissing most of them off at some stage, but as he became more intoxicated, he forgot why. Steve was in a foul mood because he had been looking forward to this night so much, as had they all. He wouldn't let them forget and lamented it all night, which wasn't helping anyone. In fact, that's what probably started Birchy's raucousness. Jonno was somewhere between pissed off and dismayed for Naz.

There was no easy solution to Naz's problem. He could never let Emily go, he loved her too much, but she came with a price. It was a price that haunted him and controlled him, yet he would never be in a position to walk away. It could be much worse. At least Jodie was single at the moment. If she were to meet someone else, there would be another man play-acting at being Emily's dad. It was foreseeable that event could occur at any time. Jonno concluded that it was probably best not to think about it, and certainly not to talk about it. They would cross that bridge when they came to it.

4 THE HOST

Birchy crumpled the letter from HMRC up into a ball and volleyed it across the room. In addition to the taxman nipping at his heels, he'd lost a big contract after the company he'd been subcontracted by went into liquidation almost overnight. It left him with unpaid bills he couldn't pay to materials suppliers, and no cash flow to buy materials for new projects. He'd even laid off the young lad who laboured for him and he was only costing one-hundred quid a week.

He knew he was sinking but it just seemed easier to keep deflecting the warning signs and carry on as normal. If he kept his eyes closed long enough, maybe everything would be okay when he opened them. He didn't feel particularly down in the dumps but was angry that he'd got himself in this position.

He sipped his coffee and looked out of his flat window. The village was busy for a Friday morning. Kids looked like penguins, huddled tightly in groups waiting for the school bus. The bakery was busy as usual, as old ladies queued for fresh bread and high-viz vested workers jostled for a breakfast sausage roll. Early morning shoppers aimlessly ambled along the street looking into store windows completely unaware of the troubles that were currently dragging Birchy down. A security guard carried two metal cash boxes from the Co-Op and placed them in the back of his van.

Poor bastard thought Birchy. *Carrying two big bags of cash in this part of town in front of the preying eyes of the local bagheads. Poor fella must be permanently shittin' his kecks. At least his wages are in the bank at the end of the month though.*

Birchy spent the next three weeks studying any early movement in and around the Co-Op. The cash was collected every Friday and was always between 8.30 and 8.40. The collection times were far from ideal due to the bustle of the village at that time. It had been the same lone security guard for each collection, and he always parked his van on yellow lines outside the store. Haldane Avenue, which was adjacent to the store, was the perfectly quiet street to leave his car while he took care of business. It looked easy.

***

Birchy was twitchy. Being in the North-side of Birkenhead when your face wasn't known was never the cleverest of ideas. The wintery day had brought the darkness in early and that made him more nervous. He looked up and down the street before rapping his knuckles on the door.

A large-sounding dog instantly went into meltdown and there was a period of shuffling and shouting as they confined the angry beast. The door flew open quickly and brought with it a waft of cannabis.

'Birchy?'

'Yeah.'

'Come in.'

Birchy followed his host into the pokey front room which was cluttered with toys and a couple of bikes. His host appeared confident, but his questioning indicated a degree of caution.

'So, you got my details off Macca, yeah?'

'Yeah mate.'

'How do you know Macca then?'

'Got talkin' to him once in *The Blood Tub*.'

The Blood Tub was the nickname of one of Birkenhead's notoriously dangerous pubs. You would not be welcome in there if you were from outside of the area and if you happened to stumble in there by accident, you would not be in there for long. Local legend had it that it had become a '*no-go zone*' for the police and any criminal activity that took place in there was self-governed by the local gangsters.

'You drink in *The Blood Tub*? You're not from round 'ere are ya?'

'I don't now—I did—for a bit. Me and me ald fella did some work on one of the local's house and he took us in there for a bevvy. I've been in two or three times.'

'And where do you live?'

Birchy was starting to get irritated with the inquisition. He equally didn't know who his host was, but he wasn't asking any questions about him. The situation was bad enough without him handing over all sorts of personal information to a complete stranger.

'Look mate, Macca told me you were sound. Are we goin' to do this or not?' Birchy said with a tad more dominance.

The host looked at him for an uncomfortable number of seconds before nodding in agreement.

'What do you need?'

'I need something tidy. Something smaller enough to conceal. It's got to look real though—I don't want anyone thinking it's a replica.'

'Give us a hand shiftin' this.'

Birchy helped his host move the tele from the corner of the room. The host pulled back the battered carpet and removed a couple of loose floorboards. He lifted up a metal toolbox and dumped it down at Birchy's feet.

'Okay, I've got this—it's a *Beretta Cheetah*. It's semi-automatic, light and can do some damage.'

Birchy gripped the handle and tossed it up and down to assess the weight.

'Yeah, I like it. How much?'

'£750.'

Birchy's heart sank, and he unknowingly let out a lung full of disappointment through pursed lips.

'Fuck me. That's too dear—I'm already struggling. 'Av ya got anthin; else?'

The host gave Birchy an annoyed look as he delved back into his toolbox.

'I've got this. It's a *Glock 17*—9mm. Semi-automatic with a magazine capacity of seventeen rounds. It's low weight and 100% reliable. There's a slight problem with it though—it's not clean.'

'What do you mean not clean? It's not a fuckin' murder weapon, is it?

'No. It's military issue that was never returned to stores.'

'How much is it?'

'You can have it for £350 but that's without ammo.'

'I don't want any bullets. It's just to scare someone. If I take bullets, I might use them and that's a whole different world of shite, innit?'

Birchy flipped the gun around a bit and wrapped his fingers

around the handle to test the value of its grip. He pointed the gun in front of him and looked down the barrel as if to check for the quality of its manufacture. He handed over the cash in used notes and the host carefully wrapped the gun into a tea towel and then placed into a *Kwik Save* bag. He looked Birchy dead straight in the eyes as he spoke.

'You do know the consequences for grassin' about where you got this from, don't ya? We've got people inside that will make your prison stay very difficult. If you get caught, you're on your own. You do not mention us. Please tell me that this is perfectly clear.'

'Relax lad. I've done time and I know the rules. You won't be hearing from me again.'

***

Birchy wasn't sure if he'd caught any sleep at all. He'd been tossing and turning all night, tortured by a racing mind that wouldn't settle down. Every eventuality had been running through his head and he was convinced that he had to have a suitable solution for any problem.

What if there was fuck all, or next to nothing in the money boxes?

What if the security guard wants to be a hero and puts up a fight?

What if I get caught and have to do a ten stretch?

The two women that had been chatting outside the store for more than ten minutes were really starting to irritate Birchy. *What the fuck have they got to talk about that takes so long, and why are they doing it in the cold?* It would be too risky to try anything under the noses of two witnesses, so if they didn't disappear soon, he'd have to postpone it.

Birchy sat and waited in his car in Haldane Avenue. His foot was nervously tapping on the accelerator and his eyes were peeled for any sign of inquisitive passers-by. As his teeth squeezed the last remnants of flavour from his *Juicy Fruit* chewing gum, the car radio churned out *Trapped* by *Colonel Abrams*. The irony of a song that contained the lyrics *I'm trapped like a fool in a cage* was too much for Birchy's paranoia and he swiftly jabbed a thumb at the radio power knob.

He got out of the car and left it unlocked. He didn't want any minor complications, such as unlocking the car door to hinder his slick departure. He pulled his dark blue beanie hat down to just above his eyes and then lifted his black scarf up to the foot of his nose. Such a large-framed man revealing only his desperate eyes would normally be construed as intimidating, but the temperature was bitterly cold and Birchy effortlessly blended in with any early morning movement.

He turned the corner where his destiny stood and was relieved to see the gossiping women had disappeared. He was deliberately a couple of minutes early. He wanted to walk up the street to take one final reconnaissance of the area. As he reached the store, the security van pulled up outside. Birchy didn't look at the van or inside the store and continued to walk up the street—the timing was perfect.

Birchy stepped into the doorway of a derelict unit which was four shops away from his target store. He knew from his surveying that the security guard always took 3-4 minutes to collect the money and return to his van. His mind and body filled with fear. He knew it wasn't too late to pull out. He could easily walk away and ditch the gun. He had a clear opportunity to avoid a lengthy prison sentence that would steal the best years of his life. He could be in his forties when he got out and would have missed so many adventures with his mates. They would all be married he supposed, and he would be left on his own, single, and friendless. *Was this really worth the risk?*

If he didn't do it, he faced going under in a life of debt and desperation. He would have to claim dole and would have no money to go out with the lads or entertain a girlfriend—the end result seemed the same.

He gripped the gun inside his coat pocket, which was still wrapped in a *Kwik Save* bag and slowly meandered towards the Co-Op. He was metres from the store door when the security guard walked out carrying two metal money boxes in either hand. He briefly glanced at Birchy but appeared to take little notice and went about his duties. Birchy strolled past the guard as he flung open the rear van doors, whilst leaving both money boxes on the floor to the side of his feet.

'Move your hand around slowly and feel what is in your back.'

Birchy planted the weapon into the lower right-side of the guards back which consequently pushed his nose against the back of the van.

'Do what I've just fuckin' told ya!'

The guard slowly reached behind himself and momentarily touched the muzzle of the *Glock* before Birchy removed his hand with a forceful jab of the weapon. The guard shuddered with fear.

'I don't wany any trouble mate. I've got kids. Please don't hurt me—just take the money.'

'You're not goin' to get hurt, unless ya wanna be a dickhead. Listen to me carefully and do exactly what I tell ya.'

Birchy shoved the guards head against the van to confirm that he had his attention.

'Show me your I.D. badge. Do it slowly.'

The guard carefully manoeuvred his badge from his front pocket to Birchy's hand.

'Right, Mister Peter Wood. Now we know who you are. Where is your next stop?'

'The Beechwood.'

'This is what ya goin' do, and if you don't do it, Petey, we're goin' come lookin' for ya. Do you understand?'

'I do. I've got it.'

'Close the van doors and leave the boxes on the floor. Get into your van. Do not radio for assistance or press any panic alarms. Drive to The Beechwood before you radio into control and tell them what's happened. If you don't do exactly what I've just said, someone will be knockin' at your door for a 4am visit sometime soon. Do you understand?'

The guard nodded.

'Go!' instructed Birchy.

The guard got into his van without turning around. Birchy casually picked up the money boxes and turned around to head for Haldane Avenue. He heard the security van pull away and he desperately wanted to run. His brain was screaming at him to *leg it* to his car, but the whole thing had gone flawlessly, and he didn't want to draw attention to himself. No one battered an eyelid as he nonchalantly walked down the street clutching the metal cash boxes whilst wearing what was effectively a homemade balaclava over his face. He placed the boxes on his back seat and drove back to his flat via an unusual route which added on an extra, unnecessary mile.

Back at the safety of his flat, he gulped down a large brandy before setting to work on the boxes.

5 OFFICE ANGEL

The alarm clock on Monday morning hurt Jonno more and more as he got older. He was twenty-three years old. *Was it really to do with my age?* he asked himself. His powers of recovery from heavy drinking sessions were diminishing by the month. He was tired, down and felt violated, as the alarm screeched a two-beat warning.

This Monday was particularly duller, and more miserable than usual because their job was in the local council offices. That meant all the usual health and safety nonsense, such as Hi-Viz jackets, no radios, no singing, no farting, no swearing, and eight hours of wretchedness. It was like Birkenhead's version of Colditz. Everyone sat in silence, badgering away in a banter-free, gloomy existence. There'd be stuffy old farts watching them all day with beady eyes, ready to report them if a brush stroke veered from the designated angle. Jonno was sure that because they wore office attire, and not overalls, they felt superior to them. He was repulsed by people *that looked down their nose at folk.* It was his biggest irritant.

Just how the company had become the approved painting contractor for the local council was a mystery to Jonno. It's not as though they were nationwide with a team of professionals and a fleet of company vehicles. They are a small team with a couple of clapped-out, old vans. Jonno assumed that Naz's uncle was greasing the palms of someone high up in the council tender process. There is no way the council would have considered them without some under-handed tactics. Special gifts and brown envelopes are rife in the building and maintenance industry, and Jonno guessed Birkenhead was no different. It's not what you know, it's *what have you got?*

The job was simple enough: a full decoration of a long corridor and the six offices branching off it. The small offices were vacant, but the corridor led to the main open-plan office which was still occupied. They were a team of four: Jonno, Naz, and two other lads. Jonno used his nous and told the other lads that he and Naz would make a start on the corridor; that way, there was more chance they would get a blimp of any decent females patrolling the corridor. *'Down there for dancing,'* as Jonno's dad would always say.

The morning was uneventful and dragged terribly. Jonno was jaded and praying for his lunchbreak and very nearly missed the sighting of something quite heavenly. Once in a lifetime you may get to see something extraordinary: a hummingbird, the aurora borealis, or the pyramids. You really wouldn't want to miss a breath-taking spectacle just because your stomach was yearning for a corned beef sarnie.

She walked down the corridor magnetising life towards her with grace and pure beauty. She was around twenty-one-years of age. Her espresso brown ponytail bounced off her very thin white blouse like a jazz drummer's brush. Her shimmering almond skin looked soft and immaculate, and her inconspicuous button nose rested just above a pouty pair of lips that were decorated in glossy pink. The shimmering diamond sparks that emanated from her mischievous, russet brown eyes made the world stop and devoured Jonno's attention.

Jonno felt like there was a divine light orbiting around her as she sauntered toward him. She seemed like a celestial miracle from a perfect world—his heart physically ached. He briefly took his eye off the ball to look at Naz for confirmation of the phenomenon. Naz winked and nodded in appreciation. Jonno was uncontrollably trembling, and his hands were clammy with apprehension. The

feeling of nervous angst you get just before you punch someone—
or worse still, get punched—was exhausting. She elegantly
sauntered down the corridor, heading straight for Jonno with a tea-
tray in her hand. He had to say something, he couldn't miss this
opportunity. Shit! He had no time to think. He had to say
something witty, yet intelligent, something a typical builder would
not say. He was useless in these situations, the circumstances
where you are forced to think on the spot. First impressions count,
and if he said something senseless, it would scupper any marginal
chance he may have had.

'Gettin' the brews in, girl?'

Jonno self-scolded his pathetic attempt. *Oh fuck! Are you kidding
me? Seriously, where the fuck did that come from? Is that the best
thing I had in my armoury?*

She glanced sideways and smiled, without breaking her stride as
she passed him. It was the kind of compassionate, apologetic smile
you would give to someone who was wearing a tasteless shirt.
Jonno could hear Naz sniggering as he fought with Jonno's shame.
*A decent mate would've helped me out there, but Naz is happier to
piss on my chips*, he thought.

'Bollocks, bollocks, bollocks!'

'Keep your voice down, you tool!' Naz warned.

'Why the fuck did I say that? Now she thinks I'm a tit.'

'Calm down, Jonno, you're going into panic mode. All is not lost,
not yet anyway. Just talk to her on the way back like a *sane* person
would.'

'Not that easy now she thinks I'm insane, is it?'

During the ensuing minutes he didn't paint a single stroke, and
scarcely drew breath. He couldn't lift his arm up, it was paralysed
with fear at the side of his body. He stood looking at the wall,
running all sorts of scenarios through his head and mumbling his
thoughts out loud—much to the amusement of Naz. He couldn't

think straight, and his hands were drenched in sweat. He wondered if he may be having a stroke and that he wouldn't be able to talk to her without slobber drooling from his mouth. *Steve would quite easily rattle off some flannel and have her eating out the palm of his hand in seconds*, Jonno supposed. But Steve and Jonno were different animals. Steve had aptitude, natural ability. Jonno had to work at everything, and this situation wasn't giving him enough preparation time to solve the conundrum.

Jonno could see that she was on her way back. *Fuck, I hope she can't sense my fear.* As she turned the corner and approached him, he was too terrified to look at her and was desperately removing gravel from his throat and searching for his voice.

'Eh, I didn't think the managing director got the bevvies in?'

'You're jokin', aren't ya? I just work on the phones,' she said. This was worth pursuing, he decided.

'Have you worked here long?'

'About four years, I think; since I left sixth form.'

He reckoned she was around twenty-two, which amplified his enthusiasm. It was shit or bust for him. He had to go for the knock-out punch, as he may never get another opportunity. Although he wasn't making her legs turn to jelly, she certainly wasn't repulsed by him, which gave him the confidence to continue.

'Does your boyfriend work here too?'

It was a cheap shot, but it was vital information that was required, otherwise he could be flogging a dead horse. She paused and sheepishly smiled before answering, which he found extremely endearing.

'I haven't got a fella, they're all losers,' she said, laughing without conviction.

Feet shoulder-width apart, knees bent, chin down, guard up, and now swing the haymaker.

'Do you fancy coming out for a bevvy with me at the weekend?'

He wasn't sure what was more uncomfortable, the awkwardness of the question or the sight of her discomposure. He'd never asked a girl out before without being completely paralytic. He got swept up in the moment, almost as if he were being controlled by a master puppeteer. He knew he had to ask her, otherwise he'd never know, but his fear of rejection was overpowering, and the pause in time was plain uncomfortable.

'Yeah, alright, then.'

Possibly through relief, or even a slight dollop of smugness, he switched his eyes from her for a second and caught sight of Naz behind her performing a doggystyle action whilst slapping her imaginary backside. He refocused and turned back to her.

'Nice one. What's your name?'

'It's Becky.'

'I'm Danny, but everyone calls me Jonno.'

'Well, I will call you Danny—Danny,' she giggled.

'Give us your number, Becky?'

She scribbled her number down and they agreed to go out on Friday night. He thought he was probably punching above his weight, but *he who dares wins*.

Following Naz doing his best to screw everything up for Jonno, he couldn't help but stand back and admire the sterling work he had just undertaken. Obviously, the *Steve Factor* was rubbing off on Jonno, only Jonno didn't have plans to make this girl love him, then drop her from a great height.

'How the fuck did you pull that off, you stuffy twat?'

'Skills, lad. Skills.'

For the rest of his day, Jonno felt like he'd had a decent win on the pools. Something was finally going right in the life of Danny Johnson. A little bit of hope for him to cling onto in this desperate town that was draining the life from his veins. He felt like he'd had won the cup, yet in reality, he wasn't even on the pitch yet. His incessant whistling all day was driving Naz crazy.

'Will ya shut the fuck up? It's like a fuckin' Tommy Steele movie!'

Jonno wasn't disillusioned, he knew she may think he was a right knobhead once she got to know him. She might think he is a knobhead now and was just being polite to get rid of him. No matter, he had a ticket, and was in the raffle. He had a fighting chance. Nobody thought Buster Douglas had a chance when he climbed into the ring with Iron Mike Tyson. *People like me don't get many opportunities, but when we do, we are prepared to fight to the death to keep hold of them*, he told himself.

Becky was something tangible for him to aim for. Something to keep him from being dragged down by the grappling hands. Everybody needs a target in life, whether it is a holiday, a new job, Christmas, a night out in *Maxine's*. Everyone needs something to look forward to at the end of a tough road—without it, we would wither away into a life of hopeless despair.

Jonno wasn't sure what made this town so desperately grey and lifeless. There are probably hundreds of towns across Britain that are exactly the same. Unemployment, crap weather, high crime rates and an ever-growing culture of life on benefits made the place rotten to the core. He had seen people's attitudes change over the years, to a point where they had just given up. Given up looking for a job, given up looking for a way out, given up trying to get out of bed. It was contagious, and he had to do his utmost to ensure he didn't fall into that trap. It was like an infectious virus sweeping across the nation. He had one thing keeping him from slipping, and that was his job with Naz. It brought him security, a reason for getting out of bed, and, simple though it may be, a purpose in life. Without it, he would be the same as the feckless free-loading zombies that paved his town's streets. The job gave him a purpose, but it didn't particularly make him happy. But now, he had something else. He had a shot at Becky, a beautiful looking woman, and he was going to give it his absolute best.

6 THE DATE

Radio City were pumping out *Club Classics* in the background as Jonno painstakingly got himself ready for his night out with Becky. His guts were playing merry hell because of nerves. He felt like he might soil his pants if he coughed too hard. He was scared to fart, or even move.

Thank fuck we're not going roller-skating, he thought.

He'd been out with girls before, but he was usually completely blotto before he'd even attempt to talk to them, and this date had him dangerously out of his comfort zone. His stomach resembled a washing machine, and he could not stop sweating. He'd already had a cool shower and rinsed his face three times, but the unwanted beads of perspiration kept appearing on his head. He was desperately trying to stop puddles of sweat form under his armpits by walking around the room with his arms raised like a pissed-off silverback, whilst blowing at them as if they were on fire.

A man who is drenched in sweat and capable of shitting himself in public is not going to be that attractive to the fittest girl on the planet. She was probably at home right now thinking of reasons not to go. I was going to make it an easy decision for her when I turned up like sweaty Lemmy from Motorhead and stinking of horse manure. Jonno was overcome with apprehension and was starting to think it may be best if he didn't go. He tried to convince himself that she must've liked him, otherwise she would have fobbed him off at the first hurdle. Yet, all the consoling he gave himself seemed to make him more anxious. *Maybe she'd only agreed to the date, through the embarrassment of being interrogated in a corridor by two hairy-arsed builder.*

He examined himself in the mirror and convinced himself that the tightly-fitted boxer shorts he was wearing were highlighting an unwanted paunch in his middle. He couldn't put his shirt on yet as it would stick to him due to the constant seeping of sweat. He sprayed deodorant everywhere, even in places it wasn't designed to go. His hair was also infuriating him. It needed tidying. If he used gel it would be rock hard and prickly, and if he used wax it would feel greasy if she were to touch it. He didn't have the time and patience for this shit, so he used a bit of both.

He had no car, which upset him from time to time, as he had passed his test years earlier, but running a motor was one expense he could do without. The bus, a lift off Birchy, or a swift walk did him fine. It would have been nice to pick Becky up in a cool car, he thought, but she didn't seem too perturbed when they agreed to meet outside the pub.

He got to The Pacific Clipper twenty minutes early but didn't want to look an idiot waiting for her, so stood on the corner where he could see the pub. He waited for ten minutes before taking up his position leaning against the wall at the pub entrance. He didn't want to go indoors and wait for her because he thought he'd look like a right loser drinking on his own, and he didn't want her to have to walk into a boozer alone.

The night was deeply dark, damp, and invigoratingly cold. The blackness of the sky sucked in strands of rope-like grey cloud into its bowels and prevented the strongest of cobalt blue stars from breaking its murky membrane. The milky moon shimmered in the depths of funeral black. The temperature had dropped well below zero and cut across the back of Jonno's newly-trimmed neck with a touch of cold steel. His toothpaste-laced breath formed grey clouds of mist around him as he struggled to find comfort in the sub-zero conditions. Only the involuntary shivering of his whole body was preventing him from dropping into a deadly, deep sleep, as if stranded on a mountain side.

She was already ten minutes late and he was annoyed at himself for ever thinking she would turn up in the first place.

I'm pissed off that I was freezing my plums off hanging on to a pipe dream. Why would such a classy, gorgeous girl ever be interested in a no-mark dickhead like me? he grieved.

He glanced down at his watch and decided he would give her another five minutes. In the back of his mind, he could hear Naz asking him how he got on and him having to tell him that he was stood up like a halfwit outside a boozer for fifteen minutes. Naz would wet himself.

Jonno browsed over his shoulder and looked into the invitingly warm pub, and for a second considered going in for a pint on his own. He then snapped himself to his senses, contemplating what was sadder, *being stood up, or drinking on your own on a Friday night.*

As he turned from gawping into the pub, a taxi pulled up and out stepped Becky looking sensational. She was wearing a tightly-fitted grey blazer over a white blouse, skinny jeans, and black high heels. As she exited the cab and took the ten steps to reach Jonno, time seemed to slow down for him, to little more than a flicker. She meandered across the pavement in slow motion, with the grace of an antelope. He was gob-smacked at how stunningly beautiful she was, and more disturbingly, that she was with him—for a night, at least.

When people experience near-death events, their life reportedly flashes before their eyes. The opposite was happening to Jonno—his future was flashing before him, or at least what he hoped it would be. He could see himself falling for this girl and spending the rest of his life with her, which he found deeply disconcerting, considering he knew nothing about her. All the irritation he'd felt thinking he'd been stood up, fluttered away in a second.

'Oh my God, Danny, I'm so sorry I'm late. I couldn't get a taxi for love nor money.'

What the fuck? This girl was apologising to me! It felt wholly wrong. It was as if the Queen was apologising to a peasant for being so gracious and beautiful. I had not only found a stunner, but she also appeared to actually be a nice person. If it turned out she was loaded, I'd try and get a ring on her finger tonight, dreamt Jonno.

'No worries, Bec, I've only just got here myself,' replied Jonno through lying, chattering teeth. If she felt the temperature of his skin, she would know there are corpses with more warmth in their blood.

'I bet you thought I wasn't coming, didn't ya?'

'Nah, don't be daft. Let's get inside, eh, before we freeze?'

The pub was fairly quiet inside. Jonno had purposely picked this boozer because it was out of town and less likely to have beer-swilling monsters in it. It was also quite fragmented structurally, so there were lots of quiet coves and corners where they could drink in peace.

He ordered Becky a large white wine and got himself a pint.

'I'll get these, Danny.'

Holy shit! Now she wants to pay for the ale. I think this girl might run off before midnight and leave her shoe, jested Jonno to himself.

'Behave, Bec. Go and find a table and I'll bring the bevvies over.'

He carried the drinks over to the table she'd picked in a secluded corner. He was so nervous of tripping or spilling the drinks, he carried the glasses as if they were a pair of nuclear missiles.

Sky Sports News was on the 50-inch plasma in the alcove where she had pitched, so he purposely put his back to the TV, to refrain from the temptation to nose at it.

Becky instantly put Jonno at ease. He found her so easy to talk to and the conversation flowed smoothly, giving each other time to talk about themselves. There was never an awkward moment, or any uncomfortable silences. He fancied her like mad, but he couldn't work out what she thought about him. It was clear that she wasn't throwing herself at Jonno, but she was friendly and talkative. From what he knew about body language, which wasn't much, she appeared quite open and relaxed. There were no folded arms or standoffishness. She was actually twiddling her hair and leaning into him when talking. Jonno thought that must be a good sign.

Their conversation was briefly interrupted while Becky made a phone call to her mum and this gave Jonno an opportunity to take his eyes off her to scan the room. It was still pretty quiet for a Friday night, which isn't a shock anymore with pubs dying left, right, and centre. Jonno did notice a couple of devotees that he'd have preferred not to have spotted. In an alcove to the left of the bar, he saw Naz's ex-girlfriend Jodie sharing a cosy chat with The Gargoyle, the very same monster they'd had a run-in with at *Maxine's* grand re-opening. It troubled him for a second or two wondering why Jodie would lower herself to go out with that abhorrent creature when she was capable of much better. He also briefly considered the chilling threat this beast had left them with the last time they'd seen him. He didn't dwell on it too long as he convinced himself Jodie was a head-the-ball and he was a prick, so they probably deserved each other. Probably best that he kept this sighting from Naz because he would only start asking questions about who was looking after Emily while Jodie was playing tonsil-hockey with Quasimodo.

Becky rolled her eyes at Jonno, indicating that she was struggling to get rid of her mum on the phone, so he thought it was a good chance to get some fresh drinks in.

'Same again please, boss.' The barman nodded and started pouring their drinks.

'What the fuck are you doing here, fag boy?'

The Gargoyle was prodding Jonno's ribs with his thumb as he interrogated him. He whispered in a low, controlled tone that gave his questioning technique more effectiveness. His warm, stinking breath skirted around Jonno's ear and chilled his bones. The jabbing into his torso shocked him and knocked the wind out of his sails. He turned to face his adversary, and in the clearer light, he could see that he was wearing more battle scars upon his face than he'd first construed. He felt openly unprotected without the backing of his boys, and this particular antagonist scared him. Not the fear that every man feels, and needs when faced with a challenge, but a deep-rooted horror, producing an advisory voice in his head that *this fucker is trouble.* This was a big moment for Jonno. He could turn away and attempt to ignore this leech, but then The Gargoyle would have Jonno over his knee for the foreseeable future. He was not only afraid, but also worried that any sort of altercation could result in screwing up his chances with Becky. He really wanted her to know that he was a decent guy and getting tangled up with *Mr Lizard Face* would kill any slim chance he had. There was a decision to make, and it had to be made instantly. Ideally, he'd like to have removed himself and sought counsel from someone wiser on what his next move should be. But he had a split-second to decide whether he should comply or die. He reached down, without disconnecting his stare from his enemy and forcefully removed his prodding trotters from his ribs. Jonno leant in closer to his rival's bulbous, zit-infected nose so that he was aware that he did not fear him. He retorted with a threat that established his antipathy but held back on aggression, so as not to escalate the issue.

'What's your problem, lad?'

He shuffled closer to Jonno, not that there was anywhere else to go, but he stood his ground.

'You're my problem, dickhead. Gettin' us chucked out of *Maxine's* with ya dead hard mates.'

'I should cut you up now.'

His tone, and his threat seemed real, but Jonno was in too deep to start swimming back to shore now. He pushed his index finger calmly but powerfully into the soft part of The Gargoyle's neck, just below the Adam's apple, and as he scuttled backwards, Jonno cautioned,

'Listen, you fuckin' tip rat. Fuck off back to Jodie or you're going to look like a right cunt lying on the pub floor.'

As he finished the warning, he fully extended his arm to push him another couple of inches away, whilst turning on his heels at the same time. Jonno headed back towards Becky, leaving his aggressor at the bar snorting with indignation.

As Jonno walked back to Becky holding their drinks, half of him thought that move was priceless, while the sensible half thought it was a death sentence. The journey back to her seemed to take forever as he was half-expecting a pint glass to be struck against his head, but he was too scared to turn around to see what The Gargoyle was doing.

As Jonno reached his seat, he heard Jodie shout The Gargoyle back to his kennel with some knobhead name like Justin or Jeremy. Whatever she called him, it didn't suit his dreadful face and repulsive personality.

'What's up Jay?' Jodie's quizzed her fiery, irate date.

'Your ex-fella's mate is over there with some tart. I've just nearly lamped him!'

'Aw just ignore him, Jay. He's alright Danny, ya know?'

'He's not. He's a fuckin' prick with no respect. They're all fuckin' pricks!'

'At least he's found a girl. It might make Naz see sense and do the same. He might stop botherin' me then.'

The Gargoyle glared over at Jonno overflowing with fury, but Jonno had his back to him and didn't turn around for the rest of the night.

They stayed for a few more drinks and the conversation continued to flow, but Jonno's night had been tarnished by the demon sitting behind him. He could feel his arctic, merciless eyes burning holes in the back of his head. He was paranoid for the remainder of the evening, waiting for a destructive response from him. He must have been fuming about the way Jonno had disrespected him and not allowed him an opportunity to counteract. The dreaded expectation of him charging over at Jonno turned his beer sour and his stomach sick.

Jonno was relieved when Jodie and her partner left before them because he didn't want them crossing paths outside the pub. Jonno was aware they were walking past him as they left but he didn't look around. He pretended to be oblivious to it. Luckily, Becky appeared completely unaware of their existence, so Jonno was happy that he'd done a pretty good job disguising any anxiousness.

They agreed to share a taxi back to Becky's and then Jonno would walk the odd mile home from her house. During the cab ride home, the two mind-controlling voices that live in Jonno's head were having a full-blown debate, which he was desperately trying to ignore, and concentrate on Becky.

Idiot No.1: '*Yer in 'ere, lad.*'

Idiot No. 2: '*Show some class and just drop the girl off home, Danny.*'

Idiot No.1: '*Why else would she be allowing you back to hers, if not to get in her knickers?*'

Idiot No.2: '*Be someone different, Danny, there are millions of twats out there.*'

Idiot No.1: '*When was the last time you had your nuts, lad? Some of the lads think you're bent!*'

Idiot No.2: '*She will remember your decorum and chivalry, Danny, not how good you are in the sack.*'

As the taxi pulled up outside her two-bedroom semi in Greasby, his brain's vocal ping-pong was interrupted by Becky.

'You know you're not coming in Danny, don't ya?'

'Absolutely, Bec, I just want to make sure you get in okay.'

Idiot No.2: '*Hallelujah!*'

They slowly strolled towards her front door. Jonno moved at a snail's pace because he didn't want the night to end, and Becky ambled because her heels would allow nothing quicker. He gently grabbed her hand. It was cold, diminutive, and lost in his warmer, much larger hand. Her skin felt like cool silk against his rough, weathered palm.

'I really enjoyed tonight, Becky. It was good getting to know you a bit.'

'So did I, Danny, you're a nice lad.'

Idiot No.2: '*Cash back!*'

'Do you fancy doing it again next week, then?' This request was much easier than the first time he'd asked, as he was now fuelled with alcohol and confidence.

'Yeah, defo. Give us a call in the week and we'll sort it out.'

Jonno didn't wait for an invitation. He reeled his neck and invaded her personal space. Her lips were cold on the outside but so invitingly warm and wet on the inside. She tasted of wine and fruity lipstick. They kissed gently for about thirty seconds—but with little passion, as this was the first fixture of a whole season.

Idiot No.1: '*Dickhead!*'

The kiss was nice. It was a taste of things to come and they both agreed it should be left there. It was left hanging in the cold, winter air, a bubble of hope that could be picked up again when they were both ready. She closed her door and Jonno got to the end of her path before he exploded the biggest fart that the bowel gods would permit. *That bastard had been trying to break down the door for the last four hours,* he revealed. Now that it was free, it disappeared into the cold, misty air.

7 HANDS HIGHER, ISAIAH

Isaiah had been banging on at the lads every week at football about a top dance night that was coming up and he wanted them all there. Apparently '*All the top DJs*' would be there, '*bangin' out the classics.*'

Birchy was well up for this and had been putting the thumbscrews on Jonno, Naz, and Steve to go and try something different for a change. There were several problems with this *top night* that made it a bit of an issue for Jonno, for all of them. The night was in Blackpool, for starters. It would also be full of drugs, which they didn't do, and finally, they weren't particularly keen on dance music, even if it was *DJ Armand van Hairyarse*.
Jonno naively put this case to Birchy; he should have known better. He had all the bases covered.

'Look boys, I'll drive to Blackpool so you lot can get hammered. The place will be heavin' with totty. All these bellends on drugs haven't got a jar o' glue what is going on. They're not arsed about birds; we can swoop in and snap 'em all up like a fuckin' herd of kestrels. The place will be full of fanny!"
Naz and Steve were sold on Birchy's inspiring pitch. They bear a resemblance to a pair of Labradors watching a packet of sausages being opened. Jonno thought it pointless explaining that he really liked Becky and wasn't really arsed about all the *fanny*. Birchy's case was too strong, and the lads were already salivating at the

prospect. He had to be careful not to be one of those people that dropped their friends the second they got a girl. Besides Naz's pathetic effort, the lads had never had any serious relationships, and this is what strengthened their bond—they were always available for each other. Jonno couldn't break that for a girl he'd only known for five minutes. He had to go.

***

The boys laughed their way up the motorway to Blackpool. Birchy had his *Dance Hits of '94* compilation CD on and their mood was good. Birchy didn't have a clue about dance music and Steve limply tried to explain to him that they wouldn't be *playing this type of shit in the club*, but as usual, he deflected any comments with obscenity. The three of them drank cans of lager to lubricate their engines, whilst Birchy stayed uncharacteristically sober because, idiotically, he had agreed to drive. Everything was good. Even Naz seemed relaxed, and Jonno subconsciously predicted that it was going to be a good night.

Blackpool had no class. Like most British seaside towns, it was in desperate need of financial injection and had become downtrodden, looking like it was in the latter stages of decomposition. Life there had become desperate for the locals and some unsavoury characters took advantage, with illegal activities and immoral behaviour. As they drove through the town centre, it looked like the streets needed a wash, and most of the pedestrians needed a fix.
This of course meant nothing to the lads. They were from Birkenhead, and Blackpool was the Monte Carlo of the North to them!

They waited in the queue for the club, tightly grasping their fifteen-quid tickets in hands. Although Birchy was the main instigator for this night out, he was still fuming with Isaiah that it cost fifteen quid to get into a club and the drinks weren't free.

What Birchy didn't know was that there would be very little alcoholic consumption in the club and the proprietor had to make a killing somewhere.

Birchy was right, the girls waiting in the queue and skulking around were on another level, compared to what the boys were used to. The atmosphere in the queue was brilliant. Everyone was friendly and chatty. Faces were smiling, laughing, and welcoming.

As the lads approached the bouncers on the door, they looked at each other and shared an approving nod. They'd rehearsed it in the car so that nothing could spoil the night. If the bouncers asked how many there was in their group, they were in two's. They didn't know the other two. If he asked them where we were from, they were from Cheshire, not Birkenhead. They hadn't actually got as far as deciding what part of Cheshire they were from but hoped they wouldn't be asked. As they stepped up to the door with their false story prepared, the bouncer looked at the four of them and said,

'In you go, lads, and have a great night.'
What the fuck? Even the doormen were friendly! Maybe we had been missing out on this dance club shit for years. Jonno thought.

As the double doors swung open, a break-out bar area was revealed which obstructed the route to the main area of the club. This is where the lads agreed to meet Willo and Isaiah, and sure enough, there they were. They went over to Jonno and the lads immediately, sweating and wired. Isaiah was electrically charged and about to blow a fuse any minute. They exchanged pleasantries and back-slaps and then made their way to the bar. Unusually, Birchy wasn't leading the way and had stayed behind to talk to Isaiah. Jonno assumed this was because he wasn't drinking and wasn't so keen to start sinking diet cokes.

They shuffled their way back to Birchy, laden with drinks and subconsciously prepared themselves to enter a whole new world. Although Idiot No.2 was screaming objections at Jonno about the whole dance scene, he couldn't help feeling excited, hearing the pounding bass coming from the gathering next door. He was intrigued and apprehensive, but the exhilaration tipped the scales.

'Right, swallow this on the sly, and say fuck all.'
Birchy pushed small, white, pills into each of their hands. There
was a momentary pause in time and sound, as the four of them
looked at each other.

'Fuck that, I'm not interested. I'm not doing that shit.'
Jonno turned to Naz and Steve for support—nothing!

'Did you two know about this?' Jonno enquired.

'We did talk about it but didn't tell you because we knew you'd
flip' Naz shamefully muttered.

'I fuckin' told you he'd act like a prick,' Birchy announced.
Naz shook his head and warned Birchy off. Jonno could feel a
shadow growing over him as he abruptly realised that he was on
his own.

'Look, lad, every fucker in 'ere is on them. They're doing loads.
You're doin' one.'
'Thanks for the education, Birch, but I'm doing fuck all, and you
can all fuck off for goin' behind me back.'

The mood darkened. Birchy fell silent, as did the other two.
Jonno's abstinence was going to spoil the whole night and he had a
serious decision to make quickly. This was peer pressure at its
most powerful. Time and time again, he had to make decisions that
he was uncomfortable with because of the unbreakable bond
between the four of them. He always got swept along on a wave of
pressure. In addition to letting them down, he was miles away from
home and couldn't afford a taxi back down the M58.

'Well...' he still wasn't sure, and he was extremely incensed at
finding himself in this predicament.

'Well, what are they like?'

'They're E's, mate. Ecstasy. They're harmless—and you are
going to fuckin' love it.'

Naz spoke from experience but Jonno couldn't bring himself to ask where his understanding had been obtained.

'Well you can't have one, Birch, coz you're driving,' Jonno questioned.

Birchy nonchalantly popped the pill into his mouth and gulped at his diet coke.

'The bizzies can't trace them, lad, and do you think I'm sitting on me arse all night readin' the fuckin' Echo?'
Naz and Steve followed suit by popping their pills and then everyone turned to look at Jonno. There are decisions you have to make in life that are sometimes wrong, and sometimes correct. We don't always know if they are wrong at the time. Jonno didn't know whether this was a wrong decision but his overwhelming love and respect for his mates misted up his sense of reality and righteousness. He nervously placed the pill on his tongue and swallowed a generous helping of lager to wash away the pill and any chance of going back.

***

They burst through the door of the main club area as if they owned the place and sauntered around until they found a decent speck where they could see the dancefloor but weren't too far away from the bar.

'Birchy, it's not working, mate.'

'Fuckin' 'ell, give it a chance, Jonno, it's only been five fuckin' minutes.'

'Well, how long does it take?'

'There is no time, mate,' shouted Steve. 'Just relax, knock ya beer back, and check out the fanny. Try to have a dance.'
I don't do dancing. I'm shite. I look like a knobhead—I've got no

rhythm, Jonno said to himself.

He picked up on his other advice, though, and knocked back his beer as he scanned the room. It truly was amazing. Two thousand people dancing everywhere you looked, not just on the dancefloor. The constant beat of the bass drum and the laser light show made them all look almost magical. Jonno caught sight of Willo and Isaiah dancing on a small stage with a hoard of extremely beautiful, glamorous looking girls around them. Everyone was happy. Everyone was dancing. The pill wasn't working but Jonno wanted what they had.

'I'm off.'

'Where the fuck are you goin?' Naz shouted, as the three of them followed him.

Jonno waded through sweaty, dancing bodies as he made his way to Willo and Isaiah. During the journey to that stage, strangers smiled at him, patting his back, or shaking his hand. He felt like *Henry Hill* in *Goodfellas*; everyone liked and respected him.

He felt a cold rush run through his veins, similar to when anaesthetic is pumped into your arm. Freezing liquid silver slipped through his venous network and the hairs on the back of his freshly-shaven neck stood to attention; he felt cold, but he was sweating. He was connecting to the music, almost as if his mind had become a computer, and he now understood the non-vocal message that it spoke. The type of music he hates. The music he had despised for years now sounded like a beautiful message from God. The constant thud of the bass drum pounded through his chest and a distant, rhythmic high-hat kept the beat invariable. He wanted to dance but didn't know how. He felt full of energy. An electrical charge had reenergised batteries in his soul that had been dead for years. He felt alive.

Jonno was confused. It wasn't like being pissed—he was spinning around in another world but was still in complete control of himself. He knew exactly what he was doing and exactly what he felt. It reminded him of the things he had read about near-death experiences. He floated above his own head with the power to return any time he chose.

A hand appeared through the dry ice and fragmented lasers and grasped Jonno's forearm.
Isaiah's face punched through an aperture in the smoke—red, sweaty, and contorted.

'You havin' it, lad?'

'Havin' what?' Jonno enquired.

'You comin' up?'

'Up where? What shite are you chattin'?'
Isaiah shook his head in submission as he grabbed hold of Jonno's arm and lifted him up to a small stage area where even more claret-faced individuals were dancing, all facing the same way. Jonno stood looking at Isaiah in the opposite direction to everyone else, with no idea what he was doing.

'Turn around, Jonno, and face the dancefloor. Move your feet and put your hands in the air,' Isaiah instructed.

Jonno turned to face the hundreds of people on the dancefloor, their faces twisted by wispy smoke, darkness, and light beams. It felt as though anti-coolant was running through his veins and he sensed that everyone on the dancefloor wanted him to join in. He couldn't help himself. His arms alternatively flicked forward like a karate expert flicking away irritant wasps, whilst his feet marched perfectly in time to the thumping bass and kick drum. The flickering strobe light made him look as though he had mastered a new dance technique, and although he knew he was only marching, he felt as if he were on a surfboard, slickly riding the ocean waves.

I've got this, he thought. *It's fuckin' easy. Everyone in the club was watching me because I was so good at dancing.*

The lads nodded appreciatively at Jonno's newfound skills, and every girl in the club desperately wanted him—he could clearly see it in their eyes. Jonno turned to Isaiah and Willo to see them smiling at him, knowing that he had wandered into his utopia. A newly discovered land where Jonno was the king.

Jonno was in disbelief at how a tiny pill could physically affect him with an injection of energy that he'd never witnessed before, and emotionally affect him, where he felt overloaded with confidence and an overwhelming sensation of contentment.

This was like a magic tablet.

The tunes were monotonous and was the main reason Jonno had disliked dance music so much. The same *thump! thump! thump!* of the bass drum and the never-changing bass riff, heavily distorted by compression. But this was addictive. The music bounced along at exactly the same tempo as his body movements. It was out of his control, but his life depended on keeping up with the rhythm. Occasionally, the DJ would do something that was absolutely mind blowing and had him begging for more. After around five minutes of continuous bass and drums, a piano would start playing a catchy tune over and over again. Quiet and distant at first, almost muted, it made you question whether it was there at all or whether your confused brain was fabricating it. It grew louder and more prominent. The transformation in the piano's intensity alerted everyone on the dancefloor, as it pushed past the dull din of the bass and drums. This caused an unconditioned, unconscious speeding up of arm movements, although the foot stomps remained at the same speed, governed by the bass drum. The music was in complete control of every dancers' body. The piano gained volume as it reached its crescendo and as it hit its highest octave, the whole room pushed a cloud of energy to the ceiling with their hands. Then dramatically, the music stopped for two full seconds, the lights went out, and the room was overcome by darkness and calm. Your mind was temporarily tricked that it was all over. Then, out of nowhere, the music kicked back in—considerably louder than before— and was accompanied by a monumental laser light show. The sensation of euphoria was colossal. Jonno could barely cope with the electricity running through his veins and the sense of freedom kidnapping his soul. This level of awesomeness had taken him to a new place in his mind and he was constantly looking around at the faces beside him to ascertain that they were in the same paradise he was.

Jonno had been dancing on the stage for around thirty minutes when he spotted the rest of the lads on the dancefloor. They looked up at him and were cheering before they pushed their way through the masses and joined him on the stage. They spent the rest of the night there, dancing and dripping in sweat. One of the lads would stick a cold bottle of water in Jonno's hand every now and then, but he never had an alcoholic drink or went to the toilet all night. He was too scared that if he went to the bar or the loo, he might miss something amazing. *The night was too good to be wasting time on trivial things like pissing and drinking.*

The girls below and to the side of the lads were all gorgeous. Everyone was gorgeous. Jonno felt an overpowering sensation of love and wanted to hug everyone, especially his mates. He was grateful he had them, and even Birchy appeared happy to hand out man-hugs. For the first time in Jonno's life he felt no malice, no worry, no fear, or anxiety. He only felt good things and thought it was amazing to be alive. He could barely contain the energy built up inside himself. He felt that he could live in this moment forever. It was the first time he felt that he had spiritually connected to something. It was euphoric.

The dancing went on for hours, but Jonno felt that the night was over in a flash. Time was stolen and wrapped into his concrete memory that would stay with him eternally. Unlike being drunk and not remembering a thing, He could recall every single detail of what had happened during the night. He felt completely in control, yet entirely uninhibited.

Jonno was heartbroken when the DJ stopped the music. His mind and body wanted to continue dancing, yet the room had fallen quiet, except for some general chitter-chatter as loved-up people made their way to the exit.
Without doubt, this had been the best night out of his life. He couldn't bear that it was over, and they were already planning their next venture before they got back to the car.

8 ZOMBIE RISING

Jonno was thinking that if he'd have known he was going to feel
so bad the day after taking a tablet, he would never have taken one.
He certainly wouldn't have agreed to take one on a Saturday when
they were all playing football the next day. They'd played
absolutely wasted on a Sunday hundreds of times, but not this.
What was this? A hangover is tried and tested, you know what
you're getting. This was a vile creature that had crawled inside him
and was determined to make him dance on the cliff edge of Suicide
Beach. It was a tenacious evil, delivered fresh from the gates of
hell, that clawed at his senses and poisoned his mind. He was
completely sapped of any energy and everything was an effort. He
deduced that his main problem was down to sleep deprivation.
Could I fuck sleep? *Regardless of how tired I was, there was a
fucking circus performing in my head all night.* Non-stop music
with psychedelic visions of an abnormal world terrorised his brain
all night. It was amazing to watch, and he was thoroughly
entertained, but it was not what he wanted at five in the morning.
The thumping bass drum that had guided him on the dancefloor
was refusing to go to sleep and continued with its thudding straight
through to the morning. Throw into the mix his incessant erection
that just would not go away despite all his usual tactics. Because

his brain was having such a great party, his mouth thought it would join in. His teeth were grinding with the persistence of an overactive pepper mill for around six hours. What a horrendous, sleepless night.

His alarm clock was screaming at him to get up but there was no fuel in the tank. He was completely dried out. He had a sausage sarnie every Sunday, it was the fuel that usually got him going, but he couldn't stomach it. The thought of food made him nauseous, and his mouth was completely parched. He hauled his limp, drained body out of bed and sat on the edge feeling sorry for himself. His eyes, through lack of sleep, felt as though they were bursting out of their sockets, pushed out by his delirious brain. Even now that he was awake, the music continued to play in his head. This was the weirdest feeling. He still felt like he had the alertness he'd experienced the night before, but it was slowly being suffocated by this overwhelming sensation of doom and nothingness. The drum and bass were still present in his head, thumping away and distracting his thoughts as he tried to make sense of what was going on. This was awful, truly dreadful.

The phone rang, and as he answered, he realised he couldn't muster the coherence and energy to speak. he could hear Birchy getting irritated that he hadn't answered instantly.

'Jonno? Jonno? Are you there, you fuckin' dickhead?'

'What?' Jonno muttered.

Birchy appeared more upbeat than he was feeling, which irritated Jonno.

'How's yer come-down, lad?'

'What's a come-down?'

'Well, how are you feeling?'

'I honest to God feel like shite, mate. I think I'm ill.'
Birchy's laughter roaring down the phone confused him.

'That's yer come down, ya soft cunt! It's like a hangover, only worse,' he said through broken sniggers.

'Get a butty down ya, I'll be at yours in half an hour,' he continued.

'Mate, there is no way I am going to footy. No way!'

'You've got to go, ya tart. We're playing The Swan, top of the league.'

'Birchy, I currently cannot coordinate the picking of my fuckin' nose. I'm not going, lad.'
Just before the phone went dead, Birchy slipped in 'Be there in half an hour.'

***

'Birchy, slow down lad, for fuck's sake,' pleaded Steve.

'Shurrup ya tart!'

Birchy was almost tackling the corner of Jonno's street on two wheels, whilst simultaneously honking his horn, ensuring the whole neighbourhood was aware of his arrival.

'We're all goin' die in this clapped-out banger,' bemoaned Steve as his shoulder bounced off the frame of the car.

'Ya can fuckin' walk if ya don't like it!'

As Jonno finished tying the laces of his trainers, he heard one of his cannabis-loving neighbours shout his disproval at Birchy's constant tooting of his horn,

'Shut the fuck up or I'll fuckin' stab ya!'

It was 10.30am. It probably felt like the middle of the night to an addict, supposed Jonno.

Sometimes Jonno preferred to jump the bus to footy which gave his sore head time to settle, but Birchy chiefly insisted that he picked them all up, and that they went together. His Ford Escort Cabriolet must have been fifteen years old and was a ghastly purple colour. The roof was down, in the middle of winter, and he had some West Coast Rap crap booming out of his speakers. He didn't even like rap, in fact he hated it, but he thought it made him look cool whenever he pulled up at a red light. It didn't. It made him look like an idiot.

Jonno slammed his front door behind himself and jumped into the back seat, where he found Naz with a baseball cap pulled down over his eyes. Steve was in the front. He always took the front seat. It was closer to the mirrors and offered his hair better protection from the wind.

The pain of Jonno's come-down momentarily disappeared when he remembered the amazing night they'd shared together.

The drive to the playing fields was relatively normal, apart from the obvious lack of energy of all passengers. There was awful music all the way there, played at a ridiculously high volume. Birchy was filling the car with horrendous, acrid odours that were animalistic, and he was producing just as much faeces from his mouth. Steve said very little and spent most of the time grooming himself in the passenger visor mirror or ogling pedestrian females. Naz and Jonno relaxed in the back making small talk about yesterday's Premiership games and the highlights of last night.

*****

Their arrival at the changing rooms saw them go through a custom, a ritual, an unwritten regulation. They were late, as usual, which was always Birchy's fault, and as they marched into the changing rooms, they would shoulder-barge or give an affectionate punch to any team-mates in their path. At least one of them, usually Birchy, would give their manager a welcome bagful of verbal abuse.

'Now then, baldy', Birchy taunted.

Dave Llewellyn had been with the club since the beginning of time and had seen many players pass through the ranks, but his patience was pushed to the brink with this current crop of reprobates that he had taken under his wing. Particularly Birchy, who bullied him in his usual meaningless, oblivious manner, which seemed to wound Dave deeper than the rest of us. Birchy loved to be the centre of attention, and if the lads were egging him on, he could be ruthless. The lads couldn't handle him, so Dave had no chance.

Dave was a placid, timid man who stood no more than five-foot-four and weighed in at around ten stone. Although not clinically proven, and more of a guess on the lads part, he suffered from depression. He was at his lowest when he was overdue for his plum rinse on his rapidly fading mullet. As an organiser and authoritarian, he was useless, but he was a gentle, kind-hearted man who put a lot of his time into the club, allowing the lads to run riot on a Sunday morning. Due to Dave's insubstantial, defensive shell, and his teetering on the brink of a nervous breakdown, Jonno thought Birchy's cruel jibes were underhand, but there was no reasoning with such a brute.

The game went well for them, with Birchy scoring one off a corner and Steve grabbing the other two in a 3-1 victory. They always went back to the pub. It was the law, regardless of how bad they felt from the punishment the night before. Irrespective of what result they'd had on the pitch. The allure of a grated cheese sandwich on crusty bread that had been in the pub fridge all night really didn't whet Jonno's appetite today and he had to make a stand.

'I'm not goin' the boozer.'

'Ya wha?' Naz looked at him like he'd asked for a kidney.

'We always go. Why aren't ya goin?'

'I'm not up to it mate. I feel proper ill. Birchy, take me home please.'

'Fuckin; bender.'

***

Jonno had been back at his house for around ten minutes and was in the middle of the longest piss in history, when the phone rang for the second time. It shocked him, causing his perfect aim to hit the toilet rim, deflecting pee all over his legs. He's ignored the first phone call because he knew it would be Birchy bullying him to go back the pub. Now he was livid with him!

'I told you I'm not going, ya fuckin' arrogant prick!'

'Charming.'
He detected astonishment and disappointment in the delicate tone of Becky's voice.

'Oh, Becky, I'm so sorry. I thought it was Birchy,' he beseeched.

'I thought you might want to go out and get a bit of breakfast or something, but I can see you're in a bad mood.'

The thought of breakfast—or any other sort of food—sent a cold, repulsive shiver through his body. He was sure that even a single grain of rice would make him baulk with repugnance. However, she had taken the initiative and called him, and he couldn't waste the opportunity.

'No I'm not. I'm fine. I thought it was Birchy winding me up. He was bein' a tit.'
He wanted to see her but didn't want to go out as the drugs and ninety minutes of football had ruined him.

'I'm not feeling great today, Bec. Think I've got a bug. Why don't you come around here, and I'll make you some toast and a brew?

'Okay, give me an hour.'

Shit! Shit! Shit!
He had an hour to go the bog, get a shower, tidy the house up a bit, iron some clobber, and eradicate this feeling of death that had overcome him. For thirty seconds, he stepped from one foot to the other as his limbs waited for instruction from his injured brain. His body and mind were ruined and were refusing to collaborate with each other. He had to prioritise, so visited the toilet first to give the room chance to air, and then had a sixty-second shower, before throwing a load of dirty washing under the couch.

Becky was ten minutes early, but it didn't matter as he was pretty much ready. He squirted air-freshener as he paced down the hall to open the door, leaving a wet cloud of *Summer Linen* behind him. He swung the door open to reveal a vision of beauty, who for some unknown reason, had an interest in Jonno. Maybe she had some sort of sick sense of humour or was carrying out psychological research and he was her laboratory chimp. *Why else would this image of pure exquisiteness be interested in a rough-arse scally like me?* With his mouth gaping open like a gormless halfwit, he looked her up and down, attempting to comprehend this complex Salvador Dali masterpiece. She had wedge-heeled shoes on that emphasised her olive-skinned legs, which had clearly been finely-tuned with many gym visits. Underneath her cropped black leather biker jacket, she wore a floral summer dress which sat just above the knee. Quite odd, he thought, considering the weather was Baltic outside, but she brought sunshine with her and brightened up the shadows. Jonno's mouth closed, as the recently sprayed air-freshener rested on his tongue and contaminated his mouth.

'You gonna let me in, then?' she probed as she removed her unnecessary sunglasses from her perfectly formed nose.

Jonno had taken Becky out maybe five or six times over the last three months, since first meeting her in the office corridor. He still hadn't got used to how stunningly gorgeous she was. He was verging on being in awe of her and hadn't yet got bored of seeing her for the first time, every time.

He beckoned her into his home. As she shuffled past him, she threw her arm around his waist, drawing him near to her, and with her other arm, shut the door in one fell swoop. She grabbed the back of his clammy neck and drew his face close to hers. His chest expanded as his heart rate increased and his breathing became heavy. She smelt inviting. A mixture of an enchanting, exotic scent and strawberry lipstick tickled his nostrils, which eliminated the cheap whiff of *Summer Linen* that had previously polluted the air. Their lips met with more passion and intensity than their previous connections. He could feel the cold of her cheek, chilled by the wintery air, and the tenderness of her inviting mouth, warmed by her sexual craving. His hand reached down to secure a firm grip of her toned bum cheeks, whilst his other hand sauntered up to caress her pert breasts. There was no resistance and it looked like all the traffic lights were on green for Jonno. She moved her hand from his neck, Southside to his groin area where she was met with a very attentive bulge that was ready for action. Becky tried to lead Jonno towards the stairs and although he was bubbling alive in a pan of passion and appetite for her body, he still had the consciousness to avert her from the bedroom where he'd lay awake earlier this morning in a puddle of sweat and lassitude. He gently swung her away from the stairs and they made their way to the couch, from which he'd earlier removed a layer of old newspapers, remote controls, and unopened post.

She pushed him into a seated position and expertly lifted her dress over her head. Jonno sat there in amazement at what stood before him. This beautiful, tanned creature, naked apart from her underwear, leant over and kissed him fervently, before gently placing herself on his lap. They kissed slowly and passionately before, and during their love-making. They rhythmically moved in unison and explored each other's body's with trespassing hands. Her slow deep breaths and occasional moan in Jonno's ear made the hairs on his neck stand up. Becky's skin had become sticky to touch through her energetic swaying, occasionally thrusting her head back to release the sweaty hair from her rosy face.

Oddly, Jonno's mind would sporadically drift, and he'd think to himself, *I should be at the pub with the football team right now.* The boys would be nibbling away at a crusty butty, and here was Jonno, in the clutches of a beautiful woman, enjoying some early afternoon, surprise sex. Their love-making went on for longer than Jonno was usually capable of due to his blood flowing with the chemicals of last night's tablet.

They spent the rest of the day curled up on the couch kissing and watching rubbish on the telly. Jonno was still suffering with the pain of his comedown, but the ordeal was made much easier by the presence of Becky.

9 THE HITCHER

Three weeks had passed since the night when Jonno was first introduced to the world of illegal drugs. The come-down from the night had been appalling and lasted longer than a single day, which Birchy had initially advised him. Luckily, he'd spent that day with Becky, otherwise, he may well still be dying on the couch.

No matter how bad Jonno's body and brain felt the following day, for him, it didn't come close to outweighing the highs of the night before. It was truly extraordinary. He'd never felt so much elation and freedom. He'd worked out why they called it *ecstasy*. He knew he wasn't a drug addict. He wasn't shaking, shivering, or looking for money to get his next fix. It had been three solid weeks since the night out and although he'd relived the actual night over in his head many times, he never felt himself pining for another tablet. It wasn't consuming him and at the forefront of his thoughts. He couldn't be an addict.

But tonight, they were at it again. This time they were off to the metropolis of all dance music cities, Sheffield! Apparently, Steve had read in a magazine that there was a massive club there that hosted the best DJs around the country and the place would be rammed. Steve even offered to drive this time and give Birchy a night off.

The drive wasn't straightforward. They hit heavy traffic on the

M60 around Manchester and then more as they entered the town of Glossop. They had a few cans of lager each, which eased the irritancy of the drive and the blaring dance music force-fed into their ears by Steve. Jonno didn't understand why he disliked this genre of music so much, yet thought it was the amber nectar when he was *off his face* on a tablet.

Once they hit the A57, the traffic eased up and they could relax a little, except for Steve who had to concentrate on some tricky, winding roads. *It's not called Snake Pass for nothing*, he moaned.

Birchy, who was next to Jonno in the back, removed his seatbelt and pulled something from his front pocket. He waved a small cellophane bag of white powder in front of Jonno's face, tapping it with his little finger to highlight the magic trick he had just performed.

'What's that?' Jonno questioned.

'Beak.'

Jonno's puzzled expression was enough for him to note that he didn't understand.

'Charlie.'
He tried again. 'Coke, ya dickhead.'

A wave of uncertainty and fear passed over Jonno and the realisation embedded itself into his psyche. Taking a tablet was one thing, but this felt more serious, more sinister—more like being a *druggy*. Birchy held the bag at an angle, tapped some of the contents onto a ten-pence piece coin, and proceeded to snort the powder up his nostril. He then repeated these steps and shoved the laden coin under Jonno's nose, as Naz watched from the front seat with a smile on his face. Jonno contemplated resisting and trying to reason with them, He really did, but he knew it was futile. Exactly the same scenario would play out as the last time he'd tried a defensive tactic. Everyone would be on a downer and hold him responsible.

Jonno pressed his index finger against his left nostril and offered his right nostril to the powder, then snorting powerfully. The white powder disappeared up his nose, drawn in by a super-charged vacuum cleaner. He was surprised to discover that it felt like most of the repugnant tasting powder had ended up in his throat, which caused his to baulk.

'Sniff up again and swallow it,' advised Birchy.
Birchy was full of great advice for meaningless shit, thought Jonno. He did as Birchy said, and the bad taste cleared. The loaded coin got passed around the car until all the lads had a Class A drug swimming in their system.

Unlike the tablet, the effects from the cocaine were almost instant. A nervous electrical charge ebbed through Jonno's body, whilst his skin was frozen with an ice-cold liquid. *This felt good, but different*. It felt quite different to the effects of the tablet. A feeling of euphoria passed over him, and while he had been feeling a little daunted about the night ahead, he suddenly felt super confident and experienced a feeling of intense pleasure. Febrile electrons formed a circuit through his body and bashed the walls of his rationality, chipping away at normality with every electrical surge. He looked around the car and could see that the boys were feeling it too. The music seemed louder and more significant, connecting them spiritually, and chemically. They chatted worthless rubbish to each other yet were hooked on every word their friends were saying.

By the time they parked the car, Jonno was a coiled spring ready to explode. As the four of them energetically bounced across the car park, heading for the queue, Birchy shoved a tablet into Jonno's palm.

'Take this now, lad, coz these fuckers will search ya.'
This time there was no hesitation, and Jonno followed Birchy's instructions without fuss.

They were in the queue for around five minutes and Jonno could feel the bass thumping through his chest, annoyingly causing him to bounce on the spot whilst he was trying to look controlled in front of the doormen.

As soon as they paid their entrance fee and paced down the corridor, Jonno was straight on the dancefloor with no knowledge of who was following him. He didn't care if he was on his own, as he had to urgently quell the overdose of adrenaline that was manipulating his body. He tried to scan his surroundings whilst pumping a fist in the air and slowing his walk to a standstill. The extravagant light display, poked through a smoke-filled dancefloor loaded with cheerful, dancing figures.

Jonno didn't think the sensation of the chemicals in his body would be as good the second time around, but this was better. This time he had no apprehension or regret. He felt like a force—as if he was better than everyone in there. Better at everything. The best looking, the best dancer, the best-dressed. The lads were laughing and smiling at him, so they knew it. They must have all agreed. Some of the girls in there were drop-dead gorgeous, but Jonno wasn't interested. Not because of Becky, she hadn't even crossed his mind. He just didn't feel the animal instinct to waste time talking to girls when there was music to dance to. They'd been there around twenty minutes when the DJ wound up the music with a ten-minute version of *Groove is in the Heart*. From this point, the lads didn't stop dancing all night as the music got better and magnetised them to the dance floor—there was no escape— flies stuck to a sticky web.

Jonno was gutted when the night was over; he was still full of beans and desperate to continue the party. It was the equivalent to going 100mph in a sports car, then hitting a brick wall. There was no slowing or sapping of energy, the night just stopped dead in its tracks. Steve put his hand on Jonno's shoulder and spun him around.

'Come on, lad, we're off.'
Jonno's mind and body were still dancing after the music had ceased but he knew it was time to head home.

Everyone was in a brilliant mood as they set off for their homebound journey. Once again, they were all chatting absolute nonsense, unmistakably high, and enjoying the love within their brotherhood. *These lads were my family—my real family*, thought

Jonno.

He left home at eighteen, as soon as he was working, and had a couple of scruffy flats before putting a deposit on his house at the age of twenty-two. He had a good upbringing, never really wanted for anything, and never went hungry. That's not entirely true, he was always hungry, but no more than a typical teenager. His mum used to call him 'cast-iron stomach'. He could eat a cow and still be hungry. If there was nothing in the cupboard, he'd have a handful of dried currants his mum used to put in her baked rock cakes or knock up a tomato ketchup butty. There was always something in, unlike quite a few kids who he went to school with who had nothing. He left home as soon as he could because of his relationship with his dad. He never laid a finger on Jonno— not after he got bigger than him, anyway. They just didn't sit right together, totally different animals. He was an extremely negative man, constantly looking for the downside and casting doubt on anything with a bit of sunshine. He never seemed happy with any of the accomplishments Jonno ever achieved and never came across as being particularly proud of him—that can really hurt as a kid. Jonno convinced himself that it made him stronger. He would get a bit of a hug and a handshake at Christmas, but he never felt as though there was real love there. He'd doubted in the past if he were his real son, but he could never believe his mum being unfaithful in the eyes of God. Besides, he was the spitting image of his dad.

As he got older and started drinking in pubs, he'd see fellas sitting there with their dads, having a pint, and watching the match. That was never going to happen to Jonno, and he knew that from an early age. His dad was executing a role, he may even have thought it was a chore, but there was certainly no vocational commitment to it. The house wasn't toxic, but Jonno reckoned it would be better if he weren't there. Similar to pineapple on pizza—it's kind of okay but it would be better if it were somewhere else, like in a pudding.

Jonno's mum was an angel, carved from diamond and abundantly filled with righteousness. Constantly worrying about other people, so much so that it kept her awake at night. She was in her sixties but still fit as fiddle and looked great. Jonno had often thought she looked fitter than some of the lads in the footy team, and in some case, could probably do a better job. She was probably happy he'd left home, not because she wanted him gone, but at least the house was rid of any tension. The lads were Jonno's family. He knew this simply because he would call on Naz before he'd call on his dad in times of trouble.

As the car reached the beginning of Snake Pass, Jonno looked out the window and blanked out the chatter endlessly flowing from the lads' mouths, and the tedious din of Steve's trance music. A dark sky had appeared from the loss of the street lighting and its blackness was only fractured by dancing, wispy clusters of ice-cold mist. The moon had been consumed by the blackness and the bare trees swayed menacingly as the venomous wind snapped its teeth at them.

Thump!

Jonno's head hit the back of Steve's seat as he violently slammed on the brakes, obscenely waking him from his inertia. The car screamed to a halt and the momentum of its passengers surging forward, then back to their original position, mimicked a terrible effort at a Mexican wave.

'What the fuck are you doin', ya dickhead?' Birchy said.
Steve thought this was hilarious and said through poorly controlled laughter,

'I've just seen a hitchhiker thumbing a lift.'
He reversed fifty metres and stopped adjacent to where an indistinguishable figure stood waiting patiently. *It must be a bird,* Jonno thought. *Why else would we be picking up a hitcher? Got to be a bird. She'd better be fit.*

'Wind yer window down, Naz,' Steve instructed.
Steve leaned over Naz to make himself visible to the hitcher.

'Where are you goin', mate?'

The weak supply of light diminished further as the figure bent down and lurched into the open window. The orange light from the car's dashboard gave the lads some idea of what the seat-stealer looked like. His head was partially covered by the hood of a yellow waterproof jacket. Piercing green eyes poked through crevice laden holes umbrellaed by wiry grey eyebrows. A stout flattened nose perched on top of an unkempt ginger beard. As he smiled politely, he presented his tobacco-stained teeth.

'Glossop will do me, boys.'
Good God! What was Naz doing? Thought Jonno. The car journey up to now had been almost as enjoyable as the club, but now the atmosphere had changed in an instant because Naz thought it would be hilarious to let a stranger share the back of the car. *I bet he wouldn't have made such a peculiar decision had it been him sitting in the back with his pristine clothes and perfect hair,* bemoaned Jonno to himself. Jonno's only saving grace was that the hitcher was on Birchy's side and he wouldn't have to sit next to him.

'Swap seats, Jonno?'

'You can fuck right off, lad.'

It was too late, the lump of a hobo was already shuffling his bum cheeks across Birchy's seat into position as Steve began to trundle the vehicle forward. Birchy's huge frame encroached onto Jonno's seat as he nervously tried to create a gap between himself and the new passenger.

'Where you been, boys?' he asked, in a thick West Country accent.

'Been clubbing, mate,' Steve responded through faint mirth.

'Where's that to?'

'Where's what to?' Steve enquired.

'The club?'

'Do you mean where was the club we've been?'

'That's the badger.'
Naz spun around and looked at Jonno with a quizzical face.

'Ah, I used to love me clubbin', I did, when I was a kiddie. Too old now. I'm in me forties.'
Fuck me, Jonno thought he was in his sixties. He didn't smell great. A blend of stale cigarettes, body odour and musty breath filled the confinement of the car.

'Ma name's Aki.'
No one cared, so no one responded. Steve's trivial attitude had changed, as the reality of the leech sitting in their car for the next forty minutes had hit home.
Aki turned his attention to Birchy.

'You're a big lad, aren't ya? Do yous go the gym?' asked Aki as he squeezed Birchy's bicep.
Birchy's face enflamed as his forehead constricted and his *'fume-o-meter'* reached explosive levels.

'Touch me again, ya smelly tramp, and I will spark you clean out!'
How honourable and magnanimous of Birchy to fire a warning shot. This was completely out of character and could only be the result of the love pill that had recently dissolved within his blood. Aki obviously had a death sentence because he continued with his *'how to chat up a lunatic in the back of a car'* campaign.

'I loves the lads that do the squats,' he confessed, as he groped the top of Birchy's muscular thigh.

Birchy flew into a rage with elbows swinging, arms flailing and legs kicking, predominantly in the back of Naz's chair. Steve thrust his foot upon the brakes and yet again, they all surged forward. At this point, Birchy, who already had one hand around his romantic predator's throat and his other on the door handle, shoved Aki forcefully out of the door, who consequently landed heavily on the tarmac. The time it took Birchy to exit the vehicle, Aki had already clambered to his feet and was abruptly met with a left hook into his ribs. The wind bellowed out of him like a slowly deflated balloon, and without chance of recovery, Birchy sealed the deal with a right cross shot to his jaw. Aki's neck tilted 45 degrees as Birchy's hammer of a fist struck the side of his face with a chilling crack. Aki's legs buckled before slumping to the floor in a seated position, eventually rolling over on his side.

A car sped past, beeping its horn in disapproval, as Aki lay on the ground unconscious and breathing heavily. The indistinct moonlight and red illumination from the vehicle stop lights highlighted a trickle of blood dribbling from his nose. The cold night air helped identify a radiant heat emitting from Aki's wilting torso, which was consumed by the more noticeable exhaust fumes from the car.

Birchy looked as if he wanted to say something to Aki as he stood over the lifeless lump, maybe another threat or a warning shot. It was useless because Aki was asleep and the only life from his frame was Birchy's shadow dancing upon him as he nervously bounced around, fuelled by adrenalin, cocaine, and rage. Birchy jumped in the car and slammed the door.

'I fuckin' warned him!'

10 THE BIZZIES

Jonno had already been up and about for around an hour when the phone rang, following another sleep-deprived night.

'Hello?'

'Have you heard?'

Naz sounded very agitated.

'The police have taken Birchy in over last night.'

'Eh?'

'Apparently, that dosser from last night was stumblin' all over the road, all dazed as fuck, and walked into a van. Dead!'

Jonno felt the blood drain out of him—he could literally feel himself turning white. He felt like he should respond to Naz, but his brain wasn't working quickly enough to compute this shocking information and come up with an intelligent retort. He wasn't sure if that was due to the shock, or the illegal chemicals poisoning of his blood.

'Wha'?'

'Somebody saw Birchy lampin' him and managed to take Steve's registration number to report it. Steve's down there getting

questioned now.'
A feeling of impending doom froze the blood in Jonno's veins and cast a shadow over his soul.

'Jonno, listen to me,' Naz continued.

'Birchy could go down for this. You've got to say fuck all, mate. Just deny everything. Say we saw the guy on the side of the road, but we were the ones trying to help him. No one hurt him.'

'But, dead, la?'

'Yeah, he's fuckin' dead, but he might have died anyway. What the fuck was he doing out there in the dark anyway? Probably just buried a body in the woods or somethin'.'
Naz delivered a parting piece of advice before the line went dead,

'Just say fuck all.'

Jonno hated these situations. There was a lot for him to consider and an awful lot for him to lose. By telling lies, he could be putting himself in real trouble with the police—he may already be in a whole host of bother. He had a lot of other dilemmas floating around his head.

I have my job to consider, a shit job, but a job all the same. They are not that easy to come by in this Godforsaken land, particularly for someone with little, to no skills. Then there was Becky to think about. If I got in trouble with the bizzies, I reckon she'd dump me in a flash. She didn't look the type who'd visit Walton prison, he pondered.

He also had his loyalty to Birchy, and more significantly, his mates in general. There are certain unwritten laws between friends that need no explanation, and which are abided by all. *You don't go sniffing around your mates' current or ex-girlfriends. You just don't do it. You also try to stay away from your mates' sisters, this is just wrong and too close to home. You always pay back any money you borrow. We were all on the bones of our arse and effectively stealing off your brothers was unacceptable in our code of conduct.* They were primitive rules, but they'd given clear guidance to friends for generations—they worked.

The epitome of this statutory instrument for friends was that you never snitched. It didn't matter if it was some council estate tip rat that had pinched your kid's bike; you never, ever told the police. If Jonno were to tell the truth about what had happened, then that would effectively be the end of his relationship with Birchy, Steve, and Naz, and would ultimately put Birchy in prison.

Missiles of stress were spinning around Jonno's head, making him nauseous, with little time to resolve the considerations, and the absence of a functioning brain, accentuated the conundrum. It had barely been ten minutes, and nowhere near long enough for him to think straight, before the phone rang again.

'Hello?'

'Mr Johnson? Mr Danny Johnson?'

'Yeah, who is this?' Jonno knew straight away who it was, but he thought he'd better play the game.

'This is Detective Sergeant Duncan Nibbs from Merseyside Police. We'd like you to come down to Mortimer Street station for a chat,' he said in a fairly polite manner, which wasn't fooling Jonno. Jonno continued with the innocence charade.

'What's it about?'

'We can discuss that in more detail when you pop down to the station, Mr Johnson.'
Pop down? Pop down? I'm not going to fuckin' Asda, mate. This is potentially life-changing here, fella. I'm not 'popping' out to pick up the fuckin' Echo! ranted Jonno to himself.

'What if I don't want to *pop* down?' he asked, without any real conviction.

'This is a voluntary interview, sir, and you are under no legal obligation to comply. However, we can arrest you in order to question you and we would then be playing a very different game.'

His reply was well rehearsed and delivered like a projectile that could not be avoided. Jonno was trapped.

'If you could come down in the next hour and ask for myself at the front desk, sir, that would be terrific.'
Terrific? I think this fella thinks we're going for a fuckin' pint and a game of darts, Jonno ranted.

***

The waiting area at the station was relatively quiet, populated by a couple of suspect drug users, an old fella, and a young mum with a toddler in a buggy. The walls were cladded in mahogany boards which were randomly decorated with *CrimeStoppers* posters. The tiled floor was battered and gave off a faint whiff of stale urine and bleach. The lighting was a sordid yellow that turned the custody sergeant into a cadaverous lemon. Jonno asked for DS Duncan Nibbs as instructed and was told to sit down and wait until he was ready for him. He left Jonno sitting there for forty minutes before he was called for. Jonno assumed that this was a technique to tire him out slightly before firing questions at him. He was shown to an interview room and told to sit down at the table.

There was a terminally-scratched metal table in the centre of the room, encircled by four uncomfortable-looking chairs. The breeze-block walls were painted a cold blue colour and the floor was a Marley type tile, coated with a thin feathering of dust. There was a tape machine on the table and a CCTV camera high in the corner of the room. Too high for a raging criminal (or bent copper) to jump up and rip off the wall. Below a grill-covered window was a large lead-piped radiator, which Jonno deduced wasn't on, due to the Baltic temperatures he was currently enduring. He sat there for around five minutes before the door opened and a pair of middle-aged men entered the room.

The first fella approached Jonno with an open hand, whilst the second copper held back and stayed close to the door.

'Thanks so much for coming down, Mr Johnson. I'm DC Nibbs, and this is DC Galway.

Nibbs was a slim man with a thick beard and curly, wiry hair which looked like it was overdue a visit to the barbers. His beard and hair had no distinguishing gap, which made his whole head look like a hairy football. He was a scruffy wretch, dressed in a beige suit with an open-collared shirt and a '70s style tie that offered evidence of his lunch. His half-mast trousers highlighted a cream pair of socks and loafer style shoes. He would be better suited teaching chemistry to thirteen-year-olds, thought Jonno.

Galway was presented in much more professional, well-groomed attire, but seemed a lot more anxious than his colleague. His bald head deflected the strong light from the uncovered tubes in the centre of the ceiling and a wispy grey moustache was collecting beads of sweat from his chubby, crimson face. He was severely overweight, but his smart, dark blue suit and matching tie distracted the eye from his obesity and laboured breathing. His polished black shoes slid across the-dust covered floor as he gently closed the door behind him.

'So, Mr Johnson, you are entitled to legal representation, but it's going to take a while to get someone down here, and we are only after a quick chat with you. If you're happy for me to proceed, we are going to record the interview, if that's okay?'

Jonno could see what Nibbs was up to. He was trying to railroad him and was popping a small cassette into the tape machine before he'd even answered him. Nonetheless, Jonno really had no desire to be there longer than he needed to be and nodded his consent. Besides, he couldn't afford a solicitor and the one they'd provide for him was probably working for them. They both pulled up a chair and sat opposite Jonno. Nibbs rattled through the persons present in the room, the time, date, and his rights—for the benefit of the tape. Nibbs was the lead, as Galway sat there staring at Jonno with protruding eyes, tapping a pen on the table as he sweated profusely and occasionally snorted.

'Mr Johnson, can you tell me your whereabouts at around 2.40am last night, the night of the 20ᵗʰ?'
Jonno thought about saying *I was in bed with yer ma*, but quickly decided that it wouldn't help his cause.

'We were on our way home around that time.'

'And who were you with, and on your way home from where, Mr Johnson?'

'We were coming home from a club in Sheffield called The Music Factory.'

'Who's we, Mr Johnson?'

He knew who Jonno was with, but he was going to make him say it,

'Steve Brookes; Naseem Hasnawi, and John Birch.'

'Who was driving the vehicle?'

'Steve Brookes.'

'Is there anything you'd like to share with us that may have occurred during that journey?'
Jonno's attention was distracted by Galway opening up an A4 cardboard wallet and shuffling a few sheets of paper about. He wasn't sure whether he actually had some evidence or if he was trying to shake him up.

'No. Nowt that I can recall.'

Galway lurched forward and cleared his throat of phlegm.

'Lucy, six.'

'Jen, nine.'

'And Annie, aged eleven.'

'Do you know these kids?'
What the fuck was Galway up to here? Did he have me down as

some sort of kiddie fiddler? Jonno nervously considered.

'Er, no,' Jonno muttered.
As Galway explained, he forcefully tapped his finger upon the paper where he had retrieved the information. These are the three little, fatherless girls of a Mr Martin Atkinson, aged 48, who was fatally injured on the A57 last night by a speeding van. The van driver is still yet to be identified, yet we have you four scroats in the area at the time of the incident.'

Galway stared at Jonno intensely, but he refused to break. There was no question, so no need to respond.

'A witness', he resumed, 'said they saw Steve Brookes' car pulled over at the mouth of Snake Pass and a large gentleman struggling to get to his feet. We presume that 'large' gentleman to be the now-deceased Martin Atkinson.'
Again, no question, so Jonno remained tight-lipped.
Nibbs took the reins.

'Look, Danny, we're not overly interested in you four. We've checked Mr Brookes' car and there is no evidence of any impact. We also know it was a transit van. We are not concerned about the traces of cocaine we found in the vehicle or the fact that you left a vulnerable man on one of the deadliest stretches of road in England.'
He paused for a moment.

'We do, however, need to find the driver of that van, and we need to know if you lot spoke with Mr Atkinson before his death.'

'Well, did you?' Galway butted in.

'No, we didn't see him. I don't know this fella,' Jonno lied.

They continued for another ten minutes with probing questions that lacked evidence and Jonno expertly deflected every one of them. Nibbs delivered the final dialogue, whilst Galway irritably grunted in the background conceding defeat.

'Don't leave town, Mr Johnson, we may need to speak with you again,' he said.

As Jonno exited the police station, the strong sunlight and crisp cold air hit him and swept away the stale, musty whiff of the interview room. A high-pitched whistle echoed from over the road and as his eyes readjusted, he spotted Naz, Steve, and Birchy waiting for him.

'C'mon, Ronnie Biggs, we're going for a bevy to celebrate your release,' roared Birchy as his collaborators chuckled with approval. Birchy pointed to the pub sign as he shouted across the street. *The Copper Pot*—Jonno couldn't believe the irony.

By the time he'd crossed four lanes of busy traffic and walked into the bar area, Birchy already had four pints lined up, with whisky chasers.

'Here he is, fuckin' Reggie Kray, Britain's most wanted,' Birchy teased as he shoved a pint in Jonno's hand.

'I kept you from being someone's wife in prison, gettin' yer arse felt every night, though, didn't I?'

The boys howled at Jonno's return.

'That's right, Danny,' said Naz, squeezing his shoulder.

'That's why us four need to stick together through any shit any fucker throws at us. We are family, and we are all we've got.'

The drinks were followed by another four pints with tequila chasers, then another four pints with vodka chasers. Jonno nipped the toilet whilst Steve was ordering the fourth deadly round of lager and optic roulette surprise. When he returned, the lads had the company of two young ladies. One of them was fairly tall, with an eye-catching '80s style short haircut. She looked a lot like the singer from Texas and had a great figure to match her fetching hair. Her friend was shorter, with copper-coloured hair, and both of them were wearing jeans, trainers, and leather jackets.

Jonno necked Steve's optic choice of gin and proceeded to take the head off his fourth pint, then removed the frothy moustache with the back of his hand.

Texas addressed him with extreme confidence and forwardness,

'What's your name, then?' she asked, patting his bum.

'Me? Jonno. I mean Danny. Danny Johnson.'

The quick succession of drinks was starting to affect his ability to talk as Birchy passed over yet another pint and a small glass of brown liquor, which he presumed to be brandy.

'Danny, eh? Handsome bastard, aren't ya?' She pulled herself closer. Jonno tried to come up with a witty, manly reply but as always, burned and sunk.

'Well, that's what me ma tells me.'

'Do you know what I do, Danny?'

'Dunno, dominatrix?'

He looked around to the boys for applause, to eye Birchy snogging *Texas's* copper-haired friend.

'I'm a professional horse trainer. I'm here for the Aintree meet.' Jonno was slightly taller than her, but she didn't have far to go to reach his ear and delicately whisper,

'I'd like to ride you, Danny.'

He was still enjoying the warmth of her breath down his ear when she unexpectedly planted her lips on his and started passionately kissing him. At this point, he probably should have pulled away from *Texas* and had a rethink about what was going on and what he had to lose. *I've a drop-dead gorgeous girlfriend that is way beyond my deservedness, and I think I might actually be starting to fall in love with her*, he considered. However, the alcohol, and the stress of the police interview had malfunctioned a circuit in his brain and he wasn't thinking about Becky in the slightest. In addition to this, attractive girls didn't usually come on to him in the middle of the day and this looked too good an opportunity to miss. He kissed her back, whilst groping her bum in the middle of the pub to the cheers of Naz and Steve. She pulled away after a couple of minutes and told him the name of her hotel, before leaving with her friend.

By the time they were on their sixth round, which was effectively the twelfth, due to the chasers, he'd completely forgotten the name of the hotel and lost the desire to pursue her.

11 STAYING AFLOAT

The week dragged horrifically, and Jonno prayed for its death so that he could welcome the weekend into his arms. He was looking forward to spending some time with Becky, away from clubs, alcohol, drugs, and dead West Country hobos. His world had been turned upside-down lately and he needed a little stability back in his life, and that came in the form of a couple of quiet nights in.

Jonno had rung Becky a few times in the week but hadn't been able to get hold of her; the phone had constantly rung out. He wasn't overly worried; they tended not to talk that much in the week as they regularly saw each other at the weekends. He'd finished early the day before and waited outside her offices to try and catch her on her way home but couldn't find her. He wasn't sure if she was off or had maybe gone out the back door and taken a lift from someone. Either way, it was Friday tomorrow, and he hadn't seen or heard from her all week, so he decided he was going to knock at her door.

It was lashing down by the time he got to Becky's street and he was soaked through. He scurried up her path and tapped at her front door. He waited what he considered a respectable time seeing that it was pouring, and then knocked again. Still no answer. He thumped the door with more purpose for a third time. No reply.

She would normally be well home from work by this time and the lack of contact, combined with the tightly closed door, disheartened him, and planted a dose of doubt. He turned on his heels and feeling dejected and soaked. It was pointless waiting for her on her doorstep because there was no cover from the driving rain, and he would look desperate sitting on her step if she did return. He found a quiet spot over the road under a large beech tree. The parked cars there, gave him cover from her view, but he could see her house. and the tree offered some shelter from the rain.

Enduring the cold air was made all the more difficult by his drenched, clinging clothes. Occasionally, an oversized raindrop that had beefed itself up would launch itself off a leaf and detonate on his head. He stood there shivering for over forty minutes as dusk crept in around him and blackened the day, before he eventually caught sight of her.

She was jogging at a fair pace, holding an umbrella at an appropriate angle to resist the force of the wind-driven rain. She was up her path and had her key in the door before Jonno even contemplated shouting her, so, he would have to knock at her door again. He could see her figure through the frosted glass side panels, trying to shake off the excess rain. He tapped on her door three times. The door flew open instantly, obviously because she didn't expect him to be standing there, and this was confirmed by the shocked expression she paraded on her face. The instant she saw it was Jonno, the door closed to leave a gap just wide enough to reveal her dampened face and storm-beaten hair.

'What do you want?' she barked.

This was a surprise slap in the face for Jonno. As he was struggling to find the words to reply, she opened her eyes to their limit and pushed her face forward, prompting him for an answer.

'What do you mean, what do I want? You haven't been answering my calls and I've no idea what's going on.'

'You're a dickhead, Danny, and you've fucked it all up.'
Not the first time he'd been called a dickhead, but he usually had at

least half an idea of what he was guilty of. Becky was on a mysterious tirade and he was defenceless in the crossfire.

'Fucked *what* up? What are you talking about?' he asked.

'You know my mate, Donna?'
He nodded.

'Well, she saw you. She saw it all!'

Now his mind was racing, looking for answers. He was trying to think of excuses before he knew what the issue was. He didn't reply with words this time, but shrugged his shoulders, offered out his palms, and wore a muddled expression.

'She was in The Copper Pot, you dickhead, when you were pissed and had your tongue down some girl's throat. She saw you.'
A cold tributary of realisation ran through Jonno's veins, causing every single hair he had to stand proud, and his tongue became dry. In the seconds that his world was caving in, he felt shame sit on his ribs, restricting his breathing rhythm, and felt guilt slowly pierce the side of his torso. There were no magic words available that would hoist him from this deep, dark excavation he'd fallen into, and he resorted to muttering,

'But Becky?'

'It's over,' she hissed, slamming the door with a venomous lash.

'Becky, I was pissed,' he pleaded, as he leant against the closed door.

'Piss off and leave me alone,' she shrieked while slamming an internal door shut.

Jonno turned on his rain-sodden trainers and commenced the long trudge home. He fell into a surreal, out-of-body state where his mind wasn't quite in sync with the current situation. The way you feel when you are delivered bad news, like someone has died or you're sacked, and you are struggling to believe it. He was still trying to process the circumstances and feebly convince himself that everything was okay. As he turned the corner, he was attracted by the green lights of his local Co-op. It symbolised a green oasis in a desert of negativity and disaster. He purchased a bottle of bourbon for 50% more than it would be in a supermarket, but he had to get the stale, rotting taste from his mouth and neutralise his brain.

When he got home, he took a hot bath and started to hammer the bourbon with no food in his stomach and no heart in his chest. His rib cage throbbed with a dull ache. He thought heartache was a fabricated fairy-tale phenomenon for little kids, but this trauma was affecting him physically, in addition to screwing up his mind. He felt low. So low. He didn't even have the safety net of blaming someone else. This was all on him. He didn't know who to feel sorrier for, himself, or Becky. He'd messed it up for her also, for the sake of a five-minute kiss with an amorous stranger who meant nothing to him.

He'd drunk a third of the bottle before he decided to ring Naz.

'I've fucked it up, mate.'

'Fucked what up? The bizzies? Have you spoken to the police again?'

'No la, not the bizzies. Becky's jibbed me.'

He struggled to talk due to his alcohol-numbed lips, and the battle to not breakdown emotionally.

'Ah,' said Naz.

'Well why? What did she say?'

'She found out about that bird in the boozer after the bizzies interviewed me.'

'Oh, for fuck's sake,' said Naz, as the penny dropped.

'Look, Jonno, you won't want to hear this now, but there's a ton of birds out there. Plenty of fish an' all that.'
Naz was doing his best, but Jonno really didn't want to hear it. He

wasn't interested in any other girls. He'd found the girl he wanted, and he was loving his life with her, and now he'd chucked it all away.

'Look, mate, I'll come around to yours. I'll be about twenty minutes.'

'I don't want you to, Naz. I wanna be on my own, la,' he confessed, and hung up before Naz could respond.

He spent the rest of the evening listening to embarrassing ballads and sipping bourbon straight, rarely moving from his horizontal position on the couch. He thought somewhere towards the bottom of the bottle, he may have tried ringing Becky again. He didn't recall a conversation with her, so assumed she didn't answer. Probably just as well, seeing as he'd lost the ability to communicate with another person many glasses earlier.

Jonno only ventured outdoors once over the whole weekend and that was to stock up on more alcohol and rubbish, comfort food. He didn't talk to anyone and ignored the phone and front door. He was broken. A lost man who had to get it straight in his own head before he could talk to anyone about it. In reality, he didn't really want to talk to anyone, including Naz.

Jonno was brought up in the 1980s, where struggling on against adversity was embedded into them. They were of tough stock and only a generation or two away from having a war mentality. They'd experienced hardship every day of their lives.

The Hillsborough cover-up was one example of such an injustice. 96 souls lost their lives, one of them being Jonno's thirty-year-old uncle. They all lost someone because Merseyside was one big family. Jonno witnessed Margaret Thatcher's force of devastation rip through the country as she shattered British industry and laid waste to communities that have never recovered. He lived in one of those communities and became a young adult with mass unemployment all around him. Thatcher caused riots, strikes and social unrest throughout their once great country, whilst nailing their coffin shut with the poll tax. Jonno had witnessed normal people become heroin addicts with all loss of morality and sanity, as the epidemic swept from Britain but hung around Birkenhead in an obstinate cloud. He'd gone into early adulthood with the constant fear of contracting AIDS or being drafted into the army to fight a plastic war that the Tories had generated. He'd watched innocent people burn at football matches, train stations and oil rigs. He'd seen people oppressed, judged, tortured, beaten, and broken. All around him were third-world people living in a first-world country, cast aside as unwanted trash. He knew there was a new wave of belief being championed, where you were supposed to talk to someone about your problems, whether they be money, girls, work, or whatever. Best to talk and get it out.

Why the fuck would anyone want to hear my problems, he thought, *when they are drowning in their own? Why would I offload my shit onto another poor fucker who is struggling in their own world?* He was a proud man, content to battle through at his own pace, using his own strategy. *If this was the wrong approach, then fuck it, things couldn't get much worse*, was his philosophy.

Jonno had done well not to answer the door until now, but Birchy's constant thumping and booming voice broke down his defence.

'Jonno. Jonno. C'mon, answer the door ya bell.'

Jonno had barely took the door off the latch before Birchy barged in and walked past him.

'Why didn't you answer the door, ya prick?'

'Coz I'm not in the mood for you. What do ya want?'

'Ya need to man up lad. Just coz ya bird's ditched ya. Fuck 'er off. They're all fuckin' murder anyway.'

'What do ya want Birch? I'm on me way to bed.'

'I want ya to mind this for me.'

Birchy presented Jonno with a wrapped up *Kwik Save* carrier bag.

'What the fuck is it?'

Birchy didn't need to answer Jonno—as soon as he grabbed the bag, he could tell instantly what it was. He'd never held a gun before, but it was an unmistakeable shape. Jonno stared at Birchy with pure terror in his eyes.

'No chance. Ya get fucked. I'm not doin' it,' Jonno said, while shoving the bag back to Birchy. Birchy kept his hands by his side and refused to take it.

'Jonno, mate, I need you to help me out 'ere. I've still got the bizzies sniffin' around over the fuckin' dead dosser on the road and I can't afford to get pinched again. I've got a record and I'll go down for a long time. It's just for a bit. Wait 'til it all settles down, then I'll come and get it back off ya.'

'Well, what the fuck has it been used for?'

'Don't be worrying 'bout tha'. It hasn't been fired; it hasn't even got a bullet in it.'

The timing was perfect for Birchy. Not only did Jonno possess a weak, impressionable personality, but he was currently at his lowest ebb. He didn't have the energy or heart to contend with Birchy and agreed to the instruction far too easily.

'Where the fuck am I goin' stash it?'

'Stick it in ya outside bog—no fucker's goin' in there are they?'

12 DOUBLE DIPPED

Three weeks had passed since Becky had dumped Jonno and he still wasn't feeling any better about the situation, but it was his birthday weekend, and the lads were insisting that he was going out.

Jonno was about to become twenty-four, he had a dull job, no girlfriend, and could see no crack of light at the end of a dark tunnel. *What else was I going to do, other than go out and get absolutely wasted?* he conceded. Drinking until his mind became numb wasn't the most sensible option, and he knew this, but it was his only option. Becky wasn't getting back with him. If she were going to, it would have happened by now. He had no desire to meet anyone else. Maybe that would come with time, but presently, the talons of guilt and stupidity were clutching at his ankles and dragging him into a wretched, hopeless abyss.

The thought of taking another girl on—and all the crazy baggage that may come with her— really didn't sound attractive to him at the moment. There was no way in the world that he wouldn't start comparing another girl to Becky, and that wouldn't be fair.

When the lads had a 'big night out', which effectively meant going to a club and not *Maxine's*, there was a bit of a ritual they had implemented. There was a small clothes shop on Matthew Street called *Drome* that they regularly frequented prior to a 'big night out.' It was actually a posh women's boutique, and they often got some rather odd stares as they entered the place like a gang of binmen. In the corner of the shop, surrounded by ladies' clothes, stood a solitary clothes rack—a beacon in the dark. The rack was loaded with a selection of men's designer shirts with price tags attached to them way above what they should be spending on a shirt. Because they were designer, there tended to be just one of them, which was great as you wouldn't see anyone else in town wearing it, but a nightmare trying to find one in your size. The lavish purchase helped Jonno's status to sink into a red pool of debt and he could hear the shrill screams from his bank account as he handed over the cash.

Everyone needed a pat on the back now and again, and this was his, even if it was self-administered. The feeling he got walking into a club wearing his new, unique, and extremely expensive shirt, gave him a confidence boost.

They stayed local that weekend, offering the ladies of Liverpool city centre their dashing good looks and an exclusive viewing of their professional dance moves. Jonno's senses were alert and sharp from the cocaine he'd consumed, but his ears pricked when they caught the delectable sound waves punching through the opaque air of this now world-famous nightclub, Cream. Dancing shapes with dinner plate eyes obstructed their corridor to the bar and slowed their progression, as they hugged and high-fived all that impeded them.

Birchy carefully placed a minuscule square of paper into Jonno's hand.

'Be careful, it's fuckin' tiny,' he warned.

'What is it?' Jonno asked, inspecting it.

'It's LSD. It's double-dipped, so just take half of it and see how you go.'

Birchy's advice fell on deaf ears. Jonno now considered himself a seasoned competitor of recreational drugs and his warning presented no fear to his subconscious, which was fuelled by the coke running through his bloodstream. He didn't know what double-dipped meant, nor did he care. He swallowed the whole tab, washed it down with a gulp of lager and hoped that the smiley face on the piece of paper would soon transform to the expression on his face.

Jonno didn't need to wait for the effects of the LSD to take hold, as the cocaine already had him firing on all cylinders and ready to cultivate a forest. They all made their way to a decent area in the club to let the magic do its thing.

Jonno was already feeling good, bouncing around to the music, and he couldn't quite pinpoint when the tab started to affect him, as he was already intoxicated by everything else. He did notice a sharp pain in his chest creeping up and starting to aggravate him. He assumed it was indigestion. His head began to spin, and his brain took a nosedive into a surreal world. This was a unique, odd experience that was slightly disconcerting, yet he decided to accept it and continued to dance as his senses became the property of another force.

The pain in his chest continued to intensify, but his mind was distracted by the visual hallucinations his eyes were introducing it to. Groups of people became vivid, colourful swirls of movement, synchronised with the cadence of the music. The experience felt good for around an hour until his visions took a dark, sinister turn and a feeling of solitude overwhelmed him.

The club was already dimly-lit, but a cloud of black mist slowly churned like a lazy twister and encompassed the room. Cheerful faces became twisted and jaded as the murky, acrid gas overcame the animated figures whilst slowly infecting his mind. His chest pain had amplified and was now causing him extreme discomfort and concern. He was puzzled how a tiny piece of paper could be causing him so much physical pain and he was beginning to worry that his rising blood pressure, which he could feel bubbling inside him, would cause his heart to burst through his chest. His brain was now battling between the horror of a having a heart attack and the spine-chilling visions that were polluting his mind. Deformed, twisted figures hobbled about to the music, which was now suppressed into the hideous bubble he had become entrapped in.

The shuffling creatures bobbed in and out of view from beyond the black haze, and occasionally, a ray of light would catch their face, revealing a scaly, reptilian demon with abnormally distended eyes. The beautiful, joyful people that had surrounded Jonno thirty minutes earlier had transformed into elderly people, pointing their creepy, skeletal fingers at him in condemnation.

He was distracted from the excruciating chest pain and his emaciated adversaries by something brushing against his legs. As he looked down to his feet, he caught glimpses amongst the blackness of vivacious pink swirls. He shook his head and blinked hard in a futile attempt to focus his eyes, but the images were beyond his comprehension and afar of his normal world. The blackness momentarily cleared to reveal a dozen pink flamingos vehemently poking at his feet and circling him in a predatory frenzy. He stepped back twice, partly in shock, and partly to create some distance between himself and the flock of exotic birds, which appeared to have a fanatical attraction to his feet. As he stepped backwards with his open palms perpendicular to him, he felt the sanctity of a wall, which offered a brief respite to the light-headedness that had previously contaminated him. Naz appeared through the throng and clenched his arm. Jonno thought he looked and sounded normal. *Maybe he was okay and wasn't enduring this living nightmare, or maybe I was just so far gone that I had lost all grip on reality*, he mused.

'Jonno, are you okay?'

'No, mate, my chest is fuckin' killin' me. I mean, like really bad, and there's fuckin' creatures everywhere. It's bad; this is bad.'

'Calm down, mate, you're just having a bad trip. I'll get you some water.'

Naz's reassuring tone fell on deaf ears as Jonno's levels of terror and paranoia intensified. His mind was now in control of everything; his eyes, the pain he was feeling, and the disabling numbness that had pinned him to the wall and was currently preventing his legs from functioning properly.

He slowly stared down at his feet with trepidation and eyed a more terrifying apparition than the tenacious flamingos, which had now disappeared. His feet were now vicariously perched on a crumbling stone ledge, revealing a sheer drop of a thousand feet into a sea of eternal darkness. He forcefully pushed himself against the wall and desperately tried to grip the flat surface of the wall with his clammy hands and fingernails. The panic was overpowering, which caused his heart to beat faster and harder, whilst his body was being eaten by paranoia and his eyes rolled around his head looking for a haven of safety. He frantically tried to make his legs move in an attempt to slide further along the ledge, but his mind was much stronger than his body and had full control of this horrific ordeal. All his intelligence, realistic thinking and valour had been consumed by a demonic episode that now had him in fear of his life.

Gigantic vampire bats rose from the black canyon below him, creating blasts of air in his face as they flapped their hideous, prehistoric wings and violently shook their fang-filled heads. The stale smell of blood and death from their unsightly bodies loaded his nostrils as they whizzed past with a formation and strategy that left no breather. Each brutal attack was accompanied with a deathly scream. He made a feeble attempt to flap them away with his hand, but then became overcome with the fear of falling off the ledge. This was dreadful.

Naz appeared and pushed a bottle of water into his chest.

'Drink this.'

Jonno took the bottle and drank enthusiastically. He was burning up and his face was on fire. Naz took his arm and guided him away from the dancefloor to a quieter, more chilled area and motioned at him to drink again. He finished the contents of the bottle and looked around at the new environment. Although he was still considerably spaced out, the hallucinations were starting to ebb away a little, although the chest pain was as strong as ever and the occasional bat whipped past him.

'I've got to go, mate.'

'No way, we've only been here a couple of hours,' Naz said, in a state of shock.

Jonno shook his head.

'This isn't going. I've got to get out of here. Tell the lads for me?'

'I can't leave you, Jonno. I'll come home with you.'

'Naz, please, I don't want any drama, mate. I'll be fine when I get outside. I'll speak to you tomorrow.'

With that, Jonno slapped Naz's arm, spun on his heels and marched towards the exit before Naz had any time to protest. As Jonno walked past the lizard-faced bouncers, he could feel their crystal, reptilian eyes burning through him. He felt as though he was walking straight and holding it together, but the voices in his head told him they knew he was as high as a kite and were condemning him without evidence. One of the lizards' opened one of the thick black double-doors to the world outside. As soon as Jonno stepped into the street, an icy burst of wind attacked him and took advantage of his sweat-soaked shirt. The merciless chill instigated its assault at his neck then patrolled his back and front with crippling frosty circles. He rubbed his body and contracted all torso muscles in a feeble attempt to fight off the chilly aggressor.

The cold was a temporary distraction from the surreal and menacing condition the LSD had put his mind in. He felt slightly more focused, but still had chest pains, a feeling of utter despair, and felt completely removed from normality.

He walked to the corner of the street and sat down on a cold, dwarf wall to gather his shit.

'Danny?'

He looked up to see that it was Maggie Layton. He'd been chasing this girl for years without success, largely due to her boyfriend being a stumbling block and the fact he was always pissed whenever he tried to talk to her. She had a head of jet-black curly hair and a smile as wide as the Mersey. She was wearing a thin, see-through white blouse that revealed a black bra, black hot pants over black tights and small-heeled shoes, the type you'd go tap dancing in.

'Hiya Maggie, what you up to?'

He concentrated intensely on not talking like a bumbling idiot, when in reality, he could barely concentrate on breathing right.

'I'm on my way home. Do you wanna share a taxi?'

Now, that was an offer Jonno couldn't refuse for two fundamental reasons. One, he was in no state to tackle the organisation required to source a ride home, and two, this was a free opportunity to get closer to a girl he'd been pursuing for a long time.

Jonno was scarcely feeling the warmth of the taxi before Maggie shifted over to him, flopped her thigh over his and planted her lips on his mouth. He felt slightly embarrassed that this was happening in front of the taxi driver, but the warmth of her raspberry Chapstick lips and slightly clammy body offered an attractive proposition. The appealing smell of her perfume filled his nose and her curly hair fell upon his face as they kissed passionately without reprieve.

By the time the taxi had dropped them off at Jonno's house, they were both highly charged and were on the floor undressing each other seconds after flinging the front door open. She straddled him, riding convincingly as he sat upright, gripping her upper ribs from either side. He noted that her body was more compact than

Becky's, more solid. There was no fat on her whatsoever, but she had quite an unyielding, robust unit that made the sex ardently physical, bordering on the aggressive. The scratches she left etched in Jonno's back would be displayed for several weeks to come. The drugs had laid him in a competitive and enthusiastic condition, and he was ready to enjoy Maggie all night. However, what happened for the next hour or so was wasted and principally deleted by his memory, due to the semi-conscious and surreal state his mind had been entrapped in. He could vaguely recall Maggie calling herself a taxi and leaving, but he was too wasted to confirm this for sure.

13 FRACAS ON THE SABBATH

Jonno woke with a start due to the banging on his front door. He instantly jumped out of bed and desperately looked for his jeans to hide the embarrassment of the wigwam that had erected itself in his boxer shorts.

He opened the front door slightly to reveal to his exhausted eyes, a strong beam of sunlight, and a slightly impatient friend.

'For fuck's sake, Naz, I was still in bed.'

'Shurrup, ya tit. I was worried about you,' he said, as he pushed Jonno backwards to allow himself in. Jonno wondered if anyone ever waited to be invited in.

'How did you get home?' he asked, as Jonno turned around to reveal his clawed back.

'Oh, fuck me! You dirty bastard!'

'What?'

'Mate, you looked like you've been attacked by a fucking werewolf.'

'Who did that?' he probed.

'Maggie Layton.'

'Get in, lad! You've been after her for years. Nice one, la.'

'Yeah, but it all felt wrong, Naz. I was proper fucked up. I can't remember half of it and I'm not even sure I wanted it. I feel shite on Becky.'

'Becky's gone, Jonno. She's not interested, and you need to move on. You're doing okay if you're bangin' Maggie Layton.'

Jonno filled the kettle, flicked its switch, and sat at the dining table, shivering slightly from the introduction of the mid-winter temperature.

'So, why are you knocking me up at the crack of dawn?'

'It's actually half-ten but I wanted to check on you after last night mate. You were really fucked up, you know? Kept bangin' on about bats and fuckin' flamingos.'

Naz's brief overview of the horrendous experience should have been quite funny, but it wasn't. It was a chilling reminder for Jonno of the haunting ordeal. The pain was still sharp in his chest and the memory still vivid in his mind. His soul had been kidnapped for a night, and his brain and body had been left scarred by a living nightmare that would stay with him forever. He took a sip of his coffee and paused before answering to allow some of the fear to drain from his thoughts.

'It was fuckin' horrible, mate. I hated it and I will never do that shit again. I thought hippies who did LSD were all fuckin' loved-up?'

'That's because you necked it all, lad. Birchy said just do half. We did, and we were all sound. You had to be *Billy Big Bollocks*.'

'Well, I won't be doin' that again. I will stick with the tablets,' Jonno said without conviction because he wasn't even sure he wanted to continue on the tablets. Maybe this thing had run its course.

Naz's voice changed.

'I need a favour, Jonno. That's why I'm here.'

'Go on then—spit it out.'

'It's my Sunday to have Emily. I want you to come with me in case that slag kicks off.'

'Ah, I dunno, mate. She might see it as if we're gangin' up on her.'

'Just hang in the background. Please, Jonno, I need this, mate.'

Why do I always find myself in these ridiculously impossible situations, caught between potentially failing a friend in need, and walking into the lion's den? Jonno moaned to himself. He wasn't bold enough to be straight with Naz and say no, and not apathetic enough not to care about any trouble Jodie might create. He had to look at the bigger picture and foresee the more severe impact of his decision. It was easy—he would stick with Naz.

'For fuck's sake, okay.'

Naz pulled his racing green Rover 200 up outside Jodie's semi-detached council house on the Whitchurch Estate with a thud, as he clipped the kerb and squashed a cheap, *Halfords* traffic cone. He removed the crushed cone that a resident had used to illegally save themselves a car speck, from underneath his balding front tyre and lashed it onto the pavement.

He rapped on Jodie's door, whilst Jonno held back sheepishly by the garden gate and tried to camouflage into the background. Jonno did a quick inspection of his surroundings. One of her neighbours was playing extremely loud heavy metal which was being painfully neutralised by reggae from over the road. There were whiffs of marijuana coming from somewhere, and an annoying nursery rhyme played from an ice cream van in the distance. The winter temperature was still bitterly low, yet neighbours sat in their front gardens on dining room chairs, smoking and chatting to each other. Jonno looked up at a tyre precariously hanging from the bend of a lamppost, which was kept company by an old pair of Diadora trainers. His eyes were momentarily distracted from the lamppost by a glistening silver jumbo effortlessly cutting through the clouds.

He still desperately wanted to be on that plane.

Naz hammered the door again, and then for a third time. Jonno looked up at the first-floor window to see the curtains moving. A hand banged on the window glass as if to confirm that they had heard the door. After a short period of shuffling and banging, the front door opened to reveal a rather dishevelled Jodie. She was wearing a thigh-high pink silk dressing gown that exposed her tanned legs, pink painted toenails, and an average portion of revealed breast. Her hair looked as if she'd just squeezed out of a motorcycle helmet, and her face brought rage and retribution.

'What?' she barked.

Naz quickly glanced around at Jonno, as if to validate the venom and condescension he tolerated every time he tried to see his daughter. This little girl was his world and made him tick. He would have long reacted to Jodie's brutal treatment and threats were it not for the fear of never seeing little Emily again. This little monkey could bring a ray of sunshine to the saddest of eyes and she was the one thing currently keeping Naz's head above the quicksand that obstructed their daily path.

'It's Sunday. I've come to get Emily.'

Emily's head appeared around the kitchen door at the bottom of the carpetless corridor and she waved to him to acknowledge his arrival. Jodie turned around to see what Naz was smiling at and ushered the child away, yelling,

'Get back in.'

Naz stepped forward slightly.

'Don't ever talk to my little girl like that again, you filthy whore.'

That was it. Naz had lost it. Things could only go from bad to worse now.

'Gerroff me, ya fuckin' dickhead,' she screeched, as she attempted to remove Naz's hand from her displaced gown, whilst simultaneously trying to slam the door in his face. Naz was quick and had already placed his foot in the threshold causing the door to continuously bounce off his trainer, no matter how many times she tried to slam it. The racket was attracting the attention of some of the neighbours and more importantly, had awoken a sleeping dragon. *The Gargoyle*, who was the obvious candidate for causing Jodie to have no clothes on at lunchtime, plodded down the stairs, a cantankerous bear arising from hibernation, made his way to the front door.

He wasn't appropriately dressed for the occasion either, naked except for a pair of dark blue Admiral England shorts which appeared to have survived the 1982 World Cup. His choice of shorts spoke volumes of the man's integrity, thought Jonno. His semi-nakedness revealed a muscular, well-toned torso which sported a three-inch badly-mended scar on his stomach and a blank panther tattoo on his right upper arm. His legs and feet were excessively hairy. His hobbit trotters received more of Jonno's attention than they deserved. His eyes were squinted, and his face reddened with rage and adrenalin when he saw that it was Jonno and Naz who were the cause of the doorstep distress. He flew to the front door, pushing Jodie aside, and inflicted a powerful jab to Naz's stomach, sending him backwards.

'Fuck off, ya pair of fucking gimps,' he bawled, his face contorted with rage.

The commotion had attracted a couple of equally ugly barbarians from the house opposite who appeared to be keen to offer their services to *The Gargoyle*. Both of them were inappropriately dressed for the outside temperature, and they'd looked like they belonged sat in a caravan parked on industrial wasteland.

As Naz recovered from the blow and readjusted his stance in order to push forward, Emily screamed from the corridor,

'Daddy!'

Jonno grabbed Naz by the jacket and vigorously pulled him backwards towards himself, to give them a moment to think. *Let me do the maths quickly in my head,* Jonno thought. *The Gargoyle* would be an awesome combatant. Heavy with muscle, scarred through battle and fuelled with an *I don't give a fuck* attitude. These elements make the most dangerous of enemies. It would be debateable whether Naz and Jonno could handle *The Gargoyle* on their own, but his two soldiers located behind the fence, made this a difficult, and one-sided affair. They were also completely unaware of what their opponents may be carrying and how many more of them would crawl from their decrepit hellhole.

The Gargoyle strode onto the doorstep, fists clenched, his woodpigeon chest pumped out, arms shaped to comfortably carry two rolls of invisible carpet. Beads of sweat had formed on his brow and ran over the protruding veins in his temple that pumped close to explosion. He bounced on both feet simultaneously to boast of his agility and handy footwork, in addition to his punching ability.

'Come on, ya fuckin' paki. Do you want some?'

This articulate young man had stepped into a new library and was now flexing his vocabulary on a different level. It mattered not that Naz's heritage was Moroccan—it would be a complete waste of time pointing this out to such a moronic bigot, whose education probably consisted of sniffing glue in a wet bus stop, thought Jonno. It didn't bother Naz. He'd heard worse and he'd heard it a million times before, but it bothered Jonno. The views and opinions of racists had stuck in his craw and he was bewildered by their judgment and reasoning. It made him sick. Naz had been oppressed all his life but his ability to let hate wash over him made him inspirational to Jonno. It clearly showed the deep-rooted class that filled Naz's personality—he was awesome! In fact, the only time Jonno ever saw Naz lose his cool, was around Jodie. She conjured up the demon in him.

Naz was born in England and knew nothing of Morocco. His skin was different, his name was unusual, but his soul was as identical as the friends that treated him as their brother.

Jonno often wondered whether he'd be so defensive if someone was poking fun at Naz because he was fat, skinny, or ginger. He supposed he would not be so offended by that. So, why did the colour of his skin upset him so much, when Naz appeared to let it sail over himself? Jodie also appeared unconcerned, regardless of the fact that her child carried Naz's ethnicity.

Jonno moved forward, shoving Naz to the left to facilitate a confrontation with the vile animal. He was no longer afraid— the burning fury that raged within him could summon the strength and speed to overcome *The Gargoyle*. Jonno's confidence rocketed.

Naz swiped his arm across Jonno's chest and pointed down the corridor to Emily. She was crying uncontrollably and screaming for her dad, but too scared to run towards him following the earlier warning from Jodie.

'Leave it, Jonno. I don't want Emily to see this.'
This would be the second time Jonno had backed down from *The Gargoyle* but they'd both been impossible situations and there was only one option available to him each time. They backed up slowly.

The Gargoyle stood proud and triumphant.

Naz kept his cool.

'I'm taking this to court—you don't deserve her.'
Naz then faced the monstrous creature that Jodie had attached herself to and left him with a parting caution.

'Your time's comin', cunt!'
The Gargoyle swiped a fresh air-kick at them, which in reality had more chance of connecting with the rose bush and left his own departing statement.

'Go on, fuck off, ya pair of shithouses. You aven't got a fuckin' clue who yer messin' with.'
They pushed past the neighbourhood back-up, got in the car, and sped off with a wheel spin.

14 THE WITCH

Monday was painfully dragging for Jonno. He was worried that now he was twenty-four, every morning would get a little harder to drag himself out of bed and to work. Maybe the pain and effort required increases a little every day, and that's why most folk are forced to retire in their sixties and spend most of the day napping he wondered. The napping in the day sounded attractive to him but it was a solid, full night's sleep he really needed. The dwindling effects of the drugs and his worries tortured his brain every night, which increased his fear of not getting up on time for work.

He'd lie in bed with a completely shot body that begged for rest, but his brain refused to quit, constantly running dramatically haunting visions, and catapulting him with unanswered questions.

The come-down from the drugs was way beyond the worst of hangovers. A hangover could be conquered in a day. Sometimes a decent breakfast and a game of football would wash away the poison. But the cocaine and tablets were powerful enough to bring down a rhino in its prime. Tenacious and incessant, it just wouldn't leave you alone and could last for days. He would suffer into the week, sometimes still feeling ill on a Wednesday, but he always started to pick up towards the end of the week as talk of another night out commenced.

I'm not an addict.

I know I'm not addict because I didn't need to take anything during the week, he convinced himself.

In fact, the thought of it repulsed him. However, the notion of going to a club playing dance music without being under the influence of a mind-numbing narcotic was distinctly more abhorrent. Drinking alcohol to dance music just didn't touch the right spots. It was a different animal. He was way beyond the effects that alcohol could offer.

The experience and the after-effects of Jonno's introduction to LSD at the weekend had caused him to reflect on his current weekend habits and he'd spent a fair bit of time mulling over quitting the whole scene. Nonetheless, the ritual had now become a way of life and a gel that connected him to his friends. Without it, he would be dislocated from the world, and, following his break-up from Becky, that was the last thing he needed.

Jonno came up with a solution that would be his point of reference going forward. He decided that the highs currently outweighed the lows. If that changed, he would stop doing it. At present, he was struggling to get through the first part of the week through tiredness, which was exacerbated by his body being under-fuelled due to appetite suppression. However, the feeling of complete freedom and ecstasy the chemicals gave him, even for a night, was worth the side effects.

Naz looked notably distant and distressed when Jonno whacked him over the head with a rolled-up Daily Star as he entered the welfare cabin.

'What's up with you, face-ache?'
Naz nodded his head sideways and beckoned Jonno to follow him to the drying room. He pushed aside a couple of paint-splattered overalls and sat down on the slatted wooden bench.

'Haven't you heard?'
This is quite possibly the most pointless question in the English language thought Jonno because no one had *ever* heard the information that followed the question. Regardless, he played

along.

'Heard what?'
Naz pinched both his cheeks together with one hand and took a breath.

'Isaiah's dead.'
It took a moment or two to register with Jonno.

'Wha? How?'

'Him and Willo went out the weekend and hammered the tablets.'

'Is Willo dead?' Jonno hoped this wasn't going to get any worse.

'No, he's fine, but he's had the bizzies crawling all over him.'
Naz computed Jonno's confused look as a request to produce more information.

'Willo reckons they'd had five or six tablets during the night. That's what he is saying now, but he could be lying. It could have been more. He said the club was fuckin' roastin' and there was sweat dripping off the walls, the whole place was on fire. Sounds like some underground hole. Apparently, Isaiah collapsed and started convulsing and frothing at the mouth. Willo said he thought it was a piss-take and was laughing at him at first. By the time the ambulance got to the club, he was stone cold dead. Gone!'
Jonno sat on the bench opposite Naz as a growing feeling of light-headedness and nausea overcame him.

'They reckon it was a heart attack. Twenty-one years old, he was.'

Jonno spent the next moment or two listening to the heated debate inside his head between the *evil, 'fuck them all'* Danny and the *caring, sensible* Danny. The news was horrific. How awful for the young lad and all his grieving family and friends he had left behind.

How was this allowed to happen?

Where was the help?

Didn't the club have a first aider?

This was the catalyst for Jonno to stop now. This was the sign, the message from God saying, *next time Johnson, it might be you.* This was the kick up the backside he needed.

Whoa, hold up there, Johnson, he counselled.

Isaiah knew the risks. He wasn't new to the game and he had blatantly pushed it too far by swallowing handfuls of tablets. This doesn't affect your tactics; you've got too much to lose by spewing it all in now. Don't do too much, stay hydrated, and continue to have the time of your life. This wasn't the time to make knee-jerk reactions.

Evil Danny made some decent points and offered up a robust defence. You have to look at the odds with conundrums like this. How many thousands of ravers were popping pills every weekend and going home safely compared to the odd one that never made it? *It was more likely that I'd get hit by a bus,* but on the flip side, *how would my mum feel identifying me on a mortuary slab?* He clearly needed more time to debate this but Naz interrupted his deliberations.

'It gets worse, lad.'
Jonno lowered his cupped hands from his eyes.

'How can it get worse?'

'Me and you have been randomly selected for an alcohol and drugs test by the hierarchy.

'Why? Do you think they know?'

'No mate, it's completely random. Just bad luck—and bad timing.'

They were working on a large chemical plant, decorating their welfare areas, canteen, control room, and a handful of offices.

'These fuckers had been proper bellends with the safety shit right from the start. It started with a day of inductions, risk-assessing farts, wearing your hard hat to go for a piss, and now drug-testing us. They are five-star generals of health and safety,' moaned Naz. Jonno hadn't touched a drop of beer since Sunday so he knew he was safe there. More concerning was the hallucinogenic, double-dipped tab of nastiness that still owned his mind and body. There was no way it was going to stay quiet, and he predicted it would sing like a canary if some safety do-gooder were to ask *is there anyone in there*?

Jonno went into instant panic mode and his brain started to flood with concerns about losing his job and them informing the police. He felt like he was under the influence again and started to have flashbacks of the vile experience he'd endured on Saturday night. He was struggling to talk properly to Naz.

'What the fuck. We're fucked. I'm fucked. What if they…? Oh, fuck!'

Naz grabbed the side of Jonno's neck, momentarily neutralising his dread and shaking body.

'Calm down, Dan. You don't even know the results. You'll be fine, mate. Get your shit together because you're gonna look like a fuckin' baghead if you go in there all sweatin' and shakin.' Naz was of course, spot on with his advice about the fashion in which Jonno was conducting himself. His confidence of the results, however, left him cynical.

They sat in the corridor, just outside the room where they were doing the testing. It was notable that they were the only two sat there and no one else from their company was being tested. Naz was called in first and it was about five minutes before Jonno was called in. Naz never came out the same door, so he deduced there was a second door for '*the accused*' to leave in shame. As he entered the room, Jonno discovered it was actually a First Aid room. It contained a padded bed, a desk with two chairs, a life-sized plastic skeleton, a modesty curtain, and several green first-aid boxes. The painted brick walls were plastered in NHS advice posters only breached by a toilet door and the second *'door of shame.'*

'Sit down please, Danny. My name is Lindsay Carrington, and I will be undertaking your test today.'
Well, wasn't Lindsay a sight for sore eyes, Jonno drooled. He guessed she was around 28 years-old. She had really fair hair with blonde streaks, a slender tall figure, and an air of confidence that augmented her attractiveness.

A radio that sat on the windowsill was playing Luther Vandross just loud enough for Jonno to distinguish the song. He wondered if that was for her benefit or an attempt to relax whatever target was under the microscope. Jonno should have been panicking as he desperately hung on to his job, but all he could think about was how attractive Lindsay looked. *There must be something wrong with me to be having visualisations like this, at a time like this. There was definitely some lose wiring in my head,* he fretted. Lindsay waffled on about some legal stuff and asked questions about the last time Jonno had eaten, had a drink and was he a substance user. He nodded and shook his head accordingly.

An overwhelming cloud of embarrassment consumed him. This would have been so much easier for him if it were a middle-aged man carrying out the test and not a drop-dead gorgeous girl. Jonno was thinking she must be judging him purely because he'd been selected for testing. He didn't see any suits in there. She removed a plastic tube from a bag and clipped it onto the breathalyser. Jonno had never been tested before but he'd seen them, and he knew what it was.

'The drink-drive limit in this country, Danny, is thirty-five micrograms. If you blow anything higher than zero micrograms, we have to wait for at least twenty minutes and then retest to ascertain if your alcohol level is rising.'

At this point, Idiot No.1 considered that sitting with Lindsay for another twenty minutes didn't seem like the worst thing in the world, and he half-hoped there was some lingering alcohol content in his blood. The loose wiring in his head led him to believe that spending a brief time with a girl that wasn't interested in him was better than keeping his job.

Knobhead No.1's sexual innuendo quotes reached *'Carry On'* status when Lindsay asked him to *give this a big blow*. Here he was, about to clip the wire to diffuse a bomb and all he was thinking about was Lindsay's completely unintentional verbal advances. He followed her instruction and blew hard until the machine bleeped. She waited a couple of seconds before checking it and then revealed that he had blown zero.

Thank fuck for that, he thought but it wasn't really a surprise. The real test was imminent.

'Right, Danny, I now require a sample of your urine, please. Could you use the toilet behind you and pee into this for me?' She handed him a large plastic beaker.

Idiot No.1 was begging him to say, *do you fancy giving me a hand with it?* Jonno managed to block out his mischief and entered the toilet, locking the door behind himself.

He stood there with his plonker in one hand and the empty beaker in the other. His brain begged the knob to perform with verses of *please come out, please come out*. However, it looked like this manhood had downed tools and really wasn't interested in playing the game. He'd been shaking it for what seemed like an age, trying to force out a pee, before there was a tapping at the door.

'Are you okay in there, Danny?'

'Yeah, I'm fine. Won't be a sec.'

He'd resigned himself to having to tell her he couldn't perform under pressure and may need to drink some water but decided to give it one last push. He closed his eyes, emptied his brain, and breathed out slowly. Finally, the valve opened, and the waters flowed. He easily filled the beaker she gave him and had to fire the remaining contents into the pan. He washed his hands way longer than he normally would in case she could hear the tap running and judged him for just giving them a quick rinse. He carefully opened the door and walked towards Lindsay with the urine-filled beaker using the same level of concentration required to carry a newly-filled ice tray over to the freezer. She sniggered as she relieved him of the abundantly filled beaker and said,

'I only needed a drop, Danny. You didn't need to fill the thing.'

'Oh shit, sorry.'

'Don't worry, everyone does it. It's my fault for not telling you.'
She slipped on a pair of disposable gloves and took out a slim strip
of paper from a box.

'Okay Danny,' she said, dipping the paper strip into his pee, 'we
are now going to test for the presence of any illegal or prescribed
substances. If we detect something during the test, we call this
non-negative. This doesn't always indicate that something is
wrong, and further analysis would need to be carried out at a
laboratory. We are testing today for the following substances:
Methamphetamine, Cocaine, Benzodiazepine, Cannabis, Opiates,
Barbiturates, Methadone, PCP, Propoxyphene, Methlaquone and
Amphetamine.'

Jonno's mind drifted and struggled to compute the words being
thrown at him before refocusing on a target word that he caught.

Shit! Cocaine.

He heard her say Cocaine.

*I am fucked! Where's LSD? Did she say that? How long does this
shit hang around in your body?*

He went into meltdown level 10. Beads of sweat invaded his
forehead, and he could feel his temperature increase. He felt weak
and shaky, and dropped into a surreal world with a mouth as dry as
a bone. He looked at her and pleaded with her in his mind to give
him a break. She looked up at him as she removed the paper from
the urine and slightly shook it. Jonno thought she could see into his
soul and could see that he was dishonest and a liar. She knew he
was a druggie, and this piece of paper was about to confirm it
whilst concurrently tearing his life apart. He felt like he was letting
her down and wanted to explain to her that he wasn't a *baghead*
and just *titted* about sometimes. He was actually a good guy who

was going through a bit of a tough time and had found some solace in a recreational scene that promoted life and love.

Idiot No.1 told him to stop whining and informed him that *she really didn't care about some prick that paints walls for a living and sniffs beak at the weekends. Her boyfriend was probably an accountant or solicitor and certainly wouldn't be some unhinged melt like you!*
She placed the piece of paper next to a colour chart and compared the various coloured stripes.

'Yes, that's fine, Danny. No issues here, and you're free to go back to work.'

'Eh?'

'You sound surprised, Danny. Were you expecting a different result?
She wasn't stupid. She must have known he was panicking and completely guilty. He stood up and started to head for the exit door. He desperately wanted to ask her out but didn't have the nerve to do it, and the timing felt all wrong anyway.

'OK, thanks for your time.'
He made a pathetic attempt to get some reaction from her, but she just nodded without making eye contact.

When Jonno arrived back at the welfare area he saw Naz sat at a table nursing a paper cup of coffee and a bad mood. He excitedly bounced over to him, elated by his recent mini-triumph, and couldn't wait to tell him how he'd duped the system.

'Smashed it, mate. Fuckin' smashed it,' he tooted whilst slapping Naz's back.

'Nice one, la, well done.'
Naz didn't look up from his cup of coffee.

'No? Surely not?

'Yeah, I failed it. Traces of cocaine,' he said.

'But how can I pass, and you fail? I was worse than you. I was off my tits.'

'Dunno, mate, but I'm fucked. I'm going to lose my job and they were talking about calling the bizzies. I've been told to wait here.'

Oh shit! This was the last thing Naz needed, the way his life had been going lately. This was going to ruin him, and maybe the business. If the business folded, that was Jonno screwed too. This was bad. Jonno didn't know what to say to the lad.

'Ah mate, I don't know what to say. Maybe the lab results will come back different.'
He put his hands to his face and started sobbing whilst hunching his shoulders up and down. Jonno put his hand on his shoulder and patted it lightly as he stood over him. He started to blub louder and some of the other contractors in the welfare room started looking over, obviously talking about him. Naz then began whining ridiculously loud and screaming. It was embarrassing and most of the lads in the room were laughing at him as Jonno tried to get him to pull himself together. Jonno could see Naz's face and neck getting redder equal to the rise in decibel levels of his crying. He put his head between his knees before slowly rising upwards and exploding into laughter. His face was crimson with joy, his eyes streaming, and he was roaring with amusement at Jonno's gullibility.

'Ya fuckin' wanker,' Jonno said.

'Of course I passed, ya tit,' he choked through tears and laughter.

They went back to work and plodded through the day. Naz lasted twenty minutes at some stages before banging on again about his master prank. *Fucking hilarious,* moaned Jonno. Regardless of the results of the drugs test, they had diced with death and Jonno found the whole experience uncomfortable. There was a big risk— and so many potentially severe outcomes. Jonno spent most of the day trying to figure out if the bad times had begun to outweigh the good. He also deduced that Lindsay probably did want him but had to remain professional for the sake of   her   career.

15 PARALYSED BY CRITTERS

Jonno wore an Adidas T-shirt and trainers and a pair of black Nike shorts. He gelled his hair to a perfect sculpture and splashed some water on the front of his chest to make it look like he'd been running for miles.

Despite his shallow victories with a couple of women since being ditched by Becky, he still desperately missed her and felt nothing for any other female. She'd left a hole in his life, and with Christmas just around the corner, the thought of spending it without her was eating him up inside.

His plan was simple. He knew what time she finished work and he knew the route she walked home. He would be randomly jogging on this route and accidentally bump into her, forcing her to talk to him. Once she saw how good he was looking and listened to his apology, he'd make her see that he was a good guy after all. That was the plan, he hadn't really prepared further than that and had no dialogue primed. He was confident that he could wing it.

As he stepped onto the street, the cold temperature filled his lungs, and his warm breath produced a cloud of icy mist when he exhaled in a mild state of shock. The mid-December sky was black and grey and rumbled angrily as heavy raindrops began to explode on the concrete paving slabs. The whine of cars on the nearby M53 rudely broke the eerie silence.

He'd been running for about ten minutes but had been taking it really easy so as not to look like he was knackered when he reached her. As he turned the corner at the foot of a mountainous hill, he saw her coming towards him cowered under an umbrella to protect her from the light sheets of rain. The umbrella gave Jonno an advantage as she wouldn't see him until he was almost upon her.

'Hiya Becky,' Jonno said as he slowly approached her before coming to a halt. She raised the pointed rim of her black brolly. Jonno looked at her intensely and marvelled at her beauty. He had no sexual thoughts about her. It wasn't that type of beauty that bowled him over. In no way, did he think about her sexually as he admired her astounding appearance and angelic face. She squinted and winced slightly as the rain struck her surprised face.

'Hiya.'
Not much of an enthusiastic response, but better than a slap or a cold shoulder, thought Jonno.

'How are you doing?' he asked, desperately trying to control his erratic breathing following ten minutes of running in the rain.

'Fine,' she said as she started walking again.
This was going to be much more difficult than Jonno had originally anticipated. He had to try a little harder but had to be careful not to come across as overpowering and desperate. It was a fine line.

'Look, Becky, I'm so sorry about what happened. I fucked up. I'm a dickhead,' he blurted out as he walked alongside her.

'Don't worry about it.'

'Well I do worry about it. I miss you.'
She continued to walk, silent and without reaction. He had one final attempt.

'I've got ya a Christmas present, ya know?'

He didn't have a present, but it was desperate attempt to pull on her heart strings and he could always pick something up if she reacted like she wanted it.

'You'd be best givin' that to the tart from the pub, Danny,' she said as she quickly looked behind her, and then crossed the road in order to put distance between them.

Wow, that hurt.

Jonno felt physically sick, and his body was paralysed, unable to move a single muscle. Reality finally right hooked him in the face; he was never getting this girl back. It really was over. His chest ached like it might collapse and his throat struggled to swallow the saliva his open mouth had created. He stood there in the driving rain for a moment or two watching her walk away, dreadfully hoping she'd turn around to check he was okay, but she didn't, and then turned the corner out of his life.

He plodded home and lay in the bath for over an hour trying to resuscitate his numb body and beaten heart. His brain and heart ached with pain and despair. He'd never experienced this feeling of loss before. He felt it was worse than losing someone through death because this person was still alive but didn't want him in their life. They disliked him so much that they never wanted to see him again, and this had truly broken him. At this point of time, it felt like he had no options, and he really couldn't see a way forward in the future.

Without Dr Emmett Brown turning up in the DeLorean time machine, I was well and truly fucked, he mused.

If I were to slip under the murky, warm waters of my bath, never to surface, would anyone ever care? A sad waste of space slipped away from the world without making a ripple.

Gloria Estefan ballads whined in the background as Jonno sunk can-after-can of lager, before collapsing onto his bed and falling asleep.

***

Getting up on a Saturday was usually difficult, but more so after the large hammer blow that had broken Jonno's mettle the night before. He had to try to put it to the back of my mind; tonight was the football team's Christmas piss-up. It was bad timing for him considering the black mood he'd fallen into, but he had to pull his shit together as this was the one night a year that they all went out together. Jonno thought about calling Naz to offload some of the weight that was burdening him, but he had enough on his plate, so he decided not to bother.

Jonno felt like one of the photographers from the 1800s who disappeared under a black sheet and removed all light from the outside world. He felt beaten and drugged by an evil spirit that had removed his energy and character with its hideous proboscis. It was slowly sucking the life out of him whilst he watched, defenceless and weak. Its hairy legs and heavy shell-like abdomen prevented him from moving as it perched upon his body gorging itself on his disabled muscles. Every tiny move and every simple thought required too much effort and energy that he just did not have. Jonno was drowning and everyone else around him was breathing perfectly fine. A supernatural force was pulling him to the dark, oily bottom of a sea of desolation and the harder he tried to reach the surface, the quicker he slipped into the depths. He felt sad, alone, and hopeless. The idea of going out with the lads filled him with dread. He didn't want to go.
As always, he was influenced and pressured by Naz, Steve and Birchy. There would be no way he could explain to them why he didn't want to go. Their persuasion had been a rescuing hand in the sea that dragged him into a lifeboat, safe from the ocean floor and a watery end. He was on the boat, but still surrounded by thousands of miles of dark waters and a strong burst of wind would have him over the edge and back in the water. For now, he felt content that he was aboard and rubbing shoulders with the people that mattered the most to him.

The Belvedere pub was situated bang in the middle of Market

Street, in the heart of Birkenhead. Hanging baskets with vivid red and striking violet flowers littered the façade, partially concealing the opaque windows and mysteries within. Roars of laughter, group singing, and compressed bass engulfed the street and drew you in with the twisted charms of a con artist. An icy breeze swept the street and cut into Jonno's poorly protected body. He hunched his shoulders and contracted his muscles in an unsuccessful attempt to defend himself.

Jonno had spent most of his teenage years hanging around outside local boozers, drenched in the smell of ale and the din of frivolity. He'd yearned to be old enough to walk into the pub with the young adults he watched enter full of life, Old Spice, and optimistic expectations.

An illuminous pink piece of card was sellotaped to the centre of the door's glass panel and boldly read in thick, black marker pen: 'PRIVATE PARTY.' This time, the lads were doing it differently. Every previous Christmas and end-of-season piss-up involved them hopping from one pub to another before the final destination of alcoholic oblivion. This year, the owners of the boozer, Ross and Sue, had organised a Christmas roast dinner, and their football manager had booked two strippers— or as he called them, exotic dancers.

The four of them piled into The Belvedere and were greeted by cheers from the lads who had already taken their seats at a long, narrow table occupying most of the lounge, brilliantly adorned with Christmas decorations.

'It's fuckin' Take That!' was fired at the lads.

Jonno made his way to the bar clutching a ten-pound note and was politely greeted by Ross and Sue who were busy behind the bar preparing for a night of bedlam and mischief. Sue was in her early forties but looked considerably younger—Father Time had been much more generous to her than Ross. She smiled when she saw Jonno and delivered a wink, which he was in no doubt had been offered to all the lads as they came in. Ross turned around to serve Jonno and greeted him with a hearty smile and a thumbs-up.

Jonno thought that Ross was a was a good guy and he had done a lot for the football team, injecting cash into the club on numerous occasions when they had struggled to pay pitch fees and registration. He also looked after the lads every Sunday, feeding them, and offering a slate for the boys who were struggling for cash until payday. He had black, tight curly hair with a receding hairline and an impressive, bushy moustache that gave him a resemblance to Groucho Marx. His enormous and rosy beach-ball face was in proportion with his large, rounded body. Jonno often wondered how Sue coped with such a large lump of a man bouncing on top of her. A short-sleeved white shirt clung to him and he had several top buttons undone to reveal a large, gold sovereign ring around a chain swaying across his hairy red chest. He offered out a chubby hand the size of a shovel, and then shook Jonno's much smaller hand with a boa constrictor grip.

'Put yer money away, Jonno lad, the first one's on me and Sue.'

'Nice one, Ross. Four tankards of your frothiest and finest ale, please, fella.'

'You watchin' the strippers, Ross?

'No, he absolutely is not!' said Sue.

'He'll be upstairs with me. Molloy will be looking after the bar.' Ross gave Jonno a disheartened look, but there was no way he would have been expecting to join them. Jonno was only asking him to wind him up.

'Not interested in any of that nonsense, Jonno, son,' he said with badly disguised disappointment.

Jonno took the beer back to the lads and parked himself between Steve and Naz, who already had paper party hats on. They had sunk around four or five pints before Sue and Ross brought out from the kitchen the most glorious roast dinners, abundantly loaded with crispy roast potatoes and succulent sliced turkey. The lads gorged themselves in-between spurts of uncontrollable laughter. They mocked each other and sniggered at stupid stories, predominantly narrated by Birchy.

Ross lined the bar with two shots each of tequila for everyone, before retiring to his first floor flat with Sue prior to the night's debauched entertainment. The combination of salt, tequila and lime took Jonno's taste buds through a rollercoaster of flavours and it felt like it was instantly affecting his sobriety. Molloy lined up another rack of shots and declared they were on the house. Jonno wasn't sure he had the authority to call this, but they weren't looking a gift horse in the mouth and bellowed with agreement, as the dancers sneaked into the pub and disappeared into the back room to get changed. They were accompanied by a middle-aged fella, in his early fifties, maybe, who sat outside the back room and waited for them. He was a scrawny costume of a man and looked as though he would offer little defence to the girls should things become boisterous with over-amorous aficionados. He sat quietly, avoiding eye contact with the lads, and slowly sipped on a straight double whisky.

Molloy cranked up the stereo system and Urban Cookie Collective's 'I've got the key' hammered the lads heads at ear-piercing levels. Dave Llewellyn stood on a chair to make himself visible, swept his burgundy mullet behind his ears and motioned to Molloy to lower the music. When the decibel level dropped, Dave clapped his hands together to get the attention of the raucous throng.

'Listen up, boys. We've had a brilliant season up to now, and we've got an important final coming up in two weeks, but tonight is about enjoying ourselves.'

'Sit down, ya fuckin' melt,' said Birchy.
Dave completely ignored his heckler and continued with his spiel.

'Will you please be respectful for our lovely dancers that have come all the way from Blackpool to entertain you tonight? Put your hands together for Denise and Sarah!'
Everyone cheered with excitement and anticipation. The door opened and out sauntered two blonde girls wearing black basques, black stockings and black heels.

'Get yer tits out,' shouted Birchy.

The older girl's thighs were littered with bruises in a range of colours and her eyes looked deprived of sleep. She poorly executed an entertainer's smile that exposed pain through its deception. She looked around twenty-five years old and appeared to be the girlfriend of the scrawny pimp, if the kiss she'd given him on the way in was anything to go by. Jonno wondered if the sadness in her face was because she was being forced to perform. He didn't know if her bony bodyguard was there to protect her, or there to ensure she delivered.

Her *dance* colleague was possibly ten years older. Her hair was tied up and revealed a face worn by alcohol and drugs. She didn't bother with the fake smile and went about her business methodically and free of enthusiasm. They spent around ten minutes gyrating close to each other and removing any item of attire they had left. Once completely naked, they navigated their way around the semi-circle of ardent young men and gave them all a short lap dance. Even Dave Llewellyn got forty-five seconds of rotating arse in his delighted face.

Birchy was being typically rowdy and verbal, and it hadn't gone unnoticed by the two experienced strippers, who made a beeline for him. The older one, who Jonno assumed was called Denise, whispered something in his ear. Jonno didn't catch what it was over the loud music and jollity of sixteen excited men, but he assumed by the thrilled look on Birchy's face that he was in full agreement with whatever had been proposed. The younger stripper stood with her back to Birchy, no more than twelve inches from his beaming smile and bated breath. She slowly bent over while her colleague sprayed a frothy mountain of shaving foam on her backside. Birchy was ordered to keep his hands by his side, but when instructed, he was to smear the foam around her exposed cheeks. He smiled with exhilaration, fuelled by the verbal backing of his teammates, and slowly leaned forward so that his face was less than six inches from her bum. At that second, the older stripper forcefully slammed her hand down onto her partner's backside causing an explosion of shaving foam that plastered all of Birchy's face and most of his unfashionable shirt. The place erupted with laughter. There were lads rolling around on the grubby, pub carpet who had lost the ability to stand up straight. Jonno was literally crying with laughter and felt like he might pee himself. Naz had his head in his hands, so choked up that he was no longer capable of observing the chaos developing around him. Birchy's fume-o-meter went off the scale. He stood up and scooped the foam from his face, desperately trying to remove the residue from his shirt. He was livid and looked like he wanted to punch someone, but due to the whole room laughing at him, he was in an impossible situation and just had to ride the wave of embarrassment. The girls got a colossal round of applause as they disappeared into the back room, collecting clothes as they retreated.

Dave shouted them all over to the bar where Molloy had prepared about thirty shots of *After Shock*, stood proudly in line. They drank into the early hours, laughing and joking, before a kebab and a taxi took them home.

16 THE QUACKS AND SMACKS

The Sunday hangover was absolutely brutal for Jonno, but it was the next few days that he would find the most challenging. His mood had slipped out of his control and he was in a very dark place. Circling black crows and dark clouds swirled above his head and obliterated any daylight attempting to fuel his day. Disturbing voices in his head constantly screamed at him,

'I am worthless. I am a shit person.'

The harder he tried to snap out of it, the worse it got, and the resulting failure increased the anxiety. He felt empty and numb; there was no emotion.

He felt as though he had a rope around his neck attached to a massive boulder and mustering up the energy to just move was hopeless. Everything he did required him to factor in this massive rock that had now become part of him. There was an important football final next Sunday and he was starting to get anxious about having no energy and doubted he'd make it.

There was obviously something wrong, so he booked an appointment at the doctors for Wednesday. He tried to assure himself,

Maybe I need a blood test to indicate a loss of iron or there was a vitamin deficiency that was eating away at my energy. They'd

probably give me some supplements and I'd be right as rain.

Jonno had to speak into an intercom and be buzzed in to gain entry into the doctors. Not really surprising, given that it was located in one of the most deprived council estates on the peninsula. He approached the counter, which was protected by a plastic screen, and waited for the receptionist to acknowledge his existence. A woman in her early sixties was sat on a tall stool in front of him scribbling away on a pad. Her stiff, tightly fitted granddad-collar matched the pursed look on her face. She knew he was there but continued to write and then picked up a ringing phone without casting a glance at him. He sniggered at the irony of never being able to get through to the doctors on the phone, yet here was *Miss bulldog features* answering it in a nanosecond as though her life depended on it. She eventually unravelled her forked tongue and barked at him to take a ticket and wait for his number to be called.

He slumped into a seat and looked down at his ticket,

Number thirteen, you couldn't fuckin' make it up.
He looked around the room to take in his surroundings. Posters for baby vaccinations, blood pressure checks, heart attack advice and prostate cancer warnings littered the walls, whilst *Radio 2* quelled the intermittent coughing. He discreetly studied the people in the room.

An elderly woman sat still and silent, seemingly content with her thoughts. An old gent of similar age flicked through *Country Life* magazine, occasionally snorting, and slowly blowing air from his mouth in disappointment and boredom. A mother kept one eye on her toddler in a cushioned playpen, whilst simultaneously enduring the constant, tedious questions from her older child. A girl around Jonno's age sat hunched like an old man and clung to a large scarf wrapped around her, evidentially protecting her from temperatures that she did not agree with. Jonno watched them all slowly disappear before fork tongued receptionist called out his number. Jonno knocked at the doctor's door and waited to be invited in. He wasn't sure if this was the standard general practitioner etiquette, but it seemed a better option than barging right in.

He was greeted with a warm smile.

'Hi, I'm Dr Warwick. How are you?'

'I'm sound, thanks.'

Jonno's stock reply didn't really work in context of the situation and environment.

'So what can I do for you, Mr Johnson?
Jonno shuffled his bum cheeks uncomfortably on the chair and exhaled forcefully, slightly embarrassed about what he was about to reveal.

'I'm shattered all the time. I've just got no energy or drive. Everything feels like an effort.'
She scribbled and nodded as she listened.

'Is there anything else that has changed about you, Mr Johnson?'
Jonno took a moment to think and considered whether or not he should tell her. It seemed the right thing to do, taking into account he was there.

'Well yeah. I feel a bit hopeless and can't really tolerate people. I'd rather be on my own. My body aches too.'
She nodded in appreciation, almost as if she were proud of herself for cracking the riddle.

'Okay, Mr Johnson. I'm going to ask you a series of questions. Please answer them accurately and honestly. You may have already answered some of these questions.'
She lay a form out in front of her with a pen in hand, poised for Jonno's answers.

'In the past two weeks, how often have you felt down, depressed, or hopeless?'
This felt like a leading question; like he'd already admitted these symptoms. The thing was, it was the truth and he had to answer candidly.

'Erm, pretty much all of the last two weeks to be honest.'

She ticked the fifth box in a row of five on her form. She moved the form from Jonno's sight when she discovered that he was watching her.

'Have you had any thoughts of suicide?'

'Absolutely not!' he snapped.

'How is your sleep?'

'Rubbish. I can't get to sleep, and when I do, I wake up about 3am with my brain flipping like I've overdosed on blue Smarties.'

'How is your energy?'

'As I said before, I'm constantly shattered.'

'Do you prefer to stay at home rather than going out and doing new things?'

'Yeah. If it weren't for my mates, I think I'd have stayed in for the last few months.'
She scribbled a few more notes at the bottom of her form while he waited patiently and tried to stop his foot bouncing up and down.

'Okay. It looks like you have depression, Mr Johnson.'
The comment whizzed past Jonno as if he were trying to identify the face of a person in the window of an accelerating train. He felt as though she wasn't talking to him, and certainly not about him. He needed clarification.

'Ya wha'?'

'I'd say you have mild depression, Mr Johnson. It's absolutely nothing to be embarrassed about.'

'No. Er, no. Is that what head-the-balls get?'
She seemed insulted by his question and shook her head.

'Look Danny, the brain gets sick sometimes, just like the rest of your body. It isn't terminal, and I'm sure we can get you back on track in no time,' she said.

'Have things been getting on top of you lately or has something happened that you would say may have affected you?'

'Well my girlfriend dumped me, and I don't think I really got over it.'

'These things take time, Danny. Your brain needs to process what has happened and work out a way to cope with the problem. I'm guessing you haven't allowed that to happen yet. We have a few options available to us.'

This was extremely difficult for Jonno to hear and he could feel his stress levels rising just listening to her. He thought depression was for nutcases and weak people that couldn't cope. Depression was for the drooling lunatics that you would see curled up in a dark corner unable to deal with the outside world and the daily hurdles we all face. There was a real stigma about this condition, and he was instantly worried about how he would hide this from his mates and work colleagues. He'd heard of people going off work with stress or depression and you'd never see them again. He used to scoff at how open they'd been telling their employer that they were suffering from something so embarrassing. He'd assumed that stress disappeared when you '*manned up*', had a bevvy, or just laughed it off. Surely this was just a mood he was going through, and it would disappear when things picked up for him. Maybe a new girl or a better job was the cure—he certainly didn't need any tablets or potions to tackle this, he just needed to get his act together and stop being such a tart. This was wholly embarrassing, he thought.

'So, have I got to go to a psychiatric ward?'
She sneered at his uneducated, inappropriate question.

'No, of course not. We could put you on a course of antidepressants, maybe Cipramil or Prozac, but these can have some uncomfortable side effects such as headaches, stomach pain, dizziness, and a general shaky, agitated feeling. However, I really don't think you have a strong case of depression and I don't want to prescribe strong medication if there are alternative options.'

'So what are the options?'

'I believe your depression is mild and I'd like to wait and see if it improves on its own, whilst monitoring you. We call this *Watchful Waiting*. I'd also recommend some lifestyle changes, such as reduction in alcohol intake and getting as much exercise as you can.'

'Well, I don't drink that much alcohol anyway,' Jonno lied, and was he hell telling her about the cocaine and tablet abuse. She slid a leaflet along her desk to him that was entitled *'Dealing with Depression'* and tapped on some phone numbers located at the bottom of the sheet, whilst continuing to talk.

'I'd like to see you again in two weeks, Mr Johnson, but if you feel you need to talk to me sooner, please call for an earlier appointment or call one of these numbers here, who can offer free counselling.'

Counselling? he thought. *Fuck that! I won't even be coming back to see you, I'm certainly not speaking to some bellend stranger over the phone.*

'OK, doctor, thanks very much.'

***

They'd all been looking forward to the final, and as the four lads entered the changing room, the atmosphere was upbeat, but serious. They knew it was game day and they had to get their *game face* on, as Dave called it. The lads all seemed cheerful, but there was no piss-taking or *titting* about. They were all up for it. Dave read the team out, which was pretty unnecessary, as anyone could predict the team every week based on who turned up.

It was a cold, grey morning and the pitch was barely playable following heavy rainfall. The lads got changed methodically and then sat quietly in preparation of Dave's battle cry. He stood at only 5'6" but gave the impression of an officious, towering figure as he pounced around the room rallying his troops before battle.

'Boys, we have worked hard to get here. We have faced adversity and oppression. People like us get fuck all for fuck all; we work for everything. We need to work hard today to gain victory. You know what this bunch of bastards are like and you know what that prick of a ref is like.'

'Who's the ref, Dave?' asked Lurch, the smallest goalkeeper in Britain.
Dave gave Lurch an exasperated look for butting in.

'It's Gorgeous Geoff, Lurch.'

Geoff had been on the local football scene since the dinosaurs and had got no better at refereeing during all that time. He was a man well into his sixties with an ignorant attitude and a deafness for listening to reason. He barely left the halfway line as his legs no longer allowed him to, and he would make decisions, usually the wrong ones, from a ridiculous distance away. Why the Birkenhead League would put this man in charge of a final was puzzling, but not surprising, given the rubbish they usually churned up. Geoff didn't like Dave, and vice versa. Geoff's attendance would almost certainly have a negative impact on the result.

'Don't bring any regrets back into this changing room. Give your absolute all. Leave nothing on the pitch. I want every shirt dripping in sweat when you come back in here—and a fucking big cup in your hands.'

'Let's fuckin' do these boys!' bellowed Birchy, followed by a rapturous roar of agreement from the battle ready warriors.

'Get them warmed up, Birchy, and let's win ourselves a cup!' snarled Dave.

The pitch was threadbare, sprinkled with patches of mud and showing signs that the winter weather had been victorious in most recent battles. Droplets of dew desperately clung onto the blades of grass in scarce supply and a thin blanket of frost covered the pitch, and partially disguised the white painted lines. The cheap polyester football shirts offered no protection from the mid-morning winter air and Jonno's nipples stood to attention. They knocked a couple of balls around to each other in order to familiarise their boots with the sodden ground and the weight of the ball.

Today's opponents, and their fellow finalists, appeared from the changing rooms and made their way to the pitch in an upbeat, confident fashion. Their adversaries, Irby FC, were somewhat of an enigma. Irby was a really nice part of the Wirral and relatively affluent, with some properties fetching in excess of a million. It has a rich history drenched in Viking roots and whilst being one of the smaller villages on the Wirral, it has a pleasant community and a low crime rate. However, the football team had dragged every low-life scumbag from all the neighbouring council estates and dumped them into the same changing room. They'd had many close battles over the last few seasons, which had always resulted in defeat for Jonno and the lads. More often than not, this was due to their superior skill, fitness, and ability to scare the life out of their challengers with vile threats and humiliation.

Today was different, though, because Jonno's teammates had grown as a team. They were now mentally stronger and would not bow to their threats of violence, and in addition, they had improved their fitness levels so that they could at least compete with them. The first fifteen minutes was cagey, as they bounced around the ring jabbing at each other and measuring distance and speed of reaction. They all knew that at some point, this bout would be toe-to-toe and the real men would have to stand up to face their demons. It was inevitable, and unavoidable.

Jonno's slippery, graceful winger, Billy Newton, flew speedily down the flank to be destructively halted by a roundhouse kick Chuck Norris would be proud of. Mayhem and chaos ensued. Every player, bar the goalkeepers, sprinted to the point of the car crash to remonstrate and push the enemy's chests with angry shoves and jabs. Birchy, of course, took it a little further and stood on players' toes whilst grabbing throats and digging exposed ribs. The referee tooted on his whistle continuously with the weak notion that the din would result in a halt to the melee. Order was eventually restored when a handful of sensible players pulled apart the aggressors and fragmented the group. The referee threw yellow cards at a couple of people, amazingly missing Birchy, and play resumed.

They got to halftime at nil-nil and Dave gathered the troops to deliver an inspiring speech whilst the lads gasped for breath and drank water from an old lemonade bottle.

'Get in, boys, get in. Fuckin' fantastic that, boys. Outstanding effort from everyone. You've got these proper worried about ya. Don't be gettin' involved in any of the shite they're creating. They're trying to wind you up and get you sent off. Keep these effort levels up and keep moving the ball around, let them do the work. 100% from everybody, and Birchy will be lifting a cup in 45 minutes!"
Everybody cheered before Birchy roared loud enough for their opponents to hear,

'C'mon boys, let's fuckin' do these twats!'

Revitalised, they entered the field of play with Dave's battle cry still ringing in their ears and an unbreakable bond that gave them the impetus to run through a brick wall for him. The first fifteen minutes of the second half were scruffy with no real clear-cut chances of any note. A poor back-pass from an Irby defender, that the goalkeeper failed to deal with, led to a corner to Jonno's team. Willo whipped in a delightful cross that was met with the head of their big centre-back, Chris Herrington. He stood 6'4" in his stocking feet but was ironically nicknamed Tattoo, after a dwarf actor from a seventies TV show. His bald head connected with the ball on its sweet spot and drove it into the net. Commotion erupted as they all sprinted towards the big man, screaming, and jumping for joy, before assembling in a swarm of hugs. Birchy screamed in the face of the centre-forward he'd been marking with venom and aggression.

'Have that ya fuckin' smackhead!'
The centre-forward convincingly pushed Birchy away in complete

shock and dissatisfaction at his ungentlemanly conduct. Birchy instantly reacted without thought or reason and slapped his antagonist across the face with a thunderous thud, causing his head to rock sideways and visibly weaken his stance. His nose started to bleed, and he retreated nervously from Birchy, who looked ready to fire off another warning shot as the red mist filled his eyeballs. Unfortunately, Gorgeous Geoff had seen the whole incident and screeched on his whistle before pacing towards Birchy, clutching a red card.

'You're off, lad!'
Birchy pleaded with the referee as Dave held his head in his hands on the side-line. His appeals were pointless as referees never changed their mind, and given Geoff's toxic relationship with Dave, he would never change his decision. Birchy trudged off the pitch shaking his head. Dave couldn't bring himself to look at him.

They now had the thick end of twenty-five minutes to hang on with ten men, and the loss of their captain and best defender. Irby brought two subs on and started passing the ball around with a swagger, whilst Jonno and his team desperately chased after it. After surviving an avalanche of pressure, a dinked ball from midfield sent an Irby attacker flying forward with Tattoo a yard behind him, frantically trying to keep up. As the forward reached their penalty area, with just Lurch to beat and five minutes left on the clock, Tattoo slid at the ball in a last-ditch attempt to stop the progression of his opponent. His timing and calculation were misjudged, and he clipped the centre forward's ankles, sending him spiralling downwards into a series of forward rolls. Geoff looked thrilled to be raising another red card and pointed to the penalty spot.

'Last man. You're off, lad.'
Tattoo looked distraught, but he'd made a split-second decision that could give them a fighting chance, even if it meant sacrificing his own attendance. Their left-back stepped forward and placed the ball on the penalty spot with care and concentration. A bony-looking boy who stood no taller than Lurch, with wiry red hair and sparrow legs.

'Bury it, Ginge,' his teammates enthused.
Lurch bounced up and down on his line trying to make himself
look bigger and clapped his gloves together, creating clouds of dry,
muddy dust. Ginge waited nervously for George to blow his
whistle, whilst Lurch growled like a strongman preparing to
attempt a record deadlift. Ginge jogged to the ball as the whistle
sounded and slotted a low, well-driven penalty to the left of Lurch.
The pocket-sized keeper took one sidestep, then jumped like a
prime Scottish salmon to palm the ball around the post for an Irby
FC corner.

*I think it was the best save I've ever seen in amateur football and
was almost unbelievable, given the height restrictions Lurch had
been dealt*, thought Jonno.
The lads ran over to congratulate Lurch and pat him on his back,
but he shoved them away and told them to concentrate on the
corner. It was all hands on deck and they were missing their two
tallest and strongest defenders. Fortunately, Irby's corner-taker
must have been overcome with all the excitement because he
ballooned the ball way over the heads of his teammates waiting in
the penalty area and out for a throw-in on the other side of the
pitch.

George managed to find five minutes of extra time from
somewhere, but there were no more scares to face, and he finally
blew the full-time whistle, which announced them as champions.
Dave ran on the pitch triumphantly, hugging every player that
came into his path and telling them how *fucking proud I am of you.*
Birchy brought the cup back to the pub for Ross to stick behind the
bar and they drank in celebration until the early hours. Birchy
repeatedly told Dave.

'I'm not payin' that fuckin' fine.'

17 THE BANK JOB

The pointed end of Jonno's triangular-shaped toast pierced the thinly protected surface of his fried egg, causing the yolk to slowly explode and impregnate his baked beans. The yellow, saturated toast was hardly in his mouth before he was shovelling a large portion of sausage into his crammed gob. They unofficially got twenty minutes for morning break and the walk to *Tommy's Café* had already wasted five minutes of it. It was bad enough that Jonno was shovelling his breakfast down his throat like a starved lunatic, but Naz was just sitting there, stirring at his fry-up rapidly losing temperature, which was really winding Jonno up.

During the three weeks since the doctor had diagnosed his depression, he'd been working hard on the good things he could take out of life. It wasn't easy because there wasn't a great deal to choose from. For this reason, he started little and low, trying to pick up on anything that was remotely positive and giving himself a massive psychological pat on the back. It may be something as daft as Liverpool winning a game or getting off work ten minutes early. They would all go into the good side of his brain and stay there for the week.

'Fuckin 'ell, lad, look at this.' Jonno shoved the half-folded newspaper into Naz's untouched plate and slanted it so that he could see what he was reading.

'That fuckin' bird that chopped her fella's knob off, goes on trial today. Listen to this.'

*The incident occurred June 23, 1993 in Manassas, Virginia.
Lorena Bobbitt stated in a court hearing that, after coming home
that evening, her husband raped her. After he went to sleep, she
got out of bed and went to the kitchen for a drink of water. She
then grabbed an eight-inch carving knife on the kitchen counter,
returned to their bedroom, pulled back the bed sheets and cut off
his penis.*

*After this, she left the apartment with the severed appendage and
drove away in her car. After a while driving and struggling to steer
with one hand, she threw it out the window into a roadside field.
She eventually stopped and called 911, telling them what had
happened and where the penis could be found. John Bobbitt's penis
was found after an exhaustive search, and, after being washed
with antiseptic and packed in saline ice, it was reattached in the
hospital where he was treated. The operation took nine-and-a-half
hours.*

'Fuck me, la, I cannot get my head around this. How the fuck
didn't he wake up when she was doing it and stop her? Why was
she holding his knob while she was driving, wouldn't you just lash
it on the seat? Imagine being one of the bizzies telling someone
what case you're working on at the minute? *"Yeah man, I'm
currently looking for John Wayne's cock in a sandy ditch!"*
Beans flew out of Jonno's mouth as he tried to eat, talk, and laugh
at the same time. Naz stared at him vacantly with an expression
that confirmed he hadn't been listening to a single word Jonno had
said. Something was obviously troubling him. Jonno clicked his
fingers in front of his face.

'Oi!'

Naz didn't blink or break from his hypnotic stare. Jonno repeated
the process and earned a limited response.

'Wha'?' he said, momentarily landing his spaceship on planet
Earth.

'What's up, mate? You're acting like a proper pot-herb.'

'It's Emily, mate.'

'What d'ya mean? Is there something wrong with her?'

'Nah, I'm just constantly worried about her living with that bint and her fuckin' ugly gorilla. I want to adopt her or get full access, or whatever it's called.'

'Well, that won't be easy, will it, mate?'

'I've done a bit of research and briefly spoken to a solicitor. There's something called The Children's Act. I can take her to court and prove that Emily isn't being cared for properly. She can come and live with me.'

Jonno instantly wanted to tell Naz to wake up and realise how difficult it would be to prove that Emily would be better off living with him, but he was so enthusiastic, he thought he'd kill him if he put a dampener on his plans. So, in his idiot true form, he told him it was a great idea. After Naz offloaded his plan onto Jonno and received his blessing, his mood directly picked up and he started to tuck into his breakfast. Jonno was gutted because he'd had a sneaky tactic to wrap Naz's sausage in a piece of toast and eat it on the way back to work, almost in the style of Lorena Bobbitt. They finished their breakfasts promptly, gulped the dregs of coffee, and left to face the driving rain.

It was only 10.30am but the thick black storm clouds cast a dark atmosphere and the swooshing wind occasionally directed the driving rain into their faces. This was a part of Wallasey that really wasn't attractive. The town had previously had so much to be proud of in the past. A regular haunt of The Beatles in the sixties, home of the famous ferry boat that linked the lads to Liverpool, and the home of the world's first ever surviving female sextuplets, born in 1983. The Liver Birds of Liverpool waterfront looked across the water at Wallasey like a disapproving older brother. This area of Wallasey was overcome with crime, house burglaries and plagued by drug dealers and drug users. The drug problem had ripped through Merseyside in the eighties, fuelled by mass unemployment, austerity, and hopelessness. A mass heroin epidemic had spread through the council estates of the eighties and left destruction and despair in its wake. The consequences of the merciless trade were still visible on the streets of Merseyside, and even ten years later, there weren't many Merseysiders who didn't have a relation or friend that was still dependant on smack.

Work was impossible to find in the eighties with massive dole queues, redundancy and YTS schemes that paid a meagre £25 a week. Weaker people needed an escape, a chance to disappear from their torrid existence, if only for a while, and enter a world of painless satisfaction. In the mid-eighties, it was estimated that there were about 5,000 heroin users on the Wirral, out of a total population of about 300,000. With the utopia came the addiction and the desire for more. Addicts would go to extraordinary lengths to get their next bag, including theft, prostitution, and violence. All reasoning and ethical thinking was lost to a bag of brown, imprisoned in the walls of Smack City.

Wallasey still exhibited the scars etched by the criminal activities of callous dealers and the desperate measures of vulnerable addicts. Used hypodermic needles littered the filthy streets, strewn with litter and dog faeces. Skeleton-like addicts with greasy, acne-covered skin stood outside video shops and pubs begging for pennies, wrapped in a story about needing bus fare or something to eat. Street corners and public parks were breeding grounds for the feckless and the feral lurking in the shadows, faces covered by scarves and hooded coats with menace and profit on their mind.

The deprived areas of Liverpool and Wirral were never given chance to recover from the heroin plague due to the introduction of house music and its associated recreational drug taking.
In 1988, Acid House swept through Britain like a tidal wave and changed the face of music and drug taking to this day. Jonno and the lads were still clinging on to the tail of it after being oblivious to the movement for six years. No longer was drug taking a dirty, desperate event, but an integral part of a night out. Some clever fiend had worked out that the synergy between dance music and the presence of LSD or ecstasy in the bloodstream created a euphoric sensation in the minds of anyone who was brave enough

to try it.

There were casualties. Jonno had heard stories and news reports of young people that had fallen by the wayside, but compared to the thousands of sweaty, ecstatic dancers taking it every week, it seemed a risk worth taking. No longer did angry lads that faced daily hardship want to leave a pub and punch someone in the face to just feel something other than numb and gloom. Strangers felt love, walls were broken down and instant friendships formed. Kissing, hugging, and high-fiving upon introduction, sometimes without spoken words became the norm.

How could this be bad?

They christened 1988 *The Summer of Love* and Jonno was gutted that it passed him by, desperately trying to reinvent it every time they popped a tablet. They were having their own party in 1994 but would never get to experience the underground raves in fields and disused warehouses, in locations protected from the police and gifted to members of a cult elite.

Wallasey and Merseyside were peppered with smackheads in their thirties, and a generation of pill-poppers in their twenties. Jonno was glad he missed the pressures and temptation of heroin and was part of a culture that glamorised drug taking and pushed the boundaries of conventional music making. Maybe in ten years, the streets would be plagued with ex-ravers begging for a quid to feed a pill habit or buy a floppy hat. Jonno knew that would never be him because he never felt like he was unable to control it, and let it control him.

'I've got to jump in 'ere, lad and get some dosh out.'

Jonno shoulder-barged Naz into the cash point and they both cowered under a thin aluminium lip above their heads to escape the incessant downpour. After withdrawing three crisp, clean tenners, and whilst waiting for his card to return, Jonno could hear some shuffling behind him and assumed a queue had started to form. Naz was still wittering on about adopting Emily and Jonno had fleetingly switched off his scumbag detection monitor and was totally unmindful of the horrors that were presently stood behind him. As they both turned around, they were met by two unsavoury looking characters that had wandered way too far into their personal space. Their path was impeded by two despicable mischief-makers, who both stood around six-foot but appeared much taller when adopting aggressive stances.

Oxygen levels became thin as the black-and-grey sky sucked breathable air into its rancid belly and blew out toxic gas in exchange. Jonno struggled to fill his lungs sufficiently with clean air and felt subsequently lightheaded as a hypnagogic bubble entombed him. The grotty figure that obstructed his way was gaunt and visibly flaunted pronounced cheek bones and a chiselled chin. He was *smackhead-thin* yet gave no real indication of being addicted to the brown. Large droplets of rain slid down his greasy shoulder-length hair before plopping off to their concrete doom. His blue, shabby Berghaus coat was drenched and clung to his emaciated upper frame. Jonno confirmed that the cobweb tattoo on his neck and inkydink tear under his eye reinforced his lack of class and solid membership to *The Scruffy Cunts Association*.

Naz was confronted by a horrid-looking creature who clearly bore the scars of epic narcotic battles. His unctuous skin was a breeding ground for yellowheads and scabs. Only his forehead showed some shame and covered its grotesqueness from the public with a cheap Everton baseball cap. His teeth looked like a row of bombed houses and the ones that remained in his insidious mouth sported different shades of yellow. His saturated denim jacket featured a patch on the arm that read *Born In The USA*. Jonno thought to himself that *he shouldn't have been born at all and was probably best washed down a storm water gulley when his mother first dragged him from the haunches of Mephistopheles and forced him into a life of depravity and misdeed.*

Jonno's assailant lurched forward and breathed his stale, tobacco-laden stench across his face.

'Give us that money or I will cut you up.'

'Fuck off, you smack-rat cunt,' Jonno replied.

He slowly raised an impressive six-inch Bowie knife that could cut a horse in half. He placed the razor-sharp blade vertically under Jonno's chin so that the point of the knife gently punctured his skin. It felt like a tiny needle prick piercing his flesh and was followed by a warm trickle of blood cascading down his neck.

It wasn't the first time he'd had a knife pulled on him, but never one so horrifying, and never in a confined space where running away wasn't an option. He really should've been concentrating on the situation at hand, but he was distracted by a police patrol car meandering past them. Jonno baulked at the ironic notion of a driver being pulled over for doing 35mph while daylight robbery with a deadly instrument went completely unnoticed.

He moved in closer so that their foreheads met and pushed Jonno's head back with his in order to fire off a warning shot. The back of Jonno's head connected with a shop window amongst a small explosion of rain droplets and a dull thud. It was not delivered to hurt but act as a blocker of bright ideas. In reality, Jonno had no bright ideas of escape or victory, and yet again, he found himself in another impossible situation that this sick-minded life continued to throw at him.

'If I have to ask again, I am going to bury this in your fuckin' kidneys.'

He pushed the blade deeper into Jonno's chin whilst delivering his latest threat. What was scaring Jonno most was the fact that he wasn't scared. Not once did he feel fear of pain or death. Maybe his heart had become so empty and hard, that he had lost all respect for his life. It momentarily felt like the loss of his life would be no great cost to him or those around him, least of all Becky. Even in this dramatic and potentially life-threatening situation, she was still on his mind. The deadness in his heart had eliminated fear, and all he felt was rage and retribution.

How could this poisonous bandit steal the cash I'd worked so hard for and so desperately needed to stay afloat, right before my eyes without resistance?
He knew deep down that there was no solution available, but he

looked deep into his glassy yellow eyes and swore to him that he would get his comeuppance. Karma would serve him a dish of revenge that he rightfully deserved, and at that moment in time, Jonno cared not whether that was someone sticking that knife into him, or him sharing a cell for ten years.

With Jonno's new method to combat depression and negative thoughts, he convinced himself that it could be a lot worse, as he was asking for the cash and not his bank card as well. He handed him the money which he snatched from him and placed in his back pocket without moving the blade from his chin. His malevolent eyes twisted to his accomplice, who took one step back and launched a brutal right hook into the side of Naz's face, producing a sicking thump. As the punch struck, Jonno moved his body forward to react, but was forced into reverse by the threat of the knife. Naz slumped heavily to the ground whilst his assailant stood over him, grinning. Jonno felt useless and cowardly, watching his best friend take a punch while he stood helpless and pathetic next to him. They were brothers, if not by blood but by bond. They were supposed to look out for one another and act as each other's protector no matter what. Yet here Jonno stood, observing a heroin-laced creature of vileness execute a kick into his brother's ribs as he lay defenceless on the floor. It sickened him. Jonno swore to himself, at that moment, that he would never let this happen again, regardless of the consequences.

He calmly removed the knife from Jonno's throat as though he had all the time in the world to toy with him and then smirked to imply that he'd enjoyed the whole event. They turned on their heels and headed for a back alley and were then lost to the dark caverns of Wallasey. Jonno helped Naz to his feet; he was shaken but okay. They brushed themselves down and headed back to work. Telling the police was pointless and taking time off work was not an option, even more so now he was thirty quid down.

'Expensive brekkie that lad.'

18 SAFETY ROZZERS

Monday mornings were bad enough, but Naz and Jonno were on a job in Grimsby and had to drive there on a Sunday. Naz's uncle had put them up in a *proper shithole*. It wasn't even a hotel, it was a boozer called The Ropewalk that had a few guest bedrooms, and Naz and Jonno unfortunately ended up in one of them.

They got there on Sunday evening and were met by a landlady called Polly. She was quite welcoming to the boys and sipped a Martini as she showed them to their room, occasionally spilling it on the well-weathered carpet.

'I've been in a right benny all day, but I feel much better now you two have arrived,' she said as she opened their room door with a dungeon key attached to a small log.

'There you go, darls. It's two single beds and there's a little electric heater there. If it gets too cold, I'm sure we can find a way to warm you both up.'
Jonno looked at Naz with a raised eyebrow and he fired back a grin that suggested he was genuinely interested in tasting the local delicacies.

'Now get yersen downstairs for a pint.'
They got the gist of what she was saying and followed her orders. Jonno noticed that she was clearly accentuating the wiggle on her arse as they followed her downstairs. Naz walked directly behind

her, performing the customary doggie-style manoeuvres whilst slapping her imaginary bum.

The pub was a typical old-style boozer with a cigarette machine close to the front door which provided ammunition to the smoke-filled room and yellowed Artex ceiling. The walls were covered with a regal style wallpaper and peppered with old bygone photos encapsulated in large brass frames of buildings and people who had left a mark on the history of this once-great fishing town. A large, teak-varnished bar protected the pumps of bitter and Guinness and poorly-upholstered stools provided roosting platforms for Sunday night revellers.

A singing guitarist in his mid-fifties sported a grey Elvis-type hairstyle and played standard middle-of-the-road classics such as *Summer of '69* and *Stuck in the Middle with You*. A group of young lads huddled around a fruit machine that constantly made annoying noises and flashed lights into the eyes of anyone who dared look at it. Pool and darts offered alternative entertainment for the folk that didn't fancy the dulcet tones of the *Silver Elvis*.

'Sit yersen down there, darls, and I'll get ya a pint,' instructed Polly.

The noise of *Silver Elvis* playing the intro to *Proud Mary* wasn't enough to conceal their entry to the bar. They shiftily sat on a couple of padded stools violated with beer stains and circular ciggie burns. The folk playing darts and pool halted their games to observe their ring walk to the designated resting area. Even *Elvis* cast his eyes over at them and then nodded to a handful of regulars stood at the bar, without breaking from his lyrics. They endured a couple of uncomfortable minutes whilst the locals examined them and tried to work out if they were a threat to them. They kept their heads down and spoke softly as to show respect before Polly returned with a couple of pints of bitter and two steak-and-kidney pies sat in their tinfoil housing. They weren't on a plate and there was no cutlery, but they were warm, and the lads were starving. They also didn't really like bitter, but there was no chance they were complaining.
They scoffed their pies and sank a couple more pints before

retiring to their penthouse suite with panoramic view, silk robes and hot tub.

Jonno woke up during the middle of the night desperately searching for his socks because his feet were blocks of ice, but it was pitch black and he couldn't see a thing. He switched on the table lamp knowing it might wake Naz up, but his feet couldn't take anymore and were faced with the threat of frostbite. As the lamp slowly illuminated the room in a classic 1970's warm amber, Jonno noticed Naz wasn't in his bed. *The dirty bastard must have got up when I was asleep and gone to slip Polly one without telling me*, he mused.

Naz still wasn't in when the alarm went off at 6.30am. The early morning February sun penetrated the flimsy, dust-covered curtains and revealed the horrors of the room Jonno had just spent the night in. The carpet looked like it had been removed from the bar at the end of its life and fitted into the guest room: threadbare, beaten, and stained. The bed sheets presented evidence that they may have been used to move a dead body from a murder scene to its final resting point. The mahogany furniture and tongue-and-groove walls were a home to stains, hair, and dead insects, and the subservient convector heater did nothing to combat the cold air. Jonno turned on the wood-encased TV and wrestled with its antenna, attempting to a get a clear picture before giving up and making his way to the ensuite bathroom. As he peed into the avocado-coloured toilet pan, stained with the last guest's dinner, he marvelled at the mould that had made a home of the badly-fitted peach wall tiles and psychedelic lino. The once-white shower curtain now showed a soiled timeline of previous inhabitants and was a key factor in helping Jonno decide that he was not getting a shower. He turned on the heavy-duty hot tap to get a swill and brush his teeth. As it slowly unwound its rusty thread, the boiler came to life, growling and moaning in rage at being woken from its slumber. Discoloured brownish-yellow water trickled from the tap with all the pressure of a hole in a bucket. The internally frost-covered single pane window rattled in its frame as a bus sped down the high street and he desperately searched for highs to place in his positive box.

Jonno heard the door slam and put his head out of the bathroom to see Naz return from his night of passion with *Polly the Pole Rider*.

'Where the fuck have you been?' Jonno asked, already knowing the answer.

'The little fella's been getting' some action, lad,' Naz replied, grabbing his crotch.

'Well, c'mon, what happened?'

'I'll tell you later, mate, we've got to get a shift on. We're supposed to clock on at 7.30.'

As they drove to the site through the streets of Grimsby, there were notable signs of this once-great town's demise, now an area of depravation and loss. At its peak, Grimsby was one of the busiest fishing seaports in the world, but the Cod Wars result of conceding 200 nautical miles of fishing territory to Iceland, had an impact that they would never recover from. Loss of business and support resulted in loss of jobs and mass unemployment. Unemployed fisherman and factory workers found refuse in pubs and bookmakers, and the weaker folk found solace in drugs. Shuttered-up shops and derelict buildings lined the empty dockland skyline and the jobless masses gathered in a shabby town centre desperately in need of investment.

It felt like a home-from-home.

The lads had been contracted by a massive construction company to paint the exterior of a newly-rendered ten-storey new build office block. They realised as soon as they pulled into the car park that the building wasn't ready for them, as it was only half rendered, and the site looked like a bomb had hit it. They were ushered into a cabin to listen to the site safety induction. They were met by a short, baldy fella with a moustache, who probably weighed in at around 28-stone. His jeans were tucked into thick, beige hiking socks and his boots were covered in dry mud that left a flaky trail as he moved around the room. Naz and Jonno were joined by half a dozen other lads and they were addressed by a thick, Yorkshire accent.

'Right, lads, settle down. Settle down,' he said, whilst tapping a marker pen against a flipchart.

'Let's do the safety stuff, lads, and then ya can out t'site and get t'work. We act safe on the site so don't be a knobhead. Wear a hard-hat all t'time and watch out for site vehicles. First aid is in my office. Any questions?'

The room fell silent as he waited for a moment or two, before ushering them out the door. The walk across site to the building they were working on was peppered with hazards and they knew they would have to stay alert. They found themselves hopping over potholes, dodging rebar sticking out of the ground, and walking past unprotected excavations. Large plant moved around the muddy site without much care and attention for pedestrians, while cranes lifted large steel beams across site with unsuspected contractors walking underneath them. The site supervisor took them up to the fourth level on the scaffold and instructed them to start painting the render white. The render hadn't set yet and this was a disaster in the making, thought Jonno.

'That hasn't gone off yet, mate, and the plasterers that are three lifts up will be splashing shit all over it.'

'Just get it done, you moaning scouse prick, or fuck off!'
Jonno looked at Naz before reacting but he was popping his eyes and shaking his head. They did what he said and started painting uncured render, with both of them knowing it wouldn't take.

'So, what happened last night, then?'

Naz naively thought Jonno had forgotten.

'A gentleman never tells,' he said in a Sean Connery voice.

'Fuck off, you always tell. C'mon, spill the beans.'

'Alright, la, pipe down.'

Jonno stopped painting so that the storyteller had the full attention of his audience.

'So, when you nipped the bog for a piss last night, she came over to me and started whispering in my ear and rubbin' her tits against me. Told me to knock on her door around midnight and she'd sort me out.'

'For fuck's sake, ya lucky twat. Was it any good?'

'Well, I was there all night, wasn't I?' he said with a dirty grin, and then they fell about laughing.

'Now get some graft done before that bellend comes back and bollocks us.'

They'd been working for two hours and were just winding down for their tea break when they heard a chilling scream from above them. Jonno instantly thought it was the scaffolders who'd been causing commotion above them all day. Following the scream came a series of dull thuds and a flash of orange flew past them, heading for the ground. Jonno first thought that some *knobhead* must have been lobbing things off the scaffold, but when he walked along the boards and peered over the handrail, he saw an image that he will never forget for as long as he lives. Forty feet below them, crumpled in the mud, lay the limp and lifeless body of a man in an orange boiler suit. Blood gushed from his head and quickly filled muddy depressions in the ground. Jonno looked upwards to see three fellas in the same orange suits. Their faces were white as snow and terror overwhelmed their eyes. Jonno looked at Naz, but he'd lost the ability to talk. Jonno went into the surreal world he often slipped into when his mind couldn't cope with what is happening in the present.

'Fuck me, I think he's dead,' muttered Naz.

His body must have hit numerous scaffold tubes and objects before landing crumpled upon the mud. The air was still and silent, as was this poor man's body. His life gone in a flash. Left for work in the morning like everyone does, and three hours later, his existence has been eradicated by some form of safety failure. They stood frozen to the spot watching the activity below which increased from mildly inquisitive to hysterical pandemonium.

'Ring a fuckin' ambulance!' screamed a supervisor as he carefully tried to lift the head of the flaccid orange body.

'Get me a first aider, now!'

'There's no first aider bringing that fella back. He's fallen close to a hundred foot there,' conceded Naz.

Jonno's thoughts were consumed with this poor soul who looked no older than thirty, yet his ashen face and broken body multiplied his years. He wondered what life, and what people he had left behind and what the impact of his loss would be.

Was he a single man who liked a bevvie every night, or did he leave a wife and children behind?

How would his family cope with the mortgage and monthly bills?

Who would tell the kids that their dad was dead and how would his parents cope with him dying before them?

Would his company pay for the funeral? It seemed there was a lot more to dying than just burying a body.

'Everyone off the scaffold. Make your way to the welfare cabins.'

The site manager had appeared and was barking orders at all of the site personnel. As they started walking down the scaffold stairs, they bumped into the lads in the orange suits who had been working above them.

'What happened there, boys?' asked Naz.
They were all in a state of shock. One of the lads was fighting the urge to vomit.

'The fuckin' scaffold failed. He leant back and the handrail gave way. These fuckin' tight bastards have killed him by doin' everything on the cheap!'
Naz glanced over at Jonno— they had both predicted that this

149

shithole of a site was capable of killing someone. They never truly believed it would, though.

By the time they got to ground level and walked past the spot where the poor fella had landed, the site manager had already covered the body with a sheet of tarpaulin. Jonno fought with the theory of this being respectful for the lads on site as they had to walk past the scene, or whether this was disrespectful, as the plastic sheet previously covering a mound of sand was now concealing the body of an innocent man. A man that had come to work in the morning to earn an honest crust and would never return home because of a greedy employer that had cut corners. Around sixty men squeezed into the welfare cabins and conversed loudly and angrily about what had happened. The site manager stood on a chair and told them that the health and safety police were on their way to investigate the accident and that the site was closing. He said they should go home until they were told to come back. A few disgruntled workers fired questions at him, but he ignored them and scuttled back into his office.

The lads went back to The Ropewalk and had a few beers before Naz's uncle told them the job had been shut down and they should make their way back home.

19 GOLD RUSH

After the long, dark days of winter, there were visible signs that the month of March had brought spring with it as a companion, shutting the door on wintertime as it made its remarkable arrival.

The warmer temperature produced clusters of golden daffodils and frothy white flowers that displaced the greyness of the ebbing season. The early morning sunlight and warm, gentle breezes encouraged the primrose to softly dance in unison. The still silence of February was lost to a dawn chorus of robin, wren, and blackbirds orchestrating rejoiceful song and delivering it to the world without inhibition. Bees broke from hibernation to busily explore the new world, while swallows twisted and dipped in a clear azure blue sky, fragmented only by aeroplane vapour trails and splatters of cloud.

The completion of days was still difficult for Jonno, but he had improved a lot since his visit to the doctors. He received a missed call from them a while back, probably about him returning and checking in, but he never went back. It was always his intention to get through things alone and he thought he was doing a pretty good job. His approach to concentrating on anything positive, no matter how inconsequential, and disposing of anything adverse, really seemed to be working for him. He was slowly climbing a ladder from a deep, dark pit rather than slipping to the bottom of the ocean. He still had bad days, but he now realised that the next day may be a little better. He still thought about Becky far too much and his heart still ached for her, but it was nowhere near as bad as it had been two months earlier. The transformation of the weather and the introduction of natural light instantly improved his mood.

Jonno tackled the walk to Naz's with an abrupt pace and enjoyed the intermittent rays of sunshine that fell on his face, breaking through the still-bare branches of the sycamore as he marched along.

Mid-morning visits to the pub were still quite novel to him but since Sky Sports had monopolised control of all football on TV, they'd found themselves in the pub watching the match on the oddest of days, and the strangest of times. Sky had convinced the football league to become the Premier League a couple of years back and had changed the face of football, sexing it up with American-style music and graphics. The downside to this was that it was *pay-per-view* and normal hardworking folk simply couldn't afford to subscribe. So they now had to watch the football in the pub. Luckily for them, landlord Ross had a dodgy TV box and satellite dish which meant he didn't pay to get the games, and they got to have a few beers whilst cheering their team on.

After two heavy knocks on his door, Naz finally opened up and popped his head out of the gap.

'Freeman, Scott and Turner!' he revealed.

'What?'

'Freeman, Scott and Turner!' he repeated.

'Who the fuck are they? Is that where you get yer cheap trainees from?'

'Come in for a sec,' he ordered.

'That's the name of the solicitors that are going to help me get full access of Emily. I spoke to them yesterday and they reckon they can help.'
They sat at his kitchen table.

'D'ya wanna brew?'

'Nah, mate, we're goin' for a pint now. So, what's the craic with these solicitors, then?'

'Well, they first came up with a load of suggestions that would never work for me and that selfish bitch. Like discussing it over a cup of tea or going to see an independent mediator.

Then they said I should keep a diary of every time she has denied me access. Well, I was already doin' that. I've made a note of dates and times. Every fuckin' vile word she's said to me. Every time she's knocked me back. Every nasty word I've heard her say to Emily and every fuckin' threat that ugly gorilla has made to me.'

'Whoa, calm down, lad,' Jonno said, trying to slow down Naz's excitement a little.

'Sorry, la. Anyway, to cut a long story short, I am going to take her to court to get better access. My uncle has said he'll loan me the money to pay for the solicitors. I've got fuck all to lose, mate.'

He was a desperate man and Jonno knew exactly how that felt. The faint hope of him seeing more of Emily was a helping hand to cling onto at the edge of cliff. Jonno feared for him. He feared it would all end up in tears, probably Naz's, but he couldn't bring himself to sound negative. Jonno had to support this pipedream that Naz had, as that is what he would expect of Naz should the roles be reversed.

'That's fuckin' brilliant, mate. I'm made up for you. Finally some good news, eh?'

***

As they entered the boozer, Jonno was surprised to see how empty it was with just an hour or so before kick-off. Ross had a redder face than usual—something must've aggravated him.

'Two pints please, Ross.'

'It's off, lads.'

'Well give us a couple of bottles, then,' Jonno replied.

'Not the beer, ya tit, the football is off!'

'What?'

'Someone's bubbled me.'

Naz and Jonno looked were confused.

'Someone's grassed me up about the dodgy dish. I've lost the footy unless I pay for it.'
This was bad. A section of Jonno's world had just caved in.

How were we ever going to watch the match?

'What the fuck, Ross? Who's done that?'

'Dunno, Jonno, some proper snidey, jealous fuckers about. I'm really sorry, lads, you'll have to go over to *The Reflection Rooms* if you wanna see the game.'
This was awful news. They could relax in *The Belvedere,* swearing and shouting without fear of upsetting anyone. Everyone in there would be watching the game, so they wouldn't be winding anyone up who was trying to have a bit of food or a quiet chat. *The Reflection Rooms* was the opposite. They would have tellies on, but the volume would be turned down and the place would be full of people eating their lunch and sipping wine.

'Alright, Ross, we'll come back in 'ere for a few after the game, mate.'

As they entered, the place was full of people having something to eat and they all turned to face them as they swung the door open. It wasn't that this place was too posh for them, it just wasn't the right type of place to watch the football. They didn't have any English lager, so Naz ordered a couple of trendy German beers in tall glasses.

'Will you be able to turn the sound up for the match love?'

'I can't, I'll start getting complaints.'

'Go on—we'll sit over there in the corner out of everyone's way.'

'Okay, I'll put it on low, but you'll have to keep the noise down.'

'Ta love.'

They sat down in the corner on a couple of fake leather chairs and had a reasonable viewing point to one of the TV screens. Naz pulled out a *William Hill* betting slip and shoved it under Jonno's nose.

'There it is, fella, 250 quid banker!'
Jonno looked down and read Naz's scrawl upon the betting slip.

Liverpool v Chelsea

Rush first goal and Liverpool win 2-1

25/1

£10.00 win

'Go 'ed, lad, I'll have a bit of that. I'll give you a fiver and we'll go halves,' Jonno proposed.
Naz seemed a bit perturbed that Jonno had gate-crashed his party, but he had to agree otherwise he'd be breaking all sorts of codes of friendship. Jonno shoved a fiver in his hand, and Naz smiled jokingly through gritted teeth.

They were just over twenty minutes in when Fowler dinked a left-footed cross which was met by the head of big centre-back Mark Wright. The Chelsea keeper made a pig's ear of the save and the ball fell to Rush. Naz gripped Jonno's arm tightly and they both slipped to the edge of their seats with bated breath. Rush poked the ball in with his right foot and they roared with excitement whilst jumping up and down and hugging each other. They had the first part of their bet up. As they sat down, Jonno looked around the room and there were quite a few diners who didn't appear overly impressed with their etiquette—but he really didn't care.

It was nearing halftime and in the 44th minute, Steve McManaman skipped down the right wing into the penalty area. He whipped in a delicious cross from the right that Fowler and John Barnes challenged for. They never made it because Craig Burley headed the ball into his own net to make it two-nil. The lads went ballistic, and beer went flying all over the table as they screamed and bounced in celebration. They sank another two pints of Germany's finest during halftime and prattled away to each other about how well Liverpool were playing.

The second half was different, as Liverpool took their foot off the gas and allowed Chelsea to start pressurising them with numerous opportunities at goal. They'd defended several chances before Burley let fly a half-volley screamer with his left foot from twenty yards out that David James had no chance of saving.

Their bet was up, the money was practically in their hands, but Chelsea continued to put pressure on Liverpool's goal, and it became difficult for them to watch. They were extremely nervous, desperately holding on to money they hadn't yet won. They let rip the loudest cheer of the day when David James pulled off a fantastic save as the game neared the final whistle. As soon as it blew, they spent the next ten minutes laughing and telling complete strangers that they'd just got a £250 bet up. In that moment, they felt special, like millionaires.

'Come 'ed, la, let's pick our winnings up and go back *The Belvedere*.'

Naz's suggestion sounded perfect to Jonno, so seven pints worse for wear, they got up and started to make their way for the door, accidentally bumping into the odd chair on their way out, causing huffs and puffs from people having their lunch. As they neared the exit, Jonno was stopped in his tracks and time came to a standstill. Although his mouth was abundantly lubricated with German lager, it became arid and choked. His throat closed and he struggled to swallow and inhale. The tightening of his throat starved his lungs of air and they instantly failed in their function to pump and provide. A cold sweat covered his face and forehead and he started to shiver in a nervous reaction to the vision that had hooked onto his eyes. There, sat with her friend, was Becky, tucking into a salad and half a glass of lager, chatting away, completely oblivious to this momentous freezeframe in time.

The light bouncing off her dark brown hair gave the appearance that it was much lighter. Having her hair tied back allowed the true splendour of her face to parade itself. She was smartly dressed in a pink woollen jumper and skinny jeans. Her black stilettos were noticeable as her foot bounced in a rhythm a metronome would be proud of. Jonno felt like he'd been sucked into an imploded watery bubble and the rest of the world had been washed away into an inane insignificance.

Knobhead No.1: 'Fuck 'er off, Danny, she isn't interested.'

Knobhead No.2: 'This might be your only chance to talk to her.'

Knobhead No.1: 'She'll jib you off and you'll look like a proper tool.'

Knobhead No.2: '*Carpe diem,* Danny.'

Jonno glanced at Naz for guidance but he was oblivious to her presence, as was Becky to his. This was it, he had to say something. In for a penny, in for a pound.

'Hiya, Bec.'

'Oh, hiya, Danny.'
He couldn't believe the reaction he'd got from her. She had acknowledged his existence and spoken to him like he wasn't a leper. Hopeful thoughts raced around in circles inside his overburdened mind— he'd assumed he was dead to her but here she was, talking to him as if he was an old friend. His body filled with hope and elation, which resulted in his heart aching when he realised that she was no longer his. As she looked up, to wordlessly enquire why he was still standing there, rays of refracted sunlight caught her hazel eyes and triumphantly showcased glassy, golden flecks.

'What you doin' here, then?' Jonno asked.

Knobhead No.1: 'What type of dickhead question was that?'
Shit! It was too late, it was all he could think of due to his racing
nerves and seven pint consumption. Becky was the epicentre of
humility and answered his daft question with grace.

'I'm just grabbing some lunch with my friend, Zara.'
He nodded in the direction of Zara to acknowledge her existence
without really looking at her or removing his gaze from Becky.

'Ah, sound. We came in to watch the game, like.'

'We know, we heard you,' she chuckled.

'Ah, bollocks, were we too loud?'

'Nah, it's just coz' it's dead quiet in 'ere usually.'

The knobheads in his brain were firing conflicting advice at him
as usual. The rush of beer in his brain wasn't helping him think
straight, either. He needed to leave this conversation in the best
possible state he could but wasn't sure how to do it. He may not
get chance to ask her out again, and this might be the only
moment, but he could also come across as being a psycho stalker
that couldn't take no for an answer. He'd tried pleading with her in
the past and it hadn't worked. Surely begging her now would make
him look like an unattractive loser desperately clinging on to the
unattainable. He had to think with his head and look at the bigger
picture.

'Apologies if we spoilt yer scran, girls. Lovely to see you, Becky.
Take care of yourself.'
He gave Naz a slight shoulder barge towards the door and they
headed for the exit.

'See ya, Danny.'
He wasn't quite sure how he managed to stay so collected and
cool, but he thought he'd pulled it off. Cold enough to not look
desperate, but enough warmth to show her he was a good guy and
may be worth another shot.

They went to the bookies to collect their winnings. The bookmakers weren't happy about handing the cash over, but they never were, and the lads didn't care what they thought.

'Let's jump in 'ere before we go back *The Belvedere,* Jonno.'

Naz pulled Jonno into *Rudi's* Chippy. An establishment of the highest order when it came to fine dining. Rudi had a scouse/Jamaican accent and offered a range of beer-soaking delights such as Chinese, pizzas, burgers, and kebabs. This epicureanism phenomenon offered tasty pleasures from around the world to satisfy the most eloquent of diners. The lads could often be found in *Rudi's* at the end of the night with many drunken locals, but because of the early kick-off, this was an unusual time for them.

'What will it be, boys?'

'Jumbo sausage and chips, Rudi lad, and two cartons of gravy, please.'

'Do ya want the gravy on the chips, boy?'

'No, la, I'm gonna drink the gravy.'
Rudi didn't bat an eyelid following Jonno's strange request and moved on to ask what Naz wanted. They sat at Rudi's plastic table and chairs and scoffed their food as though they'd just been plucked from ten years on a desert island. They lined their stomachs and were now ready for additional beers to finish off a very productive day.

As they stepped outside, they took a moment to gather themselves and work out what direction they were heading. They were confronted in the street by two wasters who blocked their path. One of them grabbed Jonno's forearm and began to question him, whist his supporting offender stood close to Naz. He stood askew to Jonno and spoke to the side of his face. His grip on his forearm prevented him from turning to face him directly and the alcohol in his blood prevented him from summoning up a counter-move. He could tell from his clutch that he possessed supreme strength.

'Do you know Sam Black, lad?'

Jonno knew of Sam Black, but he hadn't actually met him. He'd been one of the toughest lads at their enemy school and was relatively renowned in the area. Birkenhead was a small town and anyone with a bit of a name for themselves found it difficult to lie low and go unnoticed. Naz shook his head and suggested that it might be best to not antagonise this fella, so Jonno lied when he answered him.

'Never heard of him, mate.'

Like a Honda GL 1500 Aspencade Gold Wing doing 80 mph in a 30mph zone, his punch came from nowhere and smashed into the side of Jonno's mouth, jolting his head sideways and converting his legs to jelly.

'Give him that from me!'
Before Jonno had time to calculate what had just happened, they'd fled and were nowhere to be seen. Jonno ran his tongue across his newly-enhanced lip, and through the taste of warm blood, he could still detect Rudi's outstanding beef gravy. He felt shock. Shock like *what the fuck just happened*, but he felt nothing else. He didn't feel fear, or anger, or vengeance. He felt nothing. He'd become cold and hard to the dirty streets that encapsulated him. Only in dream or thought could he escape a world where looking at someone the wrong way wouldn't result in a beating. Everything he did in life had to be carefully planned or sometimes there would be consequences to making wrong decisions. The route he would walk to a shop had to be calculated, as would the way he would talk to someone or how he would react if something had wound him up. If anyone ever approached him with such an innocent request as the time of day, he would have to be cautious that it was not a decoy to a duplicitous attack. Everything had to be assessed. Sometimes, the calculations would be incorrect, and you would end up with a smack in the face, a lost girlfriend, or a P45. It was a constant gamble and sometimes your hand just wasn't good enough and you had to watch in despondency as a parasite removed your hard-earned chips from the table and tucked them into their own pocket. Jonno's world was plagued with hyenas

nicking the fresh hunt he'd ardently just snagged. Vultures circled these streets eyeing weakness and opportunity. He knew he had more to offer than what Birkenhead could give him, but it refused to let him leave and persistently removed rungs from the ladder whenever he attempted to climb from the pit. All he was left with was his attitude. He could allow this misfortune to bother him, or he could let it pass over him and carry on as normal. That was all he could do for now and a smack in the chops wasn't going to stop him having a few more pints to celebrate a great day.

20 THE TRUTH

Jonno was irritated with Steve on three counts. One, he'd asked him out for a quiet drink but didn't want Naz or Birchy there, which Jonno found rather odd. Two, he didn't want to go into town and said he'd pay for them to get a taxi to The Beagle, which was miles away, and three, it was a waste of a Friday night as this was a quiet boozer that would be dead apart from the odd local.

Jonno tried to let him know he wasn't keen but with Steve's typical nonchalance, he let it pass over his head. *Maybe it was just me?* thought Jonno. Maybe he was just in a sombre mood considering the date. He'd always struggled with the fifteenth of April, as did most Merseysiders and anyone remotely related to Liverpool Football Club. Weirdly, for a Merseysider, Jonno's dad wasn't an avid football fan and certainly didn't follow *The Reds* like he did. That deep-down passion he had for the club had been instilled by his dad's brother George, who'd started moulding Jonno when he was just three years old. Liverpool's greatness and superiority in European football ran through his veins thanks to his stories and the nights spent with him and his grandad watching games while they drank large tins of bitter. As Liverpool fans, they could walk with a swagger and always felt taller than the opposing fans that constantly tried to knock them off their perch.

Jonno loved, and looked up to George, and he'd not long turned eighteen in April 1989 when George went to a football match and never came home, along with another 95 of their brothers and sisters. The grief and trauma that cast a shadow on Merseyside was incomparable and widespread; there wasn't anyone Jonno knew who hadn't been affected by it in some way.

Lifeless, unidentified bodies were laid in a cold gymnasium, whilst medical officers sifted through them to remove the people that were still alive. One nurse reported that they had no equipment and desperately needed a pair of scissors to cut a victim's jumper in order to perform a tracheotomy. A policeman handed her a blunt knife. When the injured were removed, the gymnasium became a mortuary. *Our dead family*, lying cold and alone on a gym floor with the life squeezed out of them was only the beginning of the sorrow for Jonno's tribe.

From the filth-laden fissures of Hell, crawled out the lies, the denial, and the deflection of the truth. A tabloid newspaper whose name will never be muttered or written in Merseyside, printed unspeakable lies without shame about what had happened on that fateful day. The newspaper editor is said to have sat pondering for a while, between two front page headlines, 'You Scum!' and 'The Truth,' blatantly fuelled by the West Yorkshire Police's false report that Liverpool fans were drunk and unruly. The filthy rag went on to report that fans picked the pockets of the dead, urinated on the police, and beat them up. People were urinating, but it was through fear as the life was crushed out of them. Fans did search pockets, but only to identify the victims who lay on the ground whilst almost every police officer on duty did nothing. Liverpool fans ripped up advertising hoarding to use as makeshift stretchers and ferry the injured and the dead to the gymnasium. The editor didn't apologise, but he, and West Yorkshire Police did create something that was great and more powerful than any printed words. *They created unity.*

Jonno's dead uncle and 95 others from his sporting family were classified as accidental deaths, but they knew differently. A campaign to gain justice started, and was still going strong four years later, to identify the true killers of their family and to out those that had lied through their teeth. They had strength in numbers and a tenacious intensity that wouldn't see them stop until they got the truth, no matter how long the fight.

Naz and Jonno had stopped work at 3.06pm and observed a minute's silence for the fallen whilst everybody around them continued with their day, unaware of what they were doing. Maybe the stress of the day had put Jonno in a black mood and he was taking it out on Steve, but this really did seem an unusual set-up.

As expected, The Beagle was fairly quiet with just a couple of middle-aged regulars propping up the bar, the odd couple having a quiet drink and an old fella reading the Liverpool Echo in a corner. The pub was dimly lit, which made the whole place a bit drab and dreary. Music was being piped through the house speakers, but it was so low that you could barely make out what rubbish they were playing. Shelves filled with antiquated books lined the walls and an open fire roared jubilantly, alleviating the early evening spring chill. A small portable TV fixed on a corner bracket played *Noel's House Party* with the volume down and the smell of fish from that afternoon's lunch service still hadn't left the building and uninvitedly filled Jonno's nostrils without shame.

They approached the bar together to discover the only draught lager they had was *McEwan's*. Jonno gave Steve a *'what the fuck?'* look. As if tonight couldn't get any worse for Jonno, they now had to drink lager that tasted like a *cup of Satan's stale urine*. There wasn't even a decent-looking barmaid working that could temporarily offer a virtual escape from this hobbit hole of misery, bemoaned Jonno.

Steve seemed quite dominant about where they were going to sit and led them to a couple of battered armchairs that had seen better days, located at the back of the pub next to an unlit fireplace. Jonno didn't want to come across as a negative ogre, but he couldn't hold his tongue any longer.

'Ste, what the fuck are we doing here?'
Steve didn't look perturbed by Jonno's line of direct questioning and must have known that he would consider this whole thing a bit suspicious.

'I'm sorry, Jonno. I needed to talk to someone, and I didn't know who. I thought you'd be best coz you're straight-up.'
Jonno jumped in with his two massive, insensitive size tens.

'Fuck me, you haven't got a bird pregnant, 'ave ya?

'No, la. I wish that's all it was. You need to give me your absolute word that you will never tell anyone what I'm going to tell you. Swear to me?'

'Holy fuck, have you got herpes?'
Steve didn't look particularly impressed by Jonno's latest callous comment and it was at this point Jonno realised he was being serious. Jonno's initial thoughts were that he didn't want to hear what he was about to say and he was still wondering why he had decided to tell him.

'Swear it?'

'For fuck's sake, I swear it!'

After the build-up, he paused and looked as though he was having second thoughts about confiding in Jonno. He shuffled a touch closer to Jonno in order to talk a little softer—Jonno's only concern was that people might think they were a gay couple having a heart-to-heart.

'It's embarrassin'. I've never told anyone before,' he said, hesitantly.

'Go 'ed, la,' Jonno encouraged.

'I've been seeing a psychiatrist at the 'ozzy and she's told me that I've got Complex Post-Traumatic Stress Disorder.'
Jonno looked at him quizzingly, demanding some form of explanation to aid comprehension. He was fairly sure that's what the yanks got when returning from Vietnam. *Why would Steve have it?*

'You get diagnosed with it when you've repeatedly experienced traumatic events like violence, neglect or abuse. It's more severe if it happened in early life.'

Jonno's knee-jerk reaction in difficult situations was to make some sort of comical response. Especially if they were talking about death or dying. He always resorted to a *smart-arse* comment in an attempt to make light of any seriousness.

'The only trauma you've experienced is staying with the same bird for a month.'
The quip fell like a lead balloon and Steve looked like he hadn't even acknowledged it. He was focused on offloading his information regardless of any pathetic, unfunny attempts Jonno would make to interrupt him.

'I'd been struggling to control my emotions, breaking out into tears all the time for no reason. I constantly feel guilty and can't concentrate for very long. Headaches and tiredness keep me awake at night and I am not proud of the fact I can't keep a relationship down. I'd like to have a full-on girlfriend.'

'So you've got this post-trauma thing 'coz of that?' Jonno asked sheepishly.

'No mate, the PTSD is a by-product. There's more to it than that.'

Jonno thought it was the right time to give him a last-minute chance to pull out and not tell him what was blackening his life. Jonno also reckoned he'd be better off if he didn't tell him.

'Look, don't pressure yourself, mate. You don't need to tell me.'

'But I do, Jonno. The doctor told me I need to talk to someone about it, and you're that someone!'
There was no turning back now. They were about to be bound together by a secret, shackled together by a sinister union.

'I was sexually abused by my uncle when I was 11 years old.'

Bang! A gloveless right-hand haymaker from Lennox Lewis annihilated Jonno's jaw. It knocked him three illusory steps sideways and sent a waterfall of emotion and confusion to flood his brain.

How had he hidden this so well, for so long?

Jonno wasn't in the business of knowing what a child abuse victim looked like or how they acted, but he guessed Steve wasn't a prime example. This fella radiated confidence. He would swagger boldly around in an alpha male lion manner, occasionally allowing gorgeous females to admire his thick, lavish mane and then dropping them brazenly when they became tiresome. This was not a man who showed weakness or came across as introverted or broken. He was what they all wanted to be, and they loved and hated him for it in equal measure. It didn't seem right that the words Jonno was hearing were coming from Steve's mouth. Jonno felt himself slowly slipping into his surreal world. He really didn't want to hear this.

Steve continued to talk, which Jonno estimated had been a predetermined decision to prevent him asking any questions or judging the look on his face.

'It lasted for three years, until I was fourteen. My ma had remarried and wanted to spend time with her new fella, so she used to pack me off to me Uncle Barry's. I stayed at his house or he'd take me away to his caravan. I thought I'd packed it away to the back of my head, but all these symptoms I've been having are because of what happened. I just feel shame and isolated. It's been clinging onto my back for the last ten years.'

Jonno didn't want to push Steve for more information but there was stuff he just wasn't understanding, and he thought it was worth risking further questioning. The worst he could do would be to refuse to say any more.

'Abuse? Like what abuse?

'Proper sexual abuse, mate,' he said.

'When you got to like thirteen or fourteen, couldn't you fight him off or tell someone?'

'It wasn't like that, Jonno. I was a shy, reclusive kid, and didn't have a muscle to save my life. Who could I tell? Who would believe me? I suspected me ma knew and didn't care. I mean, who sends a teenage boy off to stay with their creepy uncle? I just buried it.'

'Well, where is the cunt? We'll go and Stanley-knife his cock off and stuff it in his mouth. Did he get punished? Did he go to prison.?'

'He's dead, Dan. He died of lung cancer about 8 years ago. He used to stink of roll-up ciggies. I could smell them on him when he was breathing on me.'

'Fuckin' 'ell, mate, I don't know what to say.'
'You don't need to say anything—just listen. That's why I am the way I am with birds. They don't mean nothing to me. I just shag them and fuck 'em off. I don't feel anything, and I know I am being a twat to them. I want to feel something, but they just serve a purpose for me and that's it. I struggle to show emotion and have become a hard, cold bastard.'

Jonno felt sorry for Steve, he really did, but now it felt that he too carried this burden—an albatross around his neck. His emotions were mixed with extreme pity and severe selfishness. He couldn't help but think, *why the fuck has he decided to tell me? How will I carry this information in my head whilst the rest of the lads didn't know?*

The feeling Jonno had of wanting to offload this to someone else must have been a battle Steve had struggled with for ten years. It was an awful, dark piece of history that Jonno was now part of. He could hardly manage the troubles that was going on in his own life, and now he had someone else's profound violation entrenched in his thoughts. He felt sorry for himself for a moment and then realised the living nightmare poor Steve had endured as a young boy, his childhood violently ripped away from him in the most macabre way by an evil, remorseless beast that didn't face punishment. Jonno could only pray that he was receiving his comeuppance in the afterlife. Steve was living his hell here on earth, and Jonno had to be the best friend he could be. If that meant just listening to him, regardless of the weight it placed on him, then so be it.

They talked about it for a little longer and Steve explained how the counselling process worked. Jonno marvelled at how honest and courageous he was and estimated that he would not have been so strong had he been in his shoes.

'I'm here if you need me, mate. If there's anything I can do.'

'There isn't, Jonno, but thanks.'
They continued to talk as the McEwan's turned to shorts, and they occasionally dipped back into the subject, but most of the night's conversation was light and blithe.

21 UNEXPECTED

The summer brought with it long sweaty days in work, an influx of annoying insects, big red noses, and the pressure to do something, rather than lie on the couch for the rest of your life. The sun was protected by a quilting of thick, interconnected clouds, but the warm breeze and flickering of yellow light submitted its presence. Jonno wasn't much of a sun-worshipper and preferred the winter months—apart from the fact that he couldn't afford to heat his house. Where darkness and anguish had once implanted itself, the fiery rays of summer scorched any misfortune, and the warm, gentle wind carried away its ashes.

The four lads sat in the Queen's Arms beer garden at 5 o'clock on a Friday evening with absolutely nothing to do. The working week was up, and they were enjoying the warmth of the sun whilst sipping pints of cold, dry cider. A Photinia Red Robin hedgerow stood proud above the coping stones of a dwarf garden wall made of sandstone and separated the beer garden from the outside world. The pub's house system pumped out *The Real Thing by Tony Di Bart*, but not at such an annoying level to affect their scholarly conversation. The pitch of a chaffinch's tweet was more distinguishable than the music and became rather irritating as it bounced around in the hedge without a care in the world and with a gob full of mayflies.

Jonno directed his face to the sun with tightly shut eyes and felt its radiated magnificence. His ears dampened out the sound of music and chitter-chatter, as his mind slipped into another dimension. He imagined the gentle, rhythmic breaking of waves on a crisp, golden shore. Annoying chaffinches turned into the squawks of seagulls, and foreign tongues politely tried to sell fresh fruit to sunbathers. Young children joyfully screamed and cackled as foamy waves took them by surprise and swished their faces. Becky gently massaged suntan lotion into his neck—the smell of coconut sunscreen filled his nose while reggae beats soaked his ears.

'This is fuckin' wank!' lamented Birchy, kicking Jonno's chair to wake him from his slumber.

'There's no totty here and it's fuckin' borin'. We're not stayin' 'ere!'

'We're in our work clobber, mate, so we can't go to town, can we?' said Naz.

'Fuckin' right we can. Shoot home. Quick scran, quick shower, and in town for eight.'

Birchy was clearly leading the way but no one had a counter argument of any value; even if there was one, it would be futile when contending with Birchy. However, Naz gave it a decent effort.

'It's always a quick shower for you. You only wash yer plums and armpits!'

'That mean we're out, then?' Birchy asked, already knowing the answer.

''Fuck it, let's do it!' Steve cried.

***

Maxine's was heaving. The warm weather seemed to bring out thirsty people and the speed they were sinking their own pints substantiated the fact. Jonno looked around the room to see that all the regulars were in. Pete was behind his DJ box with a new curly perm and vivid golden streaks. The Goths were looking as sultry and glamorous as usual. They weren't really goths, but Naz had given them that name because both of them always wore black. Jonno had noticed them clocking him and Naz for the past few months, but they'd never had the gall to go over and talk to them. There was something quite untouchable about them— forbidden fruit.

Just to the side of The Goths was the girl they called TOW which stood for The Older Woman. She was probably about 32 years old and had the most amazing physique—the boys were in awe of her. Jonno had fantasised so many times about reacting to her *come on* eyes and provocative mannerisms, but she also came across as well out of his league. Jonno wasn't sure if it was her beauty, her age, or that he was just a bit of a coward when it came to talking to girls.

The guy they called *Tony Knowles*, because he looked like the snooker player, patrolled his circuit in a black leather jacket, jeans, and *Lee Van Cleef* type cowboy boots. He was well into his forties, with a dyed black greasy mullet and a creepy marauding technique—slithering around the pub whispering to uninterested girls.

Jodie and her unattractive boyfriend weren't out which helped relax Jonno a little and there didn't appear to be any idiots in that may cause them grief. The relaxed atmosphere helped the beer flow, along with the laughs.

A couple of hours in, a woman approached them with a mousey-brown bobbed haircut.

'Is your name Naz, lad?'
Jonno thought to himself, *what the fuck has he snagged here?*

'Erm, yeah,' Naz answered with extreme caution.

'My name's Tracey. I live next door to Jodie.'
Fuck! Please don't let this go badly and spoil what has been a good night, Jonno quickly prayed. She continued.

'She's a fuckin' bint, her next door. All ya ever hear is screaming and arguing and her shouting at your poor Emily. And that fuckin' ugly prick she's moved in, is vile.'
It was plain to see the levels of anger filling up in Naz's eyes, not at Tracey, but at what she was telling him.

'Do you think they're hittin' Emily?' Naz mumbled.

'Nah, they've just got big gobs,' replied Tracey.

'She'd deffo be better off with you instead of that joke of a mother, though, mate.'
Tracey turned her attention to Jonno.

Aw, do you know what, lad, he's a boss dad, him. I've seen the way he dotes on Emily and ya can tell he loves her to bits. I feel dead sorry for him, and the kid.'

'Well, I'm trying to get full custody of her!'

Jonno wished Naz hadn't have told Tracey that.

'And I bet ya will win, as well, lad. I hope you do for that little girl's sake.'

Naz took this as a positive rallying cry. A surge to the enemy lines to conquer the evil malefactors, with all that is good in their hearts. *We will not be defeated, we will be victorious, and we will never walk alone!*

They had around six pints and a couple of shorts and then walked across the shopping precinct to *Ambience* nightclub at about a quarter past eleven. *Ambience* was notoriously difficult to get into unless you went about 10.30pm. Rocking up at well gone 11.00pm put them in the risky zone. It wasn't as though the club was anything special and only let in sophisticated aristocrats; this was in the dead-centre of Birkenhead, after all. The reason it was so challenging gaining entry was down to one man—Harry, the head doorman. He was an absolute arsehole of a human being who thrived on humiliation and intimidation, but he was the lock that had to be picked to get inside. Getting knocked back from a club was a pain for the lads and meant that they'd end up in an establishment that was further down on their wish list. They'd been knocked back from clubs before and it would almost certainly happen again in the future. It was no big deal. However, *Ambience* was different. The silverback gorilla that was Harry purposely let people into the club in dribs and drabs so that a lengthy queue formed outside the entrance. This is a common club management tactic to make the place look busy and increase one's desire to get in, although it was probably empty inside.

What made the entrance to *Ambience* so daunting was that it was at the end of a dead-end street, meaning that if Harry didn't let you in, the unsuccessful had to walk past everyone still waiting in the queue while they sniggered at your embarrassment. The lads called it *The Walk of Shame*.

Harry was a beast of man. He wasn't a typical-looking bouncer with bald head, goatee beard and a muscular body pumped up with steroids. He still had steroid-type anger issues, but his rage was produced by some deep-rooted mental screw-up and not the result of injecting synthetic testosterone into his blood.

The lads followed suit with their usual strategy, which had been relatively successful in the past. They'd hang round on the corner, out of sight of the nightclub entrance, and wait for a gang of girls to walk past. Steve would flutter his eyelids and give them some flannel, and then they'd all walk in together as a mixed group, rather than a gang of lads.

Jonno had seen swanky Mayfair Gentlemen's clubs on TV where the front door would be opened by a welcoming commissionaire, followed by a pleasant greeting and an outstretched, white-gloved hand. *Ambience* was the opposite. The queue wasn't filled with well-dressed, affluent high-flyers from Knightsbridge, but more an array of council estate residents who'd purchased their outfits from Birkenhead Market.

The two lads that were in front of Jonno in the queue, who had been relentlessly blowing second-hand *Embassy Regal* smoke into his face, which mildly masked the smell of the urine-drenched wall, finally got in. Jonno, Naz and two of the girls they'd commandeered, stood poised in front of the big, black door. The door was permanently closed and only opened when Harry allowed clientele into the club. He didn't even open the door to look at you, it was undertaken by a small sliding hatch. The door was sat on top of a single concrete step which meant Harry was always standing taller than the club-goer. Therefore, he appeared much taller than he was, not that he needed a psychological advantage.

The hatch slid open quickly and Harry's beady eyes peered through the slot. Jonno was standing at the foot of the step and that's who Harry addressed through the slim aperture.

'Have ya got I.D?' he grunted.

'I haven't, Harry.'

Jonno was taking a chance calling him by his name, as they weren't friends and were unlikely to be sharing buttered scones and a cup of Earl Grey anytime in the future. It could be seen as disrespectful, almost arrogant, but Jonno deduced it was worth the risk. The sliding door on the hatch slid shut forcefully. They had now entered the unknown zone. Harry never knocked anyone back verbally, he just closed the hatch and didn't open the door. You would wait there for ten seconds or so and if the door didn't open, you would start the excruciating *Walk of Shame*. They waited what seemed like minutes but was probably around fifteen seconds. This was a stand-off, *Western Style,* and Jonno was going to stand firm until he pulled his 1847 Colt Walker Revolver and shot him dead through the heart.

The door opened and there stood Harry in all his domineering magnificence, blocking their path to the laser lights and dry ice. He stood maybe 5'11'' but the single step gave him a gigantic uplift and the door frame was filled with his broad shoulders and silverback chest. Numerous old scars created bald gaps in his stubble and his chilling eyes were deeply sunken into a protruding

forehead. Beads of sweat upon his face and irritated cheeks were
evidence that wearing a suit and dickie bow in summer
temperatures proved uncomfortable. He lurched forward and stared
hard with one final assessment.

'Is it just you four?'
Jonno nodded in agreement, shamefully severing his knowledge of
two great friends behind him in order to gain entry to a Birkenhead
nightclub. He opened the door and summoned them in, to a
collective sigh of relief.

'Wait!'
Just as they had their feet in the door, there was now a steward's
enquiry by another bouncer who fitted the typical look of a usual
stedhead. It transpired that he also had the traditional aggressive
attitude, injected with so much indignation that he could start an
argument in an empty room.

'He's barred!' he announced, pointing directly at Jonno.

'Wha'? No, I'm not.'
Harry turned to his young soldier and requested more information.

'He was in here last week. Got chucked out for fighting.'
Harry returned his stare back to Jonno.

'I didn't even go out last week,' Jonno lamented.

'That wasn't him, Pete. You've got him mixed up with someone.
This lad's a good kid.'
*Fuck me! Harry knows my face, and furthermore, he thinks I'm
okay*, Jonno privately rejoiced. This was like getting a cuddle from
Kenny Dalglish; he almost felt famous.

It came to realisation that the asking for I.D through the hatch
was just a big coercion exercise because he knew who Jonno was
and that he'd been in the club many times. Jonno suddenly saw this
big, bullying beast of a brute in a different light. It felt like this
fella had his back and he had a bit of authority around the joint. He
felt like *Henry Hill* in 1965, taking Karen to *The Copacabana*,
ushered past the queue by the chief of security and sat at a newly

planted table, right in front of the stage. A crooner belted out *The Good Life* by *Tony Bennet* and Martinis were instantly placed on their candlelit table, whilst fellow guests looked on aghast.

'I'm keeping a fuckin' eye on you, gobshite,' whispered the goatee-bearded bouncer into Jonno's ear through mists of spit.

There was a break-out area with a bar as soon as guests walked into the club, with the main dancefloor and louder music upstairs. It was still early, and they needed more lubrication, so they hit the optics at the downstairs bar before being joined by Steve and Birchy and heading upstairs.

As they walked up the stairs, *Mr Vain* by *Culture Beat* bled the ears, and colourful, sweeping lights and lasers splintered the darkness and the mist. The place was jam-packed. A circular dancefloor was the club's centrepiece, with people heavily populating its borders. The lads found a suitable speck and skimmed the room for any female delicacies.

The poppy, mainstream dance music was less intense than what they were used to, but it still caused overactive electrons to dance upon the hairs of Jonno's neck and arms. These occasions were the only times he wished he had illegal substances in him, so that the pulsing beats meant so much more. Tonight, he was powered only by alcohol, but he had managed to develop a technique where he could artificially transport himself to a time where he'd been off his face on a tablet. It didn't feel the same, but it was better than the groggy draw of alcohol.
He swept the room with predator eyes and caught sight of his nemesis bouncer on the door glaring over at him—a coiled spring waiting for one of them to step out of line and he would be over with the breakneck speed of *Linford fuckin' Christie*.

Jonno averted his eyes to the dancefloor, and through the darkness and haze, he caught sight of Becky dancing with a friend, and a couple of lads hovering around waiting for their perfect moment. His instant thought was to fly over to her and eradicate the two parasites waiting to feed on her beauty and loveliness. Then he remembered she wasn't his girlfriend and it had nothing at all to do with him. His heart sank. He didn't think she'd seen him, so he acted oblivious and continued to laugh and talk to his mates. He tried to keep it to more than a minute, but every few seconds he found himself slyly looking over to see what she was up to. Even though he was intoxicated, he kept telling himself that this was not great behaviour, and she would like him better if he showed some maturity and acted in a civil fashion.

'Come 'ed, Danny, it's half one. We've got to get on the dancefloor before there's only munters left,' Steve declared as he grabbed Jonno's arm.

Jonno didn't dance. He hated it. He felt like an idiot and that was why taking ecstasy had been like opening a Kinder Egg and finding your favourite toy. A toy that teleported you to a new world of confidence and opportunity. Alcohol didn't do that for him and every time he tried to dance, he felt awkward and disjointed. Steve shoved him into the centre of the dancefloor into a pot of speculators, opportunists, and targets, all being slowly stewed in a pan of *Show Me Love* tangy sauce.

Jonno had a hidden agenda and unknowingly marshalled Steve to the spot where Becky had been roosting all night. He wasn't sure Steve even spotted Becky before he'd accosted her friend. That left Jonno and Becky facing each other.

'Hiya, Bec, I didn't know you went to Ambience?'

'I don't, my mate wanted to come,' she shouted in his ear over the thud of the bass.

'Are you ok with me dancin' with ya? I'm not bein' a pest, am I?

'No, Dan, coz we're mates, aren't we?'
Jonno hated that word when referring to girls. They weren't mates. He didn't want to be her mate, he wanted her to love him. To feel like he did. He didn't want to talk to her like a friend or act like her friend. It had to be all or nothing. At this moment in time, this was all he had, and he had to play along with it.

They danced for a bit. Well, she danced, Jonno just moved his feet side-to-side, occasionally singing the wrong words to an odd chorus and trying to clap in time. The DJ pulled the dance tunes up and expertly bled in the introduction of *Where Do Broken Hearts Go* by Whitney Houston. Some clubs had started moving away from ending the night with slowies, but *Ambience* had stood firm and still finished the night with one slow song.

This was a torrid time of the night for every single man. It was four minutes of sheer panic and desperate decision-making that could make or break you. A man could come out the other side of *The Erection Section* a valiant knight on a white steed with a beautiful damsel on his arm, or the beer goggles could take control and he could get shackled with a lady that would scare kids away from the fireplace. It was stressful and chaotic, and any spadework a man had put in for the previous twenty minutes could become undone in a nanosecond with no time left to readjust and find a suitable substitute.

'See ya, Danny.'
Steve was already playing tonsil hockey with Becky's mate, so she had nowhere to go and Jonno had nothing to lose. He grabbed her wrist to gently prevent her from moving.

'Stay, Bec?'

He pulled her towards himself, with little resistance, and placed both his hands on her hips and she coupled her fingers around his neck as they completed the standard *slowie* position. He tilted his head and delicately kissed the soft skin on her neck, moving slowly up to her ear. Her perfume was perfectly conservative, and her hair smelt of fresh linen and cleanliness. His eyes were closed as he moved his mouth towards hers, while *Whitney* bellowed completely pertinent lyrics in the background. They kissed tenderly, and in well-rehearsed union, despite his overwhelming desire to accelerate the passion. Her lipstick tasted like fruit and he desperately wanted to be back in her world. He could feel energy leaving his body and he wanted it to enter her heart; to feel the same as him. He removed his right hand from her hip and caressed her perfectly-formed bum as the kissing intensified. It was as if the passion control knob had been turned up a bit and then, to his absolute disappointment, the song ended and so did the kissing. She slipped from his grip—a lucky mouse escaping the constrict of a boa and was free of him in an instant.

'We're not back, Dan. This was a one-off. Take care of yourself.'

And then she slipped away into the crowd.

22 THE SHOCK

The violent hammering on Jonno's front door was causing his head to throb. He glanced at his watch.

Who the fuck was knocking at my door at 8 o'clock on a Sunday morning?

The banging continued and he could now hear muffled shouting to add to the commotion. He stuck a T-shirt on and slowly trudged down the stairs, muttering *shut the fuck up* to himself. He opened the door to Naz who was frantic and spluttering nonsensical words. His face was white, and he was bouncing around anxiously. He grabbed Jonno's arms and shook him.

'Come. Come. You've got to come with me.'

'Mate calm down. What is goin' on?

'Come. Let's go.'

'Naz, you're not makin' sense, mate. Slow down and tell me what's up.'

'Emily's in hospital. Her neighbour, Stacey. Tracey. She rang me.'

'What's up with her? What happened?'

'I don't fuckin know, Danny! That's all she told me!' he screamed.

'Get in the car. I'll stick my jeans and trainees on.'

This was the point Jonno really wished he'd have had enough spare money to take driving lessons. They were on the way to the hospital, but he wasn't sure whether it was going to be in Naz's car or on a stretcher in the back of an ambulance.

'Slow down mate, you're gonna get us killed.'

He was dodging in and out of traffic, undertaking cars, doing sixty in a thirty zone, and

consistently beeping his horn to anyone and everything that obstructed his path. At one point, he nearly went through a zebra crossing and if Jonno hadn't have screamed at him, he'd have clipped some old lady. He was in a really disturbed mood. He had a face like thunder and was continuously muttering obscenities about Jodie under his breath.

'I'll fuckin' kill her. I'll fuckin' kill her if she's hurt Emily. I fuckin' knew it. I knew this would happen. The fuckin' slag. I'll fuckin' kill her.'

'Naz, calm down, mate. We don't know anything yet. It might have nothin' to do with Jodie.'

'Fuck off! Of course it has. She's in her fuckin' care!'

They sped into the hospital layby and hit the kerb with an almighty thud. He just left his car on yellow lines. They ran in to the A&E department and approached the lady at reception.

'Emily McAnally. I'm her dad,' pleaded Naz.

'One moment, sir.'

'Naz!' shouted a voice from behind them.
It was Tracey from next door who had rung the ambulance. She scurried over to them. Naz decided to skip any pleasantries.

'What the fuck has happened? Where is my baby?'

'I don't know, Naz. I'd heard Emily crying and screaming all night. I think she was on her own. About six this morning, there was an almighty bang and then just silence. I knew Jodie hid a front door key under a plant pot, so I let myself in and Emily was unconscious at the bottom of the stairs. I followed the ambulance up here, but they won't tell me anything coz I'm not family.'

Jonno had never seen Naz's face like this before, and he knew him better than anyone. It was twisted with anger and depleted with sorrow. The whites of his eyes enlarged themselves in a bid to hear the words that his ears could not accept. He stopped bobbing and stood inert as if cast from stone. The weight of Tracey's words injected concrete into his veins and paralysed him on the spot. He stood motionless, and emotionless, in a state of shock and incredulity. Jonno's heart felt heavy, and an icy chill ran down his spine. The room darkened as he began to realise the severity of the situation. He wanted to slip into his surreal world to escape the horrors of the truth, but he forced himself to stay focused because Naz was currently unstable and unpredictable.

'Mr McAnally?'

The reception snapped Naz back into reality.

'No, it's Hasnawi. We're not married. McAnally is her mum's surname.'

'Emily is in ICU. Go through the double doors and follow the blue floor tiles down the corridor. It's the last door on the right.' Naz was gone in a flash and Jonno thanked the receptionist on his behalf.
They flew down the hospital corridor, but when they tried to get through the door to the intensive care unit, they discovered it was locked and had to press the intercom button. A nurse in her mid-fifties opened the door to them.

'Emily McAnally?' Naz bellowed.

'Okay, just calm yourself down, sir. There are a lot of sick people in here and I would be grateful if you could lower your voice and show them some respect, please. I appreciate that you must be worried, but there are other people in here.'

Naz nodded and accepted the verbal slap in the face.

'Now, are you Emily's dad?

'Yeah, I am. Naz Hasnawi.'

The nurse wore a different coloured tunic to most of the other staff and generated an air of authority, so Jonno assumed that she was some sort of head nurse. She talked softly as she led them down the corridor.

'So, Naz, don't be too alarmed, but Emily has got some tubes in her, so she won't look herself. She is quite poorly, but she is in the best place. We have the most brilliant medical team here.'

'But what happened to her? How did this happen?'

'There's a police officer over there who may be able to give you more details. I can only tell you what we know. She was brought into us in an unconscious state. She has since woken up, but we have sedated her, so she is currently asleep. She has second-degree burns to her fingers and the palm of her right hand. These are swollen and very painful and is the main reason we have sedated her, in addition to her not knowing where she was. However, the burns are not the reason she was unconscious.'

'Well what was the reason, then?' demanded Naz.

'She was found at the bottom of the stairs with a teaspoon close to her.'

'A spoon?' Naz quizzed.

'Yes. The police think she may have stuck the spoon into the wall socket. The electric shock has burnt her hand, jolting her backwards and down the stairs. As soon as she came in, we did a full body CT scan and discovered that she has a linear fracture to the skull.'

'Linear? What's that? Is it bad?'

'Look, it's a closed fracture and she is going to have a sore head for a few days. Her burns are badly blistered, but we've cleaned them, and dressed them. She doesn't need a skin graft and we expect her to make a full recovery. The police will want to talk to you about how this happened.'

'It's that fuckin' bitch! I don't live with Emily. It's her fuckin' oxygen thief of a mother!'

'Sir! Keep your voice down— and mind your language. This is a paediatric intensive care unit full of critically ill children and they, and their parents do not need to hear language like that! If you swear again, I will have to ask you to leave.'
Jonno put his hand on the top of Naz's shoulder and squeezed it firmly.

'Come on, mate,' he implored.

'I'm so sorry. This isn't like me. I'm just so upset over all of this. Sorry.'

'That's fine, Mr. Hasnawi, I completely understand, but we have a duty of care for everyone in this hospital. Now, you can see your little girl, but your friend will have to wait behind the window.'

Naz walked into her room and softly closed the door behind him. Jonno could see him approach the bed slowly as he looked through the viewing window. Emily lay still, propped up by pillows in a junior bed with side rails. Pieces of white tape securing tubes broke up the beautiful olive complexion of her face. Her curly locks of golden hair were controlled by a thick, pink Alice band and she looked comfortably snug in lilac *Rugrats* pyjamas. Naz pulled up a chair close to his daughter and delicately lifted her hand into his. Her chest moved slowly as she breathed at a placid rate; it was the only movement her little body offered. Naz gently tickled her tiny ears and wept uncontrollably like a man who'd lost everything. He muttered in unheard words that Jonno estimated was prayer.

A male and female police officers approached Jonno as he stood outside Emily's room.

'Mr Hasnawi?'
Wow! You're not the sharpest tool in the shed, are you? Do I look like a Mr Hasnawi, you fuckin' thick fuck? This fella was in contention for Chief Superintendent with investigative skills like that, Jonno raged to himself. However, he managed to hold his tongue of its sarcastic venom and answer him politely.

'No. Here he is now,' Jonno said, as Naz left the room looking like a shadow of himself.

'Naseem Hasnawi?

'Yeah, that's me, officer.'

'I'm PC McGovern and this is WPC Samuel.'

McGovern was a skinny, stretched man, not much older than Jonno but had a good four inches on him, even without his helmet on. His greasy face was barraged with acne and Jonno thought that his wispy moustache made him look slightly creepy. His tone made him sound like he been bullied in school and was now gaining vengeance with the world by being a petty, pedantic arse of a man. Jonno didn't have a great deal of time or respect for the boys in blue. He'd grown up in the eighties and every time he saw them on the telly, whether it was the Toxteth or Brixton riots, the miners strikes or Broadwater Farm in Tottenham, they always seemed to be beating some poor person up or shafting someone with lies and corruption. He hadn't had any serious run-ins with the police, but he'd heard stories from people he'd grown up with. Bent coppers in black Maria vans pulling some half-innocent kid in the back and kicking *seven types of shite* out of him. The police were above the law and answerable to no one. They used force and intimidation and if you didn't like it and showed an attitude, you'd end up with a stick to the head.

Jonno heard from a friend who had a brother in the force, about the misdemeanours and brutality the Operations Support Group police used to administer. The OSG were specialist trained officers empowered to deal with public order offences like riots or carry out drug raids. The problem was when there was nothing for them to do. It would result in six pumped-up-with-steroids coppers in the back of a van who were trained to fight and had no fight available. The second someone farted in the wrong direction, they'd be out that van and kicking the life out of someone without a single question asked. Of course, not all coppers were like that, and Jonno was sure there were some lovely overweight sergeants in the hamlet of *Heartbeat* that knew all the villagers by name, but those fellas weren't stationed in Birkenhead.

WPC Samuel was a pretty little thing. She was a mixed-race lady with a beautiful complexion, glassy blue eyes, and inviting lips. Jonno was concerned that he was having sexual thoughts about a copper at such a distressing time. It could be the uniform, but it was more likely that the link to his brain was wired up wrong. *There is definitely something wrong with me*, he conceded.

'Are you the father of Emily McAnally?'

'Yes,' Said Naz.

'Where were you on Saturday night, sir?

'I was at home, watchin' telly.'

'Was your daughter with you, sir?'

'No. It wasn't my weekend. I had her last week. I'm trying to get full custody, though. I've got a solicitor.'

'Do you stay at Miss McAnally's house much, Mr Hasnawi?

'No chance. I'm not allowed in. I pick her up at the doorstep, and if I can get away with it, I'll wait in the car away from that psycho.'

WPC Samuel took notes as McGovern continued.

'Are you aware of anyone else other than your daughter and estranged partner living at the house?'

'Yeah, the gargoyle. Well, I don't know if he lives there, but he's there a lot.'

'The gargoyle?'

'Her boyfriend. An ugly fucker.'

'Ah, that must be Mr Julian Thorbinson.'
Jonno looked at Naz and sniggered. Even bang in the middle of a dramatic event, they still couldn't help sneer at his name.

'Okay. That'll be all for now, Mr Hasnawi.'

'Whoa, hang on! You've got to tell me what you know. What happened to Emily?'

'Look, Mr Hasnawi, I can't tell you too much, as it is still under investigation. Jodie McAnally was arrested for neglect early on Sunday morning.'

'Neglect? Why?'

'We believe the child—sorry, Emily— was in the house on her own at the time of the incident. There are also some additional factors that I cannot disclose at present.'

'The fuckin' whore left my baby in the house on her own and went out on the piss with the gargoyle?'

'Keep your voice and language controlled please, sir. I appreciate this may be disturbing news, but you are in a hospital.'

'So what happens now with Emily? Can I take her home? She can't go back to her mum after this, can she?'

'I'd estimate that she will be in hospital for a couple of days, but that is really a question social services would have to answer, sir.'

'Well, what usually happens, officer?'

'I can't answer that, sir.'

'Fuckin' lot of use those pricks are,' Naz said quietly as the two coppers walked away.

Shite, mate,' Jonno consoled.

'Listen, Jonno, you get yourself off, mate. Thanks so much for coming with me. I was off my head.'

'What are you gonna do?

'I'm gonna stay with Emily, la, at least until she wakes up. I don't want her to be on her own and I don't want that fuckin' reptile anywhere near her. I'll wait and see what the 'ozzy say about me taking her home.'

'Okay, mate. Take care and give her a big kiss from me,' Jonno said, as he gave Naz a hug.

23 FROM MAKER TO TAKER

Naz didn't make it to work on Monday but he was ringing Jonno's phone the second he got in from work.

'Hello?'

'Have you read it?

'Read what?'

'The Liverpool Fuckin' Echo! There's a piece in there about Jodie. Page five.'

'I've only just got in from work, Naz. I haven't even looked at the sport yet.'

'Read it now and ring me straight back.'

'OK. Let me get my dirty clobber off and I'll ring you back.'

Despite Naz's desperation for Jonno to read the article, he still turned to the back page first. He wished he hadn't. It was all about Everton's escape against Wimbledon and how their fans cheered them to victory. An absolute travesty in the world of football. Everton were two-nil down after twenty minutes before Hans Segers started diving in the opposite direction to all Everton shots, which ultimately kept *The Blues* in the Premier League. The glory and celebration of Everton staying in the division put Jonno off reading the sport, so he flipped the paper over and flicked through to page five to discover the *Jodie* article.

Young Mother Arrested After Child Suffers Electric Shock

A mother left her three-year-old child in their home while she went out clubbing with her live-in partner.

Jodie McAnally, 24 of Vyner Pine Close, Birkenhead, was arrested and charged in the early hours of Sunday morning and will appear before Magistrates on Tuesday at Birkenhead courts.
She will be charged with child neglect and abandonment under The Children and Young Persons Act and has currently been released with no bail requirements.
Reports say that McAnally left her home at around 8pm on Saturday evening with her boyfriend Julian Thorbinson, 27, and left her three-year-old daughter asleep in bed.
A witness said they heard the toddler crying around 9.30pm but didn't think too much of it, as there was often a lot of noise from the house.
The toddler allegedly poked a metal teaspoon into an electric wall socket and received burns to her hand, and head injuries from the resulting fall.
During a search of the property, police discovered a large quantity of cocaine stuffed into an opening in the child's mattress. The cocaine is estimated to have a street value of around £8,000.
Both McAnally and Thorbinson will be investigated for procession of class-A drugs, separately to the neglect case.

Ms McAnally was not available for comment, but a
neighbour did say, 'It doesn't surprise me.'

The phone rang again.

'Ave ya read it yet?'

'Yeah mate, just read it.'

'Fuck me, Jonno, that is some heavy shit that, innit? That fuckin'
trollop has allowed the ugly fucker to stuff cocaine in my baby's
bed. He's got to pay for this, Jonno. Anything could've happened.
Emily could have opened one of the bags and taken some of it.
He's got to pay. We've got to do him.'

It felt fundamentally wrong to Jonno being so opinionated and
disproving about the dirty life of drugs. He'd guessed that the
narcotic undergoes a long, dissolute journey from its maker to its
taker. Possibly spending time near many innocents, including
children. He envisioned families and neighbours picking leaves
from cocoa plants amid the lush greenery of northwest Colombia,
and how the process must be an *all hands on deck* operation.
Young brothers, Juán and Alejandro harvesting cocoa leaves, then
passing them to their father, Santiago, who would mix the crop
with chemicals in a clandestine, primitive laboratory. These people
were tiny cogs in a massive machine driven by cartels, local
militia, and corrupt police forces.

He wondered how many children would be directly, or
vicariously involved in the movement of that paste once it was
processed, and then trafficked through Mexico to be smuggled into
the United States, and then finally shipped to Europe or North
Africa. How many people would be bullied, threatened, arrested,
maimed, or killed for the drug to reach its final destination? How
many hands had it passed through, and how many times had it
been cut, before ending its journey with a nefarious monster like
The Gargoyle? The Gargoyle, who then feeds off vulnerable idiots
like Jonno and the lads, serving out exhaustively mixed powder
packets for extortionate prices.

Even though Jonno tried to make himself feel guilty, he was still not in the same division as what *The Gargoyle* was doing, and Jonno was quick to back Naz up.

'It's fuckin' outrageous, mate.'

Although Jonno was upset for Naz, he didn't feel the rage he was experiencing. He supposed this was a defence mechanism that only a father could feel, although it had bypassed his own dad. Most fathers would run into a burning building to save their kid or take a bullet for them. That feeling that the child's life was more precious than yours and that you were prepared to die on the spot if it meant the child could be saved. Jonno reckoned that his own dad didn't have that deep, embedded instinct—he'd certainly never shown it. Jonno didn't feel it either. —not yet. He didn't know that feeling and was dubious that he ever would. Maybe that is something that just creeps up on you and develops without you even knowing it, he supposed. It must have something to do with a child being innocent and defenceless and that caveman instinct to protect what is yours kicks in. He wasn't a caveman yet.

There were, evidently, potential consequences of that uncontrolled desire to protect and punish those that harm your offspring. The erupting fury that churned around Naz's psyche was clouding his composure and decision making. People say *I'll kill you* all the time as a flippant comment, but Jonno thought Naz was genuinely considering this as a viable option and anticipated himself masterminding it with him. Jonno shook his head. There was no way he was getting involved in any featherheaded idea to attack *The Gargoyle* that would result in him doing time. He really wouldn't be able to handle prison. He wasn't sure exactly what it was like on the inside, but he'd heard stories that proved he was not cut out for it. He once asked Birchy what it was like and he replied, *you couldn't handle it.*

Jonno had been in loads of scraps in his twenty-four years and very rarely walked away from a fight, although that irresponsible attitude was dwindling as he got older. He didn't consider himself a hard case and he knew he would not be able to deal with the crazed lunatics that frequent prisons, and the nonsensical politics.

A lot of these men were more than just hard knocks that could fight; they'd lost the fear factor through drugs, mental issues, or burning rage. That made them the most fearful opponent. A man who does not fear death or consequence, is a life-threatening obstacle that must be avoided, especially in confined spaces.

The rules of mainstream society don't apply when you are banged up and the tales he'd heard of brutality could send shivers through the most hardened of souls. It was difficult to decipher what was fact and was fiction, but the stories narrated by ex-cons served as a perfect deterrent to Jonno. Stories of bullying, beatings, extortion, humiliation, and rape from screwed-up, crazed psychopaths who had taken leave of their senses and were on a road to destruction, not caring about who stepped in their path. Jonno knew that if he were to be locked in a world where suicide, shanking, scalding, and complete isolation from ordinariness were the norm, he would die internally before any eye-bulging maniac could hurt him physically. There was no way he was going to get involved in any reckless plans Naz was hatching and he didn't want him involved either, so he had to be the voice of reason.

'Naz, mate. I know you're pissed off, but you need to think about Emily. You're going through the courts to get full custody of her, and you could get collared doing something you will regret for the rest of your life.'

'I won't get caught!'

'Naz, you're talking shit. You're not a criminal mastermind. You will get caught. The bizzies and social services already know what's going on with you lot. If anything happens to *The Gargoyle*, whose door do you think they will knock on first?

There was a silence down the line, except for an annoying cackle, which indicated to Jonno that the penny had dropped and hit Naz's thick skull. He continued his lecture until he accepted the facts.

'If you go to prison, who's gonna look after Emily? She might end up in care. Jodie is in a pile of shite at the minute, and that puts you in prime position. Why would you risk that?'

There was a slight chuckle in response which suggested he'd taken on Jonno's advice, so he decided to change the subject quickly.

'So are you still out on Saturday for our end of season piss-up?'

'Of course I fuckin' am!'

'Sound. Ross is doin' us a brekkie, so we're all meeting in The Belvedere at ten.'

'Sound. See you in there, Dan. Oh, and Danny?'

'Yeah?'

'Nothin', doesn't matter.'

***

A baked bean managed to escape Birchy's plate and was making a run for it, to make a better life for itself and its baked bean family. A short run down the polished mahogany path to freedom and bean utopia. Unfortunately, Birchy spotted the tomato sauce-drenched fugitive and flicked it at Naz, scoring a direct strike on the arm of his dark-blue suit jacket.

'Fuck off, Birch, ya prick!' Naz protested.

'Well, fuckin' snap out of it, then! Sittin' there like a bird on the rag.'

'Leave it, mate,' Jonno said to Birchy, whilst shaking his head to discourage the lampooning of a broken man. The state Naz was currently in, giving him any sort of grief would be plain wrong. Besides, there's banter, and then there's outright stupidity. Flicking beans at someone who was *suited and booted* for a day at the races was plain idiotic.

It was ten in the morning and they were all drinking pints of lager to wash down a fantastic breakfast that Ross and Sue had prepared for the whole team. They all looked a million dollars in their suits, ready for their end of season booze-up at Chester races. Jonno was just about to violate his egg yolk with a round of toast when Birchy jumped up to attention, knocking crockery and cutlery everywhere, in a one-man mission to wreck everyone's suits before they'd even left the boozer. He squinted his eyes to focus on his prey through the sections of the window that were not opaquely etched.

'What the fuck? Is that *The Gargoyle*?'
The three lads spun around in their chairs to face the same direction and then bobbed their heads to avoid the frosted window film. There was *The Gargoyle*, trudging his malodorous trotters right past their pub carrying a Woolworth's bag, without a care in the world. Jonno's brain hadn't had time to even register what was going on and Birchy had already left the pub, leaving the door swinging as if it belonged in a Wild West saloon. The three lads jumped up to follow him, chased by a couple of the other lads that were interested to see what all the commotion was about. Birchy sprinted towards *The Gargoyle* and performed some sort of flying Jean-Claude Van Damme kick into the small of his back, which sent him tumbling onto the ground with a low-pitched groan. He got to all fours, still not facing his adversary, and took a moment to analyse what had just happened. Snot dripped from his pig snout and he snorted with anger. His *Parklife* by *Blur* album had escaped his *Woolies* bag and skidded a couple of paving stones away. He turned to face them, still on all fours, ready to expel toxic fire at his enemy, and then stopped dead when he saw what was facing him.

Birchy stood over him with a clenched right fist and he probably looked eight foot tall from *The Gargoyle's* grounded position. Birchy was supported by five proponents dressed in dark suits. It looked like a scene from a Mafia movie where you could cap someone in the street, and if you were wearing a suit, and in the family, everyone would look the other way.

Naz stood aslant of Birchy with a poisonous look of revenge and hate. Jonno stayed focused on him in case he lost it and did something stupid, risking his chances of custody. *The Gargoyle* clambered to his feet and stared for a second at the six of them. *Surely, he was not sizing up his chances?*

No words were spoken. It didn't seem necessary. He knew, and *they* knew what this was about. This was a clear message to back the away from them or chance the consequences. *The Gargoyle* lowered his eyes from their stare, and then to the ground to pick up his poor taste in music. As he trotted off down the street—scolded and humiliated, Jonno couldn't help but think that this would serve as lighting the touch paper, rather than a lesson learned.

They trudged back into the pub. No one congratulated Birchy—it didn't seem like a victory worth celebrating, more of a chore that had to be completed. Jonno was glad that it was Birchy who did it and not Naz. Dave Llewellyn gave out the end-of-year trophies. There were no surprises, really; Birchy won everything except top goal scorer, and that was because he was a defender! That trophy went to Paul North, their five-foot-six striker who'd bagged 32 goals that season. Jonno was happy for Birchy, and he deserved his haul, but he didn't look at the victory the same way as he would. Jonno would have had his trophies on the telly or the living room mantlepiece, but Birchy will probably lash them in the loft or in his shed. Jonno's life wasn't filled with praise or accreditation, so if he was ever lucky enough to be recognised for something he'd done, then he would cherish that.

The coach trip was as manic as they'd expected. They'd already had three pints at breakfast and the coach was awash with lager cans. They'd all splashed out with tickets for the County Stand at the course and it felt great to rub shoulders with people who had a few quid; Jonno was discreetly disguised in his suit as something he wasn't. He wasn't too fussed about gambling but stuck a couple of fivers on a few races with no real success. He was there for the beer, a craic with the lads, and maybe a touch with a classy Chester lass.

They bumped into a Birkenhead lad at the course who was now playing for Wimbledon Football Club in the Premier League. He was with a couple of first-team players and they hung around together for a while. It was a very odd situation that made Jonno feel uneasy, but he was loving it just the same. Here he was, a nobody from Birkenhead who didn't have two pennies to rub together, dressed in a suit and mixing with Premier League footballers. He felt fake but was willing to wing it. The lads made them feel comfortable, though, and although two of them were cockneys, they blended right in with their Merseyside wit.

Jonno looked around at all the lads and everyone was smiling or laughing. Naz had forgotten about his troubles with Jodie for a while, Steve appeared to not be thinking about his horrific childhood, and Birchy had forgotten to bring his brain cell out with him. The sense of unity and camaraderie Jonno felt with these boys was at its strongest right now. It felt stronger than you could experience with family, and he could never see this bond breaking. They were united in a world where they had to work for everything they had, and that was always accomplished easier if they did it as a team. They had each other's backs, and even though they all got on each other's nerves at times, Jonno loved them all dearly.

24 SNOW IN THE DASH

Since the fleeting snog with Becky, she'd been back on Jonno's mind constantly. After all the trouble he'd been through at the doctors and finding his own methods to concentrate on the good stuff, she was back, bang in the centre of his head, living rent-free. She consumed his mind and it felt like he couldn't go more than a few minutes without thinking about her. He was starting to worry about himself because this now felt more like infatuation rather than love.

Where could this go?

Was I capable of kidnapping or murdering her unless she met my demands?

Did he have the capability to be a Mark David Chapman or a Lee Harvey Oswald, so obsessed with their subject that only murder would satisfy their fascination.

If I couldn't be happy, why should she?

Maybe one murder was the start of something bigger—he could get a taste for it, possibly even start to enjoy it, and find himself prowling the streets like Peter Sutcliffe in the shadows looking for a soft touch. Living without her did seem impossible, so maybe the solution was to not let her live?

Fuck me, get a grip of yourself, Jonno!

He had to give himself an imaginary slap in the face. Of course, he couldn't hurt a hair on that girl's head. All the same, it didn't feel like it was over. It never felt over, he was just keeping his distance because it was over for her.

The kiss in *Ambiance* had changed all that. He speculated that she must've still had some feelings for him. How could you kiss someone that you absolutely despise, someone you never want to talk to or see again? You just don't entertain that type of person. She'd walked away that night and said it meant nothing, but Jonno knew Becky was more intelligent than that. That really wasn't her style. She wasn't drunk and she wouldn't do that type of thing out of vengeance, so there must have been something there. Some tiny inkling of hope. He deduced that it must be worth a phone call.

He paced the room for an hour running everything through his head. He wrote the lines and ran through every possible twist in his mind. There was no way he was going to get caught out; he had to have an answer for everything. It was nearly 8pm on Wednesday. She was always up early for work and there was no way she would be out, so she'd have to answer. It wasn't too late for the cut-off point, either. The point where you say to yourself, *who the fuck's this, ringing at this time of night?* and expecting bad news. No—it hadn't entered that zone yet. She could hang up straight away, he supposed. That would be the final nail—there'd be no coming back from that. He couldn't see her pulling a nasty trick like that, especially if he were being nice to her. She didn't have a noxious streak like that. He had to do it. It would eat away at him all night if he didn't.

The phone rang three times before she picked up.

'Hello?'

'Hiya, Becky, it's me.'

'Who's tha'?'
For fuck's sake, this wasn't the best of starts.

'It's Danny.' he wasn't saying his surname. *If she needed that, she could sod off.*

'What do you want, Danny?'
She certainly didn't sound like she'd be welcoming him home with open arms anytime soon.

'I just wanted to give you a bell, you know, about the other weekend.'

'What d'ya mean, Danny?'
Fucking hell, she is going to make me say it. This was definitely some sort of power trip she was on. She was almost ridiculing me, he grieved.

'You know, in *Ambience*. The kiss.'

Becky knew exactly who it was, and exactly what he was referring to. He'd let her down and broke her heart and there was no way that she was prepared to be overly nice to him—why should she? She felt like a fool—she stupidly thought that Danny was a little bit different to most of the idiots that Birkenhead had to offer. She was committed and willing to offer her heart to this lad, but he flushed that down the toilet for a two-minute fumble in a pub. So, why should she make it easy for him?

'I told you on the night, Danny, it was a mistake. You shouldn't read anything into it. It was nothing.'

She bit her lip. Her words to Danny hurt as they were delivered but she had to stick to her guns. She had to be true to herself. There was an awkward silence as Jonno tried to find valuable words.

'It didn't feel like nothing to me.'

'Well you need to wake up then, lad. There's no coming back from what you did to me. You showed your true colours.'

'But you've never let me explain, Becky, or apologise. I was absolutely leathered, and I just had a quick kiss with some nothin' bird. I didn't know what I was doin' and regretted it straight away.'

'I'm not interested, Danny.'

'Look, I'm so sorry I've hurt you. I made a mistake. A big mistake. It'll never happen again, I promise you.'

'You're right, it'll never happen again coz we're never getting' back. It's over, Danny. Please don't call me again. There's nothing to talk about. Take care of yourself.'

The line went dead.

Well, that couldn't have gone much worse. He didn't have time to start experiencing the pain of the cold steel jabbed into his heart when the phone rang almost instantly after he'd put it down. *Maybe she'd realised how harsh she'd come across and wanted to thaw out a little, and offer me another chance,* he ridiculously fantasised.

'Hello?'

'Who the fuck have you been on the phone to? I've been ringin' for ages. Have you been ringin' those Thai Lady Boys on an 0898 number again?'
Perfect timing. Jonno currently felt like jumping off a tall building and ending it all and the most arrogant, unemotional Neanderthal rings him.

'What's up, Birch? It's not a good time.'

'Jonno, I need a favour.'

'I've got no money, Birch.'

'It's not money, ya prick!'

'Go on then, what is it?'

'I can't tell ya on the blower.'

'Fuck off, Birch, the fuckin' FBI haven't bugged me phone, ya know?'

'Can't talk on the phone. I'm on me way round to yours. Be there in ten.'

What the fuck did this loon want now? Jonno's life was a non-stop ride on the Waltzers—his head was forever spinning. Just when he thinks he's got things back on track and the ride is slowing down, a crazed fairground worker spins his car around to make it go faster.

What trouble was Birchy about to lay at my door? It wouldn't be good news, because it never is, and it wasn't straight, because he was acting like a ludicrous version of James Bond. Jonno could feel the storm clouds rumbling.

'Two sugars in mine, sweetheart,' he said, as he barged into Jonno's house and down the hall.

'Fuck off, Birch, I'm goin' to bed soon. I'm up early for work.'

'I need you to come on a little errand with me, Daniel.'

'Are you serious, Birch? It's half-fucking-eight. I'm not goin' out now.'
Birchy stopped inquisitively picking things up and stomping around Jonno's living room for a second to face him.

'Look, we're all out on Saturday for my birthday, aren't we? The big twenty-five!'

'So?' Jonno didn't want to play his cryptic guessing game.

'So, Daniel. We're gonna need some beak to loosen us up and get the party goin', aren't we?'

'And?'

'And where do you think it comes from, you fuckin' knobhead? I haven't got a cocaine tree in me garden.'

Jonno really wasn't arsed about snorting cocaine in whatever grubby club Birchy was going to drag them into. Jonno, Naz and Steve liked to dress up when they went to a club and show a bit of class, even if it was above their station. Birchy, however, preferred his feet to stick to a tacky carpet in a cattle market full of sexual predators and easy prey.

'But you usually score the shit, Birch, why do you need me?'

'That's fuckin' right. I do get it, taking all the fuckin' risks while you melts just get off yer tits on it and do fuck all.'

'So why do you need me?'

'Because I'm gonna score off a new dealer. It's a bird. A friend of a friend. I don't know what I'm walking into and I don't want to get fleeced with five-hundred quid in me pocket.'

'Five hundred? Are you openin' a fuckin' shop? What are you getting that much for?'

'Because I'm sick of doin' this every two weeks, so I'm gonna get enough to last us for a bit.'

'Well, I'm gonna be no good to you if it all kicks off.'

'You're not there for that, Dan. Just keep yer eyes open and keep yer wits about ya.'

Jonno really, *really* did not want to do this, but he would never win in an argument with Birchy. Here he was again, being dragged down into the pit of scum and depravity. There just didn't appear to be any viable options in his life. He was a good man being beaten back by demon giants all the time. The world was bereft of angels and only devils ever tiptoed into the waters of his life. Impossible situations and optionless decisions were the only menu he ever had presented to him, forcing him to feed on sustenance that would only ever do him damage.

Jonno climbed into Birchy's new Mitsubishi Colt and they headed for Birkenhead town centre. He was psychologically shackled by duct tape and gagged with an old sock. He tried to visualise the journey, but his sight was hampered by the surreal Hessian sack placed over his head. He screamed—loud, but his cry was muffled by the sock.

They pulled up into a car park at the back of a small block of flats. Jonno was relieved that the car was off the main street, protected from prying eyes, in a somewhat decent area. It wasn't the downtrodden ghetto type of street he'd imagined drug dealers to live in. It looked like sheltered accommodation; somewhere your nan might end up in her later years.

Birchy's new contact answered the door and invited them both in. Jane had shortish blonde hair and looked physically fit—gym fit. Jonno estimated she was a year or two older than him but was extremely easy on the eye and not how he'd imagined a Birkenhead drug dealer would look. They were introduced to her flatmate, Lynne, who was equally attractive. Under normal circumstances, Jonno's mind would be running wild, being in the same room with two beautiful women, but the drama of the situation was quelling his romantic side.

Birchy handed over a fat roll of ten pound notes. Jane passed back to him a significantly-sized plastic packet of white powder. Jonno had only ever seen cocaine in a line, or on the back of a twenty pence coin, so the size of the package shocked him a little.

'Now be careful. This is really strong stuff. Make sure you cut it down with something,' warned Jane.

'Yeah, yeah. Don't worry about it, girl,' replied Birchy in a typical cavalier fashion.

As they walked down the stairs heading for the car, Birchy pushed the packet of coke at Jonno.

'Hold that, while I get me car keys out.'

'Fuck that, I'm not touchin' it!'

'Fuckin' get hold of it and keep yer gob shut!' he threatened whilst forcefully pressing it into Jonno's stomach.

Yet again, Jonno was forced into an impossible moment. Now the packet had his fingerprints on it and there were traces of coke on his clothes that a sniffer dog would detect in a sandstorm. There was no way he was keeping hold of it once they got into the car. He'd throw it out the window first and face the wrath of Birchy, or a beating if he had to.

As soon as he was in the car, he passed it back to Birchy as if it were radioactive. Birchy pulled down the glove compartment and then flicked a clip that Jonno thought was a hinge. It revealed another compartment, into which he stuffed the coke.

'What the fuck's tha'? Did you have that compartment made?'

'No, did I fuck. It's on the car. It's a secret compartment, I dunno what it's for. It's where the beak is goin' for now.'

Although Birchy's new wheels were a good fifteen years old, Jonno was rather impressed with this Japanese advancement in technology that would aid drug trafficking worldwide. They'd barely pulled onto the main stretch of road that runs straight through the centre of Birkenhead, when blue flashing lights from behind them filled the car and the following police officers intermittently sounded their siren. Jonno's nervousness must have magnetically drawn the police to them, he reckoned. He looked to his left, and the sweeping blue lights bounced off the memorial stone of Diane Sindall. Diane was just twenty-one years old in 1986, when she was dragged into a dark alleyway and beaten about the head with a crowbar by *The Beast of Birkenhead*, Peter Sullivan. Six years on, her memorial stone was positioned on a small patch of grass and served as a stark reminder that life is delicate and can be snatched from you in a flash.
The irony that Jonno's life could be over in the next few minutes, in exactly the same spot as the murder, was wasted on him.

He nervously turned to Birchy as his stomach was throwing cartwheels and ice was running through his veins. He felt as if he may throw up right there and the presence of his spew would easily prove his guilt. The thought of trying to keep it in was making him all the more nauseous.

'Keep a lid on it, lad. We're on our way home from a football meeting.'

Birchy's story sounded reasonable. Jonno needed more information, but there was no time to deliver it as the copper had arrived at his window and was signalling him to lower it. Jonno had no time to worry about what Birchy was going to say, when he jumped with a start because the copper's partner was tapping on his window with his truncheon. Jonno wound the window down about a third and a policeman with a magnificent build and a moustache a cowboy would be proud of peered in through the gap. The flashing blue lights reflected off his eyes and gave him an inhuman, robotic look.

'Get out the car.'

'Have I done something wrong, officer?'

'Yeah. You didn't get outta the car when I fuckin' asked ya. Get out!'
Jonno slid out of the door, which wouldn't fully open because the police officer wouldn't move enough out of the way. Jonno put his back against the car, and the cop lurched in with his nose no further than six inches from Jonno's. He could see the memorial stone over his left ear as he turned his head slightly to avoid the copper's breath.

'Where are you goin'?'

'I'm goin' home. We've been to a footy team meeting.'

'Where was it?'
Jonno suddenly realised that Birchy hadn't given him enough information for their fake alibi and there was a good chance that Birchy could get the same question but give a different answer. Jonno's eyes wandered over to Birchy in a plea for help, but the angle was too acute, and the copper spotted his ineffectual attempt.

'Don't fuckin lie to me, coz you're on the wrong end of this fuckin' stick, lad.' He carefully placed his baton under Jonno's chin.

Here was yet another policeman, fuelled with steroids and desperate for a fight, thought Jonno. He towered over him by a good five inches, was as wide as a bus, and had a meaty fourteen-inch wooden cosh pressed to his jaw. He was desperate for Jonno to give him a *smart-arse* answer just so he could release some of his pent-up anger on his ribs. Jonno was more intelligent than that, though. He wasn't just some *baghead dickhead* who didn't know how to play the game when faced with a rabid dog. He kept his cool and complied with his aggressive questioning technique.

'The Belvedere, on Market Street.'
He paused and stared right into Jonno's eyes, reaching deep into his soul to see if he could find a lie. Jonno stood firm and stared back at him. He removed his stick from his face and waggled it to his left.

'Stand over there while we search the car.'
Jonno stood next to Birchy and the other copper, while *PC Gobshite* pulled out his torch and started scampering around the vehicle, desperate to feed on any old turd he could find. A white Fiesta shot past them doing about 50mph, with the passenger hanging out the window shouting,

'Ha! ya fuckin' knobheads!'
It was unclear if his descriptive analysis was directed at the lads, or the police. Either way, Jonno had bigger concerns.

The copper was on all fours in the back of the car searching every crevice and Jonno's stomach was having a party. Sweat dripped down the side of his face as he battled with the mid-summer evening heat and the chance that he would find the coke. They had rolled a ball on the roulette table and this was going to be a binary conclusion. He'd left the glove compartment 'til last, possibly because it would be the last place anyone would consider hiding a packet of Class A drugs. He poked his torch inside the compartment and removed all its contents, lashing them on the floor without a care. Jonno held his breath in an attempt to stop him screaming. He considered taking flight and leaving Birchy to it. The copper hadn't taken his name and it was all Birchy's idea that he was there anyway. He could run for it and take his chances that he wouldn't snitch. It wasn't what they did, though. They were family, and faced adversity together, regardless of its origin.

He pulled his bulky frame out of Birchy's car and shook his head at his colleague indicating that he hadn't found anything.

'Go on. On yer way, lads.'

The experience had been traumatic for Jonno, and this was not a world he wanted to be living in. He could see himself being an early candidate for a heart attack or a nervous breakdown. He didn't know if it was due to nerves or relief, but when they got back in the car and looked at each other, they burst into roaring laughter.

'Fuckin' dickheads!' bellowed Birchy.

25 THE SEA OF DEPRESSION

The summer sneakily slipped out the back door, as the onset of winter approached from green, to brown, to grey. As mist and darkness descended on the peninsula, smiling faces turned to frowns as people realised the challenges that they would face during the coming winter months.

Gaggles of Canadian and Greylag geese flew high in the stone-grey sky in perfect formations, while plunging, heavy fogs carried pollution and the reek of manure from local farms with them. It got harder for Jonno to raise his weakened body from his pit. His flesh and bones ached. The cold mornings brought darkness, depression, and submission with them, and it was easy to understand why more people died during the winter. Maybe they just got tired of trying.

The inside of Jonno's single-pane windows were coated with a half an inch of frost, and the icy draughts that circulated around his bedroom warned him that it would be foolish to remove himself from the warmth of his bed. He'd been going to bed earlier because he couldn't afford to light the fire all night and the house was freezing. He'd give the fire a blast for an hour or two when he got home from work, to enable him to eat his tea with a modicum of comfort. He couldn't be sure if it was the extra sleep he was getting, the sub-zero temperatures, or his aching body that was preventing his getting out of bed, but it had become a real challenge as the mornings got darker. The introduction of the winter had hit him hard, and he was struggling to stay afloat. Naz's uncle was battling to find new contracts, and that hit Jonno and Naz quite badly. He was still doing his best to find them work but occasionally laid them off for the odd week, and when you live your life on a weekly basis, that can make survival almost impossible.

He was doing his best to find bits of work whenever he was laid off. He painted the external walls of Steve's mum's house and he'd wallpapered a couple of neighbours' living rooms, but it wasn't enough. Naz kept saying to Jonno, *Tough times don't last, but tough people do*. Jonno thought inspirational quotes like this were great at the end of arduous journey, but offered absolutely no help when you were stuck in the middle of it.

The constant worry about money and keeping hold of his house had made him anxious and fretful. It kept him awake at night and refused to let his exhausted mind rest. He was so tired, physically, and mentally, but the worry kept nibbling away at him. The battle to ensure he had enough money in his account at the end of the month consumed him to the point that it was in his forethoughts with every decision he made. Putting the fire on, buying fresh meat, and wearing new clothes had become unattainable luxuries.

Unemployed, lazy slobs in his street had decent cars, Sky TV, and a cigarette permanently in their mouth. Jonno struggled to comprehend why he was eating beans on toast in an igloo, and they were living as *Richard Branson* in a system swindle that was oblivious to the authorities. It didn't seem right, and it stuck in his craw. He would go to work at six, graft for ten hours and pick up just enough money to survive. He had no luxuries or extravagant spending sprees.

There was a fella down the street in his early thirties who hobbled around on a pair of crutches all the time. The poor blighter looked as though he'd been crippled with a degenerative disease and faced a daily uphill struggle. You'd look at him from the outside and think, *that poor fucker's got no life, probably can't even wipe his own arse, or put his socks on*. Yet every Sunday morning, Jonno watched that *bent-over insect* straighten himself up and get picked up for football by his mates, swapping his crutches for football boots and half-volleys.

Jonno couldn't live like that. Constantly watching your back and praying that no one was going to snitch to the authorities about your parasitic scamming of the state system. It was honest working folk like him that were paying to uphold the affluent lifestyle these charlatans kept. The constant acting and paranoia would eat away at him and the strife didn't appear to outweigh the benefits. He would rather struggle in a dishonest world than live a fake existence. These people were breeding and filling his society with their lies and illusions. When Jonno left school, the advice was to find a job or join the forces. If he hadn't been lucky enough to get a start with Naz's uncle, he most certainly would have joined the army, he presumed. It wouldn't have been his first option, but it would have been better than spending his days lying on the couch eating *Sayers* sausage rolls and watching *Kilroy*.

Being a drain on society and milking the system was now a viable career option for some of these blood-sucking school leavers, he mused. He had a mental battle with himself every time he went for a pint with the lads or bought himself a new shirt. But without that, what did he have? If he gave up the odd night out with the lads, he'd have nothing. he'd just be existing. He'd worked hard to get his own home at such an early age and moving back to his mum's wasn't a practical option, so the monthly payday battle became a regular occurrence in his lifelong struggle to stay afloat in a holey boat on *The Sea of Desperation*.

Jonno felt like he'd only been asleep for five minutes when a noise from outside woke him. At first, he thought it might be Ronnie, the milkman who likes to wake the street with his incessant whistling and clinking of bottles. He glanced at his clock radio and realised that 4.10am was way too early for Ronnie. He lay in bed in a paralysed state, trying not to breathe in case the noise from his respiratory cycle prevented him from identifying a repeat noise from outside. He wasn't sure that the crackly hum he could hear was coming from his ears or from his drowsy mind. He remained frozen and channelled all his concentration into his ears, awaiting a repeat noise.

Warm air formed slowly from his mouth as he expelled it with complete control and purpose. His body was stiff as a board, ears pricked, eyes bulging, and head tilted forward. He lay poised, awaiting the next instruction.

He heard it again.

It sounded like breaking glass. This time he sprung out of bed and darted to the window. He meticulously peeled back the corner of the curtain and peered out into the darkness. It took a second or two for his eyes to correctly focus to the blackness outside, but he eventually identified what the noise was.

He could just make out a hand, knocking off the broken glass he'd cemented onto the top of his back yard wall. He watched in astonishment as the hand swept left to right with a metal implement, possibly a screwdriver, removing his homemade burglar deterrent. He continued to look through the crack of the curtain and watched a pair of hands appear on the wall and then the slow appearance of a woollen beanie-wearing head. His eyes peered over the wall and examined Jonno's back yard for any signs of life or inconvenience. As he hauled himself up to the top of the wall, Jonno's initial reaction was absolute rage.

How could this fuckin' scruffy bastard break into my property while I was asleep in bed? I work harder than a Blackpool donkey and I've got nothing to show for it. Now I have a cockroach in my yard attempting to take what I have scrimped and scraped for over the last seven years, which incidentally, wasn't very much.

What the fuck did he think he could steal from me? Jonno fumed.

He had nothing, nothing of any value. He had his dad's old AIWA video recorder that wouldn't be worth a carrot sold second-hand, and a ten-year-old PYE telly that had seen better days and would take three men to carry the massive thing out of the house. He had no jewellery, a tin of corned beef in the fridge, and about eight quid in his jeans pocket.

Why the fuck would they be robbing my house?

Jonno wished he had a big dog for these situations, but he was at work all day and it would be unfair to leave it on its own. So, he had a Plan B, just in case this situation ever presented itself. To the side of his bed, he had the bottom half of his dad's old pool cue. If this horrible bandit thought he could break into Jonno's castle and violate his privacy, he was going to meet Mr Pool Stick, up close and personal.

He flopped off Jonno's wall into his yard in a crouched position, scanning his surroundings with menacing eyes that were illuminated by next door's security floodlight. The fire inside Jonno burned and he desperately wanted to hurt this dishonest crook if he attempted to get into his house. Jonno didn't care if he was bigger than him, had a knife or was Bruce Lee, he was going to get his pool stick full-throttle across his empty skull. Logical reasoning had taken a vacation from his mind and his inner warrior had prevailed. He was about to hammer on the window with the pool cue and warn this filthy thug of what he had coming to him, when to Jonno's horror, another pair of hands appeared at the top of the wall.

A darker face, maybe Asian or mixed-race, popped up over the parapet and rested his elbows on the top of the glass-strewn wall. They communicated with each other with pointed fingers and nodded heads, and although Jonno's hearing was impressively bionic, he couldn't hear a sound.

This changed things. The situation had altered dramatically, and the odds were no longer attractive. The sensible part of Jonno's brain had returned and was working out a few mathematical equations with the voice of reasoning. It was an intelligent conversation, and he paused for a moment to listen to their academic analysis.

In the red corner, fighting out of Birkenhead Boxing Club and weighing in at 177 pounds, with 26 fights and 19 wins, it's The King of Chaos, The Destroyer Employer, Danny Johnson!
Fighting was in his blood. It was an unavoidable challenge that

littered everyone's Birkenhead childhood. It was how they settled things whether you wanted it or not, and most of the time, Jonno didn't really want it. But he knew the rules, and that's how they did it. A dirty look, a bad tackle, an ill-spoken comment, or a barrage of *piss-taking* pushed too far would all result in a primitive instinct to hurt your adversary. The rate of fights slowed down when he reached his twenties, but as a teenager, he would regularly be involved in some form of street combat, and more often than not, his opponent would be a friend or a known face from the neighbourhood. Fighting with your friends appeared quite odd now that he was older, but back then there was a burning desire from everyone to know where you fell in the hierarchy. This uncertainty created tension, so even the most trivial of incidents were dramatically magnified in order to create a fight that really wasn't necessary. Jonno couldn't remember having a fight with a friend and not talking to them within minutes after its conclusion, more often than not, continuing like nothing had happened.

The ironic thing was, he wasn't very good at it, but not fighting at all was a worse fate than getting beat. Weak and spineless people give off a scent that can be detected by bullies and opportunists who will drain your self-respect through their hideous proboscis, like a ravenous mosquito gorging on your blood. Blindly entering a battle against hopeless odds had been a burden on man since the beginning of time and Jonno wasn't going to be the coward that broke that historical chain.

In the blue corner, fighting out of the Shameless Stable, weighing in at around 230 pounds, with an unknown record, it's the Thief of Oxygen, Mr Scumbag! And with an interesting twist, ladies and gentlemen, Mr Scumbag is part of a tag-team, his weight is unknown because his body is disguised by red engineering brick, please be outstanding for Mr Vile Creature!

And there lay the real problem. Jonno had no idea what type of opponents he was facing and to what degree of depravity they would descend, to get their hands on his tin of corned beef. They could be addicts, who would be prepared to kill someone or face life in prison for twenty quid. They may have a knife in their hands and a brain full of fizzy brown, intent on causing damage and anarchy.

He slowly replaced the curtain and tiptoed over to the bedside phone.

'Emergency, which service do you require? Fire, Police or Ambulance?'

'The police, please,' Jonno whispered.

'Can you tell me what has happened?'

'There's two bagheads, I mean two men in me yard. They're trying to get in the house.'

'What is the telephone number you are calling from?'

'Why d'ya need to know that?

'In case the call ends before it should, and I need to call you back.'

'652 8597.'

'What is your name and the exact location you are calling from?'

'Danny Johnson. 48 Mallory Street, off Laid Street.'

'So, you say someone is trying to burgle your house, sir?'

'Yeah. Ya better get the bizzies 'ere before I tackle them meself.'

'Under no circumstances, Mr Johnson, should you confront the burglars. We have a unit in the area, and they will be with you immediately. Please stay calm and quiet.'

Jonno put the phone down with the meticulous accuracy of a surgeon placing the cowboy hat on the loaded rump of the donkey in a game of *Buckaroo*. He tiptoed back to the window and slowly pulled the curtain back. Nothing had changed. He was still creeping around his backyard while his accomplice was hanging over the wall, keeping an eye out. He skulked over to the outhouse, possibly hoping it contained a decent bike or tools, but all it possessed was a faeces-stained toilet that hadn't been used since the sixties, and a load of old junk Jonno couldn't be bothered taking to the tip. He glided across the concrete to Jonno's backyard door, silently and effortlessly, and from Jonno's elevated position, he lost sight of his hands, but he could see his shoulders shuddering and heard a rattling as he repeatedly tried the door handle.

Regardless of what the operator had said, the situation had escalated, and Jonno wasn't prepared to allow this scrote into his home. He wrapped his fingers around the butt of the pool cue and mentally prepared himself for carnage. He was about to let go of the curtain and go downstairs to meet the feckless home invader, when he saw the wall at the end of the entry illuminated with a blue light. The operator had been telling the truth and the boys in blue really were just around the corner. He settled in and smirked as he began to watch this real-life scene unfold of *cops and robbers* in his own backyard.

The loathsome lowlife hanging off his wall was completely unaware of the flashing blue lights and the two closely approaching officers of the law. The other toerag was still jabbing away at Jonno's door, completely oblivious to the fact that his collaborator was Britain's lousiest look-out.

Jonno watched open-mouthed, as the two bizzies crept down the entry, nearing the idiot on the wall. They must have created some sort of noise as Jonno spotted him look swiftly to his right and desperately leap off the wall. He darted across the cobbles at the speed of light and already had a fifty-metre advantage before the pursuing officer took flight. While Jonno's eyes had been averted by the action, the burglar that had been tugging his door handle, had completely disappeared into the darkness. Jonno scurried down the stairs to meet the remaining policeman. Before he unbolted the back gate, he wanted to make sure the copper knew that he was the homeowner and wouldn't put his cosh over his head as soon as he saw him.

'I'm gonna open the gate. I live here. I'm the one who rang you.' As Jonno reached down to release the tower bolt, he discovered that he hadn't locked it the last time he put the bin out. He was angry at himself for being such a imbecile, but then found comfort that the two halfwits had clambered over his glass-laden wall when the gate had been open all the time.

'Are you okay?' the officer enquired.

'I'm fine, mate, but they've got away.'

'No, my colleague has chased after him. He'll catch him. He's like shit off a shovel.'

I doubt that, Jonno thought, considering the start he had on him, but this copper was missing some vital information.

'There's two of them! He was in my yard, trying my door.'

'Where did he go?'

'I dunno. He disappeared.'
Jonno opened the gate fully to allow the copper access into his yard. He turned his torch on and had his truncheon in the other hand. He slowly moved to Jonno's outside bog and opened the door. He wasn't there. As the torch lit up the outhouse, Jonno noticed the five stolen radiators he'd bought from a fella in a pub a while back with good intentions of treating himself to central heating one day. The copper either didn't see them or wasn't interested and had his sights firmly fixed on the Birkenhead *Harry Houdini.*

They both walked to the back gate and the copper shone his torch in both directions of the entry. Other than a manky cat tearing away at a bin bag, there was nothing to see.

'Where's the little bastard gone?' he grunted, his face a picture of disappointment and irritation.

The silences of the night consumed the conversation. The uncomfortable, hushed pause was broken by a heavy thud. They were reunified by astonishment as they observed the burglar hop down into the entry, two doors down from Jonno's house, completely unaware that he was under the nose of a pursuing copper.

How stupid could one man be?

If he'd have waited five more minutes, the police would've been gone, and he'd have been free to ransack someone else's belongings. The copper couldn't believe his luck and sprinted at him with the pace of a young Jurgen Klinsmann. He bowled the unsuspected criminal over with an *All Blacks* game changing tackle and had him in handcuffs before he knew what'd hit him. He frogmarched him back towards Jonno whilst talking on his radio. Jonno assumed he was calling the arrest in, but discovered he was talking to the other copper.

'We got the other one. I told you my mate was quick.'

'Nice one. Well done.'
Jonno couldn't believe he was praising a bizzie, but hats off to them, they had a job to do, and they'd executed it perfectly.

The shackled prisoner held his head low and avoided eye contact with Jonno. A poor excuse of a man, he should've been thankful he was met by the copper and not the heavy thrash of a pool cue.

'I'll just lock this fella in the van, and I'll be back to take a statement, sir.'

'No worries, I'll put the kettle on.'

26 UNHAPPY BIRTHDAY

As November gave birth to December, equal portions of despondency and hope wrestled with each other. Naz's rollercoaster life appeared calmer. He finally had Emily under his care, or at least his mum's when he was working, and they hadn't heard much from Jodie and her feral friends. The rumours knocking about said that she and *The Gargoyle* had got off with the discovery of the cocaine stash in her house. Jonno had no idea how, but neither of them was in prison. Maybe the trial had been delayed, or they'd come up with some elaborate fabrication. People like that are like *Teflon* —nothing sticks. You would think karma would catch them up and hand over their comeuppance, but it never does. It always seems like the good guys permanently get the dirty end of the stick.

Naz's uncle had acquired a long-term contract with a local house builder called Indigo Living, which gave the lads a steady income for the foreseeable future and a shed load of overtime whenever they wanted. It kept the saliva-drenched fangs of the wolf from the door and helped Jonno sleep easier. Steve hadn't mentioned his traumatic childhood since the night he'd told Jonno about it in the pub. In fact, he appeared more confident and carefree than ever. He was a difficult character to read. It was hard to know whether he'd genuinely made steps in getting over the whole horrific ordeal, or was just putting on a show, to throw Jonno off the scent and convince himself that all was good. He lived his life behind a mask, and Jonno doubted that anyone would ever see his real face; God knows, plenty of girls had tried.

Jonno's head felt like it was in a better place, and although the murk of winter was looming, he'd made great strides since the doctor had told him he was depressed. He wasn't naive enough to think he'd become some sort of Mary Poppins who may spontaneously erupt into song at any time, but he was plodding on, and he was content with that. He still had ambitions to break free from his town and the hopeful thoughts swirled around his head and consumed large chunks of his time. His brain told him he had more to offer than ten-hour shifts with a paintbrush. That said, he felt he might be falling into a rut and had become comfortable trudging through the mud of normality.

Maybe this was me for the rest of my days?

People from his area didn't have encounters with fairy godmothers or magic genies offering them wishes and promises of fortune. They worked for everything they had, and that's why they were defensive of what they had, including each other. They had nothing but wouldn't allow anyone to ridicule the fact. They were proud people and would not suffer insulting remarks from the forked tongues of folk who looked down their noses at less fortunate people.

He thought about Becky a little less. She hadn't left his mind and he guessed she'd always be there, but he no longer spent hours thinking about her. He'd *kopped off* with a few girls on nights out in town, but nothing serious. He felt nothing for them and certainly didn't want to start seeing someone seriously.

As Jonno shut the front door and headed for Steve's house, the cold slipped into his shirt. The icy air surprised him, and he took a sharp intake of breath as a natural defensive mechanism. He plunged his clenched hands deep into his pockets, whilst trying not to crease his perfectly ironed shirt, in an attempt to fight off the bitterness. The final rays of light from the disappearing sun revealed a miserable grey sky, fractured only by the plumes of steam from the power station. This was no weather for dawdling.

Only his legs moved—his torso, arms and head remained stiffly set, in fear that any sort of movement would allow more icy streams of cold air into his shirt. His breathing was short and rapid, as too big a breath could fill his lungs with frosty air.

His nose sucked in the aromas of his neighbours' teas as he passed their homes. Aromatic clouds of onions, curry and fish filled his nostrils and saddened his heart because he'd quickly rushed a cheese and crisp butty down him. This was a stodgy food time of year. A large bowl of scouse with crusty bread, sat in front of the fire was the working man's dream. It was that time of early evening when folk hadn't decided whether to close their curtains or not. Jonno knew it was rude, but it was impossible not to peer into people's living rooms as he marched past and grasped a brief insight into their life. Flashes of electric blue light danced off their living room walls as blurring televisions broke the darkness of the room.

Dog crap and litter peppered the street, and the occasional carrier bag was whipped up by the icy eddies of wind to perform a dramatic, airborne foxtrot. It was unusual for Jonno to be heading out for a drinking session at this time, but this was no ordinary night out. This was the first Birthday party since *Maxine's* had reopened a year earlier and promised to be a brilliant event. They planned to have a few drinks at Steve's before getting to the pub early, to guarantee their usual speck next to the DJ.

Jonno hammered on Steve's door with the rhythmic ability of a military drummer and with enough energy to attract immediate attention. Jonno deduced that if he knocked hard enough, he would react quickly and remove him from the frosty world he was currently imprisoned in. It was a futile attempt. Steve was so laid back, he was almost horizontal and even if the police were charging at his door with a battering ram, he'd probably still finish flicking his hair into a perfect position. The door eventually flung open and there stood Steve, as expected, nowhere near ready, with nothing but a towel covering his hairy, ape-like body.

'Alright, ballbag?'

'Let us in, it's fuckin' freezin'!'

'Some lucky lady's getting it tonight, lad,' he said, proudly swinging his tackle from side-to-side.

Jonno pushed past him and left him to his mating display of masculinity. Naz was already in the kitchen supping on a can of lager.

'Grab that, bollocks,' he said, chucking a can at Jonno.

'Where's Birchy?' Jonno asked.

'Probably lookin' for his pair of brain cells,' said Steve, who had now removed the towel and was parading around in his boxer shorts. He then meticulously ironed his shirt while they waited for him.

Birchy arrived fifteen minutes later than the time they'd agreed and made a dramatic entrance, wearing a shirt that would embarrass the majority of earth's habitants.

Who the fuck dressed you, yer ma?' Jonno fired at him.

'You look like a fuckin' seventies porn star,' Naz spluttered, through sprayed mists of lager.
They all roared with laughter at Birchy's expense, and his defensive response was typically unintelligent and aggressive.

'What the fuck do you bellends know? This is fuckin' designer!'

'Fuckin' might be in TK Maxx, lad,' screamed Steve.
They all fell about with laughter. Steve was doubled up on the floor with tears in his eyes as though someone had just punched him in the ribs. Birchy headed to the fridge to help himself to a beer and made sure to crumple up Steve's half-ironed shirt on his way, muttering under his breath.

'C'mon, mate, we still love ya, even if you look like a camp version of George Michael,' Naz poked as he hugged Birchy. Steve pulled a bottle out of the cupboard and slammed it down on the worktop along with four shot glasses.

'Wait 'til you try this, it'll blow your mind!' he teased.

'What the fuck is it? Looks like liquidised shite!' Birchy shook the bottle for signs of life.

'Me ma brought it back from Tenerife. It's caramel vodka. It's forty percent and a little taste of heaven in your mouth.'.
He filled the four glasses with the potent brown liquid, and they all simultaneously clinked glasses while shouting cheers in a made-up foreign language.

Wow! This stuff was dangerous, thought Jonno. It tasted like a mini-dessert but had the force to paralyse a bull elephant. They were the worst types of alcohol; the ninja types that silently and unknowingly ruined you. They sank another three cans and a couple more shots before taking the short walk to *Maxine's*.

Craig and Gary, who usually run the door, weren't there, and had been replaced with a couple of different bouncers. They looked like clones. Both had bald heads, a goatee beard, and wore long black trench coats. They looked like they were juiced up with steroids, unless they were eating fifteen chickens a day.

'You all together?'
You can look us up and down all you want, you prick. The clothes we are wearing would buy and sell you, except for Birchy's, of course, raged Jonno before answering.

'Yeah. It's our local.'

'No trouble tonight, boys, yeah?'

He stepped aside and opened the door. None of the lads responded. It rubbed them up the wrong way though.

Why ask such an antagonising and presumptuous question? Would he say the same thing to a group of girls or a bunch of college boys that had been dropped off in daddy's Mercedes? Would he fuck! fumed Jonno. *He assumed and was looking down his nose at us. A typical dickhead bouncer looking to wind someone up and create trouble when that's exactly what he was employed to prevent.*

The pub was fuller than they'd expected for such an early hour and Jonno cursed that they'd wasted half an hour waiting for Steve, although they were already six drinks in, thanks to his cans and caramel vodka. DJ Pete punched the air, indicating he was ecstatic to see them, and then metamorphosed his raised arm into a sleek dance move with an energetic swish of his dyed blonde perm.

'Now the boys are here, we can really get this party started. Welcome, everyone, to Maxine's Birthday party. The number one venue in Birkenhead. Let's drink, dance, and have a cracking night. I'm here until twelve with all the hits and your requests. Put your hands in the air, like you just don't care,' announced Pete over the mic in a fake Fluff Freeman accent that only a time-served DJ can produce. He expertly morphed the end of his narrative into the synthesizer intro of *You've Got to Let the Music* by *Cappella,* which filled the room like a soul-stealing poltergeist and injected liquid energy into the once-motionless inhabitants.

Jonno looked around the room as Birchy passed him a pint of lager and they headed over to their perch. The Goths were dancing to Pete's gamechanger and flashing Hollywood smiles of perfect teeth. They danced as though they'd rehearsed, moving in unison like a pair of swans in love. It was sexual, sensual, and untouchable. Jonno smiled at them and mouthed a *hiya* as he passed but still didn't have the nerve to talk to them—they scared the life out of him.

By the time they'd sunk another two pints, the pub was absolutely heaving. Maybe the two new bouncers were letting more people in, but Jonno couldn't remember it having been this packed before. He could see from his elevated position that the crowd mimicked the way a gentle tide licks the sand, swaying to and fro in a collective manoeuvre. The Goths kept looking over at them while they performed their seductive wriggles in tight black dresses. Jonno wasn't sure who they were looking at, but it was definitely one of them.

'Come 'ed. Let's go and talk to them,' insisted Naz.

'No fuckin' chance,' replied Jonno.

'Why not? They're always lookin' over, and you obviously fancy them. What have you got to lose, mate?'
Naz always made things sound so simple, but it really wasn't that straightforward for Jonno. There were unrecoverable losses at risk that he wasn't prepared to gamble with.

'The shame, mate,' Jonno shouted into his ear as he fought against the formidable noise machine that was Pete Crystalline.

'What do you mean, shame?'

'If I go over there now and get knocked back, that's it forever. It's not like being embarrassed just for a night, they're in here all the fuckin' time. I'd have to walk past them every time we came in here knowing I was jibbed. I can't do it. I'd rather have the fantasy and never know the outcome. It would be like shittin' on your own doorstep.'

'Fuckin' 'ell,' Naz said.

Jonno was sure his explanation was too profound for Naz to comprehend. It was unarguably a coward's option, but he'd never been drunk enough in *Maxine's* to take the chance. If he'd seen The Goths on neutral territory for the first time, he'd have been over to them, but too long a period of him gawping at them had passed. They'd become untouchable.

Pete changed his tactics and put on American Pie, which was a *Maxine's* anthem. If you were a local, it was a necessity to know the lyrics to the whole song. That lads were blessed that the lager and vodka had gifted them excellent singing voices and they were not ashamed to use them. They sang along to the verse, word-perfect, before hitting the crescendo of the chorus.
So, Bye, bye Miss American Pie
Drove my Chevy to the levee but the levee was dry
And them good ol' boys were drinking whisky and rye
Singin' this'll be the day that I die
This'll be the day that I die

They clanked their glasses together and sang with deep, manly voices; a battle cry instilling fear into their enemies. They grabbed each other's shoulders forming an impenetrable circle and sang as Vikings celebrating a religious festival. The bond between them was as strong as ever—and right now, in that moment, it felt good.

'Hold this, la, I'm goin' for a piss,' Jonno said, shoving his near-empty pint glass into Naz's chest. From where they were pitched, Jonno only had two options to get to the toilets. One option meant walking past the bar, which was currently a shark-feeding frenzy and there was a chance he'd never return. The only other option was to walk straight past The Goths. All the other lads wouldn't even consider this an issue and would march right past them, but he'd built up this little problem in his head and it was now affecting his decision making—even with the trivial things, like how to go for a pee. He held his breath and headed straight for them. There was no gap for him to pass and he had to move one of them out of the way. He gently placed his hand on her hip, which allowed him to sense through her black dress that she possessed a trim figure.

'Can I just squeeze past there, girls?' Jonno said, while tenderly manipulating her out of his way. She unquestionably pushed her bum back towards his groin as she swung around to face him.

'Ooh, are we dancin?
Her reaction was an unexpected but a welcome surprise and it caught Jonno on the back foot. Now that he was quite close to her, he could see how pretty she was. Heavy, dark eye shadow emphasised her deep brown, sultry eyes, and blemish-free skin. Her perfect smile was encapsulated by inviting, kissable lips. As he brushed past her, he discovered that her hair was freshly shampooed, complimenting her subtle perfume. He was annoyed at himself for never having the courage to talk to her and just assuming he'd be on the receiving end of a cold shoulder.

'Yeah, I'm deffo up for a dance. I've just gotta go for a pee.'
As he turned away from her, he thought he was Muhammad Ali standing over a canvas-licking Sonny Liston. He was unbreakable. It was obvious to him that he had developed an intoxicating

hormone that made him irresistible to women and he could probably pull any girl in here right now if he wanted to.

He stood in front of the mirror in the toilets, looking deeply into his eyes and running the forthcoming conversation in his head. He went over a couple of lines he was going to say to her before charging through the door. As he re-entered the pub and left the stench of stale urine behind him, he had one of the biggest shocks of his life. He felt the life being sucked out of him as air rapidly evacuated his lungs and left him breathless. A sinister icy fluid ran through his veins, freezing his skin in seconds. His eyes bulged to take in additional light and confirm the images his brain was receiving. He was paralysed to the spot, his legs unable to move as he stood there drowning in disappointment. His heart hit the floor as he realised the night was over when he saw *The Gargoyle* scoffing with his mates and blocking his path back to the lads. Just when everything was going great and they didn't have a care in the world, the rug was pulled from underneath their feet.

Time stood still as he watched him in the centre of his circle, strutting around and devouring attention and applaud. His dull, low-pitched voice cut through the tinny din of Pete's nineties classics. His booming laugh was the indicator for his sycophant admirers to laugh in harmony. He danced around his circle of shameless bootlickers, swinging hooks and uppercuts as he told anecdotes of mindless battles. His group of five equally ugly mates hung on the troll's every word as his leathery, vile tongue spun yarns of viciousness and grief.

Why did the Gargoyle have to live in my town? Why was he out tonight? How was I going to get past him and get the lads out of Maxine's before he spotted us? Why was I forever sinking in quicksand?

Jonno instantly sobered up as happiness vacated his body and was instantly replaced with fear and anxiety. He needed his brain to function properly, and it could not do that with a flow of intoxicated pleasure. He blinked hard, shook his head, and calculated his life-or-death route. The rush of adrenaline made him feel sick. He only had one option, and that was to walk right past him. He skulked behind dynamic bodies, creeping slowly closer, while plotting his approach with the stealth of a Bengal tiger. He deduced that none of his posse would know him and it was only *The Gargoyle* that he had to avoid, to return to the safety of his haven. This would be a simple exercise faced with a normal person, but he was bouncing and spinning around as he squeezed the reverence from his aficionados.

He crept closer. He had to go for it. *The Gargoyle* had his back to him, but the gap between the bodies was constantly increasing and decreasing as he swayed to and fro. The gap grew larger as the group leaned in to swallow shots. To Jonno's horror, he stepped back at the crucial time and he was jammed. Without another thought, Jonno tapped him on the shoulder to let him know he was passing through and successfully forced his way through the crevice without making eye contact and made his way back to HQ.

27 BATTLE OF MAXINE'S

Jonno marched towards the lads with a determined stride and didn't look back in case he saw the lizard hybrid trying to work out if he knew him. Just ten paces away from reaching the sanctity of the lads, a hand wrapped around his elbow and stopped him in his tracks.

'You took yer time goin' the bog, didn't ya?'

Shit!

It was The Goth. He'd forgotten about her. He didn't have time for idle chit-chat and flirting, so gently, but firmly pushed her aside.

'Sorry, babe, something's come up. I'll catch ya later, yeah?
He left her with a winded gut and an irate face before snatching his pint back off Naz.

'You okay, lad?'

'Yeah, yeah. Just thirsty.'

Jonno frantically downed his pint. Fear and panic overcame him, and the thoughts of the potential forthcoming massacre consumed him. His foot tapped uncontrollably, and his head started to shake in denial. His eyes twitched and rapidly changed direction from a fuming goth, *The Gargoyle,* and his unsuspecting mates. He computed the chances that both parties would fail to see each other and that he could continue this charade that everything was fine. It wasn't fine, though. He'd become cold-stone sober and was awful at acting drunk and happy when he really wasn't. He prayed that *The Gargoyle* and his trough of slimy ass-lickers would leave before anyone noticed them. He prayed that none of his mates would need a pee whilst the group of ophidian behemoths blocked the path. And he prayed for a sprinkling of luck.

Hey, big guy. I ask for fuck all. I've got fuck all. My life hasn't been easy, but I've just got on with it and played the cards I was dealt. I don't whinge to you and ask for treasures and pleasures, I just survive. If it's true, if you're up there in the sky, do us a favour, fella, and shine some of your magic light on me right now. If you think I'm a prick and don't deserve your divine intervention, then do it for Naz, who has had a lifetime of grabbing the shitty end of the stick. Help us out, mate?

Jonno wasn't much of a praying type of person, or a firm believer, but by asking for help, it gave him some hope that there may be another potential outcome to the one that was frying his brain.

'Come on, your round,' Naz said whilst gently shoving Jonno.

'Wha'?'

'Get the ale in, ya tit! Are you okay?'

'Yeah, sound. Alright, I'm goin'.'

Naz knew. He didn't know what, but he knew something was up with Jonno. He had *Spiderman* senses and could see into his mind. Apparently great white sharks can detect a drop of blood up to three miles away, well, that was Naz when he knew Jonno didn't have his eye on the ball.

Jonno headed to the overpopulated bar. As he cut his way through the hordes of intoxicated revellers, he kept looking back at the lads to see if they'd spotted the enemy.

'Tony! Tony! Four bottles of Miller, please, mate.'

The lads were regulars and didn't have to queue with the rest of the disadvantaged, waiting to be served. Besides, Jonno was desperate to get back to the lads to try and cover up the biggest unexploded bomb since the blitz. He bobbed his way through the crowd and handed the lads a beer each, but the mood had changed and was strikingly evident upon his return. Black clouds had formed over their heads. If Jesus was trying to help him, his rays of righteous light could not penetrate the barrier of fate that entombed them. The music ebbed away to the level of an annoying train passenger's headphones, chitter-chatter became white noise, and Jonno felt himself being sucked into an inhospitable bubble. It was as though the mighty Moses had parted the crowds of people that had previously hidden both war parties and pushed them into the corner of the room. All that was visible was *The Gargoyle's* militia staring at them through a smoke-filled room. *The Gargoyle* squinted his eyes from the midday Tombstone sun, dug his teeth into his half-chewed cigar, and then drew back his woollen, Aztec-patterned honcho to reveal a shiny Smith and Wesson, sat snug in a sun-bleached leather holster. Ennio Morricone's musical pocket watch jingle was the catalyst for shop owners to close window shutters and for folk to take cover behind whisky barrels. Conflict was imminent.

Jonno was right in Naz's face in an attempt to appeal for peace, but it was too late; his mind had gone. This had gone past the point of arbitration and Jonno now had to prepare himself for battle. Darkness consumed him and shut out all light and noise. He was drawn into a bubble of fear and anticipation as the rest of the room became a blur. His engine pumped adrenaline through his veins, reaching all extremities, until his body shook with readiness and overwhelming strength. He clenched his fists and shook them slightly as he admired the tungsten hammers that they had forged into. He was sure he could break through a brick wall, and any fear that had loomed was now tucked away in his pocket without a chance of escape. Alcohol masked any insecurities and fuelled his fighting prowess.

The enemy flew over towards them, knocking unsuspected revellers aside and smashing glasses in their wake. They stood firm on their perch: poised, ready to protect their land and honour. Punches flew and arms flailed as the two adversaries collided in an uncontrolled mess. Onlooking lads protectively pushed their girls behind them, while others pumped out their chests and watched tentatively in case the chaotic battle moved towards them.

Jonno was unsure whether it was a shove or a punch in his chest, but a form of energy sent him hurtling backwards and crashing over a table before unflatteringly landing on the sticky carpet. He sprung back to his feet and searched for a way back into the fray. He spied an opening where he could unsuspectingly land a right-hook on one of the antagonists. It was underhanded, but necessary in a battle without tactics or planning. He charged three steps forward with his hand already positioned so as to save time wildly swinging. His brain filled with all manner of devilment and destruction. As he squeezed the trigger to offload his tungsten hammer, a powerful force pulled him backwards, away from his target. One of the bouncers dug his four sausage fingers deep into his shoulder and wrapped his other hand around Jonno's belt. He picked him up and frogmarched him towards the door. Jonno quickly decided not to upset the chunky tank of muscle and offered no resistance as he was ejected from the pub.

As he was propelled through the doors, he tried to turn around to see the carnage behind him, but his forehead cracked the architrave, sending his head spinning. If he hadn't been so dizzy, he may have landed on his feet, but he met the ground with a crunch. He gingerly picked himself up and looked around, but the world had changed to a vision of rotating neon lights and a burnt tangerine streetlight mist. He held his hand out to an imaginary object to steady himself as his balance worsened and his vision became uncertain. He stumbled to a shop doorway and sat on the step to give his eyes and brain chance to catch up to each other. He could hear shouting and screaming around him, but he kept his head planted in his hands to give his brain time to stop revolving. A hand clipped the back of his head.

'C'mon, get up.'

He looked up to see Birchy offering him his hand.

'Me 'ed is spinnin', mate.'
He lightly kicked his ankle a couple of times and hoisted him upwards.

'C'mon, get up. Let's stay together.'

They both looked over in the direction of a high-pitched whistle and saw Steve with Naz, who had flagged a black cab down and were waiting for them with the car door open. As they approached the cab, they caught sight of *The Gargoyle* and his cronies mimicking them with wanker signs and flapping their arms like chickens. The visual abuse continued as the taxi drove past them.

'Stop the car!' screamed Naz. 'Stop the fuckin' car!'

'What are ya doin?' Jonno asked.

'This has got to end now. We sort this now or it'll go on for fuckin' ever,' Naz blustered.

Jonno really wasn't on board with this idea, but everyone else roared with agreement, and as usual, he was dragged along unwillingly. His mood blackened again as he tried to sober up quickly and prepare himself for combat. They walked with pace to where they were stood, just 800 metres from *Maxine's*. Jonno held back a bit, his head still spinning, so that he could assess the situation.

Naz charged right at *The Gargoyle* and Jonno was astonished to see him instantly release a thunderous right haymaker, before his lizard-like opponent had a clue about what was going on. His punch connected with the Gargoyle's jaw to a sickening crunch, and he collapsed to the ground. Jonno was so proud that Naz had that rage in him, but absolutely amazed that the disfigured lump of muscle and abhorrence had hit the ground so easily. *The Gargoyle* coiled up in a hedgehog defensive ball, trying to shield Naz's size 9 volleys.

Jonno's attention was taken away from Naz's contest when a cloud of air and energy flew past his nose. His head instinctively rocked backwards to avoid the punch one of *The Gargoyle's* soldiers had just thrown at him. In front of him stood two challengers who appeared to have been beaten with the same ugly stick as *The Gargoyle*. Bouncing up and down on the spot, they goaded Jonno with destruction in their eyes.

'C'mon then, you cunt!' one of them said, beckoning Jonno forward with his fingers.

'Fuckin' bang him, Sonny lad!' encouraged his cheerleading mate.
Sonny swung a cross right at Jonno, but he saw it coming and sidestepped its potential. Whilst Sonny was off-balance and within firing range, Jonno offloaded a straight right into the side of his neck and sent him backwards. His newly-discovered fighting skills injected a confidence overdose, and he attempted a *Chuck Norris* snap kick at Sonny's mate. He got the distance calculations all wrong and while one foot swiped at fresh air, the other one gave way, causing him to nosedive to the ground. It was at this point that Sonny and his accomplice decided to run in and kick him. An excess of alcohol, adrenaline and stupidity forced Jonno's beaten body back to his feet, when he probably should have just curled up into a ball and protected himself. Sonny and his mate seemed shocked that Jonno wanted more, and they took a nervous step backwards. As Jonno moved forward, he caught sight of the boys getting stuck into the rest of the gang. *The Gargoyle* was back on his feet and trading punches with Naz. Jonno took a deep breath, clenched his fists, and started a front leg bounce towards Sonny. He was about to start swinging uncontrolled punches when he heard *The Gargoyle* beckon his posse to retreat.

'C'mon, we're done!'

Sonny and his mate backed up slowly, then spun on their heels and legged it. Jonno couldn't believe it. He couldn't believe they had overpowered these thugs with little effort and that they'd run away with their tails between their legs. He went over to meet the rest of the boys and everyone was buzzing with their triumphant victory. Against the odds, they had pulled off another underdog victory. They were ecstatic in their conquest and the fact that it was over *The Gargoyle* made it that bit sweeter. They high-fived and hugged each other in a united, victorious circle. An impenetrable circle of friends that could not be broken by man nor beast.

28 THE BATTLE WITH THANATOS

Bonded by friendship and triumph, there was nothing that could
break down the concrete wall that protected the lads. Jonno
grabbed Naz by the waist and pulled him closer to him to
celebrate. Jonno's hand felt wet and warm, as if Naz was saturated
in sweat, which was unlikely given the time of year. He brought
his hand up to his face. It was covered in blood. Jonno looked
down at Naz's pristine white shirt and a patch of red blood to the
right-hand side of his stomach was rapidly getting bigger. Jonno
stepped back in disbelief. His brain went into shutdown mode as he
looked at his hand and his shirt repeatedly. He refused to compute
the visual images—he didn't want to believe what he was seeing.

'You've been stabbed! Fuckin' 'ell, mate, you've been stabbed!'

Jonno probably could have found a better way to inform Naz of
his injuries, but his mouth just thoughtlessly uttered what was in
his brain. Everybody stopped jumping and cheering and looked
down at the diffusion of blood through Naz's cotton shirt. He
obviously felt no pain because his face was of pure terror when he
saw the amount of blood he was losing. His complexion turned
ashen as the blood drained from his body out of the freshly-opened
gouge. There was panic in his eyes, and he started to shake with
fear at the realisation that *The Gargoyle* had shanked him. He put
his hand on his wound, exhaled deeply and then drew his hand to
his eyes to confirm the redness was really his blood. The whole
side of his body was now covered in it and his legs started to

buckle. Birchy caught him under his armpits as he collapsed to the floor.
Birchy lay him gently down onto his back and screamed to anyone who would listen.

'Get an ambulance! Get a fuckin' ambulance!'
Naz's eyes started to flicker, then close. His breathing was laboured, and his body looked limp.

'Stay with me, mate. Stay with me.' Birchy said, gently slapping Naz's face.

'Get me a fuckin' ambulance!'

Jonno slowly trudged over to Naz. The shock had filled his shoes with concrete and his legs refused to comply with his brain's instructions. He stooped down to his friend and placed the palm of his hand to the side of his face. His eyes fluttered as he fell in and out of consciousness. Jonno didn't know what to do or what to say. He felt useless in situations like this, he always thought it was best to pretend like nothing was wrong and act normal. He wanted to believe that this made the victim feel better, but in reality, it was a selfish, cowardly move. He can recall his dad hearing the news that his mum had passed away. Instead of hugging him and passing on words of condolence, he started yapping on about Liverpool's result in the football.

Jonno pressed his hand against Naz's wound, desperately trying to push the rapidly exiting blood back into his body. It flowed through his fingers and down the side of his hand.
Jonno felt no rage or hate towards *The Gargoyle*. He didn't think of revenge. His only thoughts were with his brother in life who lay upon the cold Birkenhead concrete with his life dripping out of him. He knew this was bad, but he knew they'd pull through, they always did.

Jonno looked up at the boys. Birchy had turned away, unable to look at the horror unfolding before him. Steve was screaming for an ambulance, but Jonno heard no noise coming from his mouth. He wasn't sure if his brain had dampened out all noise or whether

Steve couldn't muster the energy required to shout. Jonno felt empty. At that exact point, he felt that it would be easier for him to die than face what this screwed-up world had in store for him. This life had taken everything from him; Naz was all he had.

What benefit could be gained by snatching my friend, my brother from me?

Jonno looked down at Naz, who had started gurgling. He was pallid and lifeless. A tear fell from his eye and exploded upon his cheek. It mixed with droplets of blood and ran down his face. He momentarily opened his eyes and smiled at Jonno with blood-saturated teeth. He looked briefly content, without pain.

'You're alright, lad. You're gonna be ok.'

Jonno's words of encouragement were wasted as he once again closed his eyes and fell into a slumber. His face intermittently turned blue as the reflection of the ambulance lights bounced off his face. A male and a female paramedic approached them with a large medical bag.

'Who have we got here then?'

'It's Naz. It's my mate, Naz. Please help him,' Jonno pleaded.

'Give them some fuckin' room!' roared Birchy as he swept up the front row of a small gathering of nosey onlookers satisfying their morbid curiosity. The male medic cut open Naz's shirt with a pair of scissors to analyse the extent of the wound, while the female medic started emptying equipment out of the large medical bag. He firmly pressed a pad of white gauze against his wound to stem the flow. The pad rapidly became saturated in blood.

'Hi, Naz. Can you hear me? My name's Mike and I'm gonna fix you up, son.'
Jonno was stooped next to Mike, who chose to direct his questions at him.

'How old is Naz?'

'He's twenty-four. Is he gonna be okay?'

'Do you know what happened? How was he wounded, was it a knife?'

'I think so. *The Gargoyle* stabbed him.'

He looked at Jonno with a confused expression but decided to ignore his revelation and continue with his investigative questioning.

'Do you know if he has any other injuries? Is it just this stab wound?'
Jonno shrugged his shoulders.

'Do you know if he has any allergies?'

'I don't know, mate. I don't think so. Is he gonna be okay?'

'We're doin' our best, son.'

While Mike was desperately working to reduce the bleeding, his female colleague checked Naz's airways, breathing and circulation. She inspected his head, neck arms, legs, chest, and stomach for further injuries.

'Checking for additional bleeding, bruising and swelling,' she said, as she prodded and inspected Jonno's unresponsive friend.

'We've got a twenty-four-year-old unconscious, hypovolemic male with post-stab abdominal injuries. GCS3. ETA 12 minutes. Stand-by,' she informed her control centre on her radio.

'She looked at Mike and said, 'Scoop and go?'

He nodded in agreement. She ran back to their vehicle and returned with a board shaped like a stretcher. They gently eased Naz's inert body onto the stretcher and carried him back to the ambulance. The lads looked at each other with a haunting fear in their eyes, then followed the medics over to the emergency vehicle. They loaded Naz into the ambulance and placed straps around his chest and legs. The shiny ambulance floor was splattered with thick, dark red blood.

'Can we go with him?' Jonno asked anxiously.
She momentarily looked up from her duties.

'One can come. Just one.'
Jonno turned to Steve and Birchy. They nodded and gave him their blessing.

'We'll follow you up in a taxi, mate,' Steve announced.

As soon as they got in the ambulance, she started working on Naz, hooking him up to a saline IV and desperately trying to control the copious amounts of blood flooding from his body. She removed the red-drenched gauze her colleague had secured and threw it upon the blood-spattered floor. The random droplets and curvy swishes of deep scarlet upon the chartreuse vinyl flooring looked like a Jackson Pollock masterpiece. Swabs saturated in toffee apple red blood littered the bed and floor. Each drenched pad contained part of the only person Jonno had ever relied on. He watched the female medic as she methodically worked, blinded from distraction and fearless of pressure of failure. She was in sole control of saving an innocent person's life, but she undertook her duties as if she were tying her shoelaces. Meanwhile, Jonno's brother was battling with Thanatos, The Pale Horseman, for his soul.

'ETA, Mike?'

'3 minutes,' shouted Mike, over the haunting screeches of the ambulance's two-tone siren.

'We're losing him!'
A high pitched monotone came from the machine Naz was connected to and the energetic digital line went flat. The paramedic connected her hands and started pumping up and down on Naz's chest.

'What's goin' on?' Jonno screamed.

'He's gone into cardiac arrest. Let me do my work,' she snapped.

Jonno's whole life was sucked into this moment. His blood-drenched friend was now relying on the hand pumps of a paramedic to ensure his heart was performing. She systematically carried out her duties with the concentration of a champion chess player, and by the will of God, his heart started beating again. The green line was again active, and the continuous din became an intermittent beep.

Jonno thought, *there was a story Naz will be telling people in the pub for the rest of his life.* How he died and came back to life. How he'd had one foot in utopia but decided it wasn't his time and returned to a dystopian world of greyness. How the big guy with the grey beard had shook his hand and welcomed him to paradise, but then allowed him to return to a life of knocking back tequila in *Maxine's.*

The ambulance pulled up at the front of A&E and the doors were opened from the outside, to reveal a crash team of medical staff waiting. They transferred Naz onto their stretcher while the paramedic relayed information to them regarding his injuries. They worked on his wound as he was being pushed through the hospital doors and down the corridor. Jonno followed the stretcher as the team charged through the congested corridor. He tried to get close to Naz to hold his hand and tell him that he'd be fine, but he couldn't get around the medical staff working on him. The front of the stretcher burst open a set of double doors, and Jonno went to follow the team, but a hand grabbed his elbow and pulled him back.

'You can't go in there, mate. Authorised personnel only.'
A security guard spun Jonno around and ushered him over to a small waiting area. Jonno couldn't sit down and patiently wait. He wasn't sitting on a beach waiting for the sun to come up. He was waiting on his best friend pulling through this terrible scare. When he wakes up, Jonno was going to give him one hell of a rollocking for scaring them all. Jonno's brain wouldn't sit still. There were so many thoughts passing rapidly before his eyes, that they all became a dizzy blur. He paced the small waiting area for around twenty minutes before Steve and Birchy arrived.

'What's happening, mate?' Steve asked, breathlessly.

'I dunno, mate. Fuck all. They took him in there ages ago and I've 'eard fuck all since.'
The three of them stood in the corridor, frozen with fear, afraid to speak in case it was the wrong thing to say. They were all trapped with their own thoughts but too scared to express them. A male doctor dressed in scrubs appeared through the double doors.

'How is Naz, doctor?' asked Steve.

'Are you family?'

'His uncle is on his way up, but we are his mates. We were with him when it happened. Is he okay? Please tell us,' Jonno pleaded. The doctor looked at each of them and must have seen the desperation in their eyes. He shook his head before speaking.

'I'm sorry lads, but we lost him. The knife punctured his pancreas and he'd lost too much blood before he arrived. We did everything we could. I'm truly sorry.'
He placed a hand on Jonno's shoulder before disappearing back through the double doors where their friend lay dead. The noise from a busy A&E department compressed to silence and the busily moving figures became motionless stone statues. The world stopped. No one reacted or spoke. They all needed a snatch of time to understood what they had just been told. This didn't feel real to Jonno. It was like a dream, or a joke, or a mistake. It was anything but real. He initially felt sorry for himself.

How could Naz leave me like this?

He was angry that he could do that. They'd been together too long for him to just sod off without saying goodbye. Then Jonno's selfishness waned, and he thought about his brother lying on a slab, soaked in blood, his life stolen from him at twenty-four years old. He was alone and had died with strangers by his side. Jonno convinced himself that Naz would have known nothing of what was going on since losing consciousness outside *Maxine's*.

This wasn't how it was supposed to be. They were supposed to get old and sup pints together, talking about their escapades in the nineties and how, if only for a moment, they'd ruled the world. Jonno thought about Emily. Who would tell her, and *how*? He felt hollow inside, as if nothing else could hurt him. If he were to be set on fire right now, he wasn't sure he would feel anything.

'For fuck's sake. The poor fuckin' lad,' Steve lamented as he plummeted into a chair and rested his head on his hands.

'We're gonna kill him. I'm gonna get the shooter and we're gonna kill him,' growled Birchy, through gritted teeth.

'Shut the fuck up, Birch,' snapped Steve.

'Naz is lying in there in a pool of blood and you're talking shite about revenge. Just let the police sort it and concentrate on the fact that we've just lost our best fuckin' mate!'
Birchy looked shocked at Steve's tirade, but didn't react and sat down next to him. It was just Birchy's way of saying he cared. Jonno stood over Steve and Birchy. There sat his two friends, when only hours ago it was three. His heart felt so heavy that he didn't have the energy to utter a word, but he felt an overwhelming need to speak.

'I don't know how to get through this, but we've got to do it together.'
It was harder than he thought, and his voice started to break as he continued.

'We've got to do what's right by Naz, and his family. Think about his poor little girl who has lost her daddy. We're not goin' after *The Gargoyle*. Let the bizzies deal with him. Right, Birchy?'
He ignored Jonno.

'Birchy?'

'Alright, Jonno, but he better go down for a long time, coz I'll be waiting for him.'
Jonno wasn't convinced Birchy was sincere, but it was as good as he could hope for right now. The doctor who'd delivered the horrendous news ten minutes earlier, walked past then lads.

'Doctor! Can I go and see him, please?'

The doctor spoke as he was walking,

'One of you can go in. Check with the nurse first.'
Jonno didn't wait for the lads' approval and marched right through
the double doors. The nurses were still mopping and tidying up,
but he could see Nàz lying on the bed in the centre of the room. He
approached him slowly, still unsure that he wanted to put himself
through seeing him like this. A tiny flame in his heart still flickered
that he may still be alive. That they'd got it wrong, and he'd pulled
through. The devil blew that flame out when Jonno saw his face.
He'd lost his glow and looked like a portrait painted in shades of
cold blue and grey. He seemed to have been drained of every drop
of blood. There was no resemblance to the lively character Jonno
knew. His eyes were closed but he didn't look like he was
sleeping. He was gone. His soul had left his body and left behind a
shadow of the person Jonno loved. Jonno picked up his hand that
had flopped over the side of the bed and placed it next to his hip.
He was surprisingly warmer than Jonno had expected, which made
his heart heave, as he realised that not that long ago, he would have
been breathing.

Jonno's heart felt like it was going to burst through his ribcage
and his head felt faint as he struggled to cope with the grief. He
looked at his lifeless brother and wondered how he could ever
recover from this loss. Jonno put his forehead against Naz's still-
clammy forehead and whispered to him.

'You'll never walk alone, brother.'

Murky mists encircled Jonno's head, and the lights dimmed as the
darkness encapsulated him. The theatre lights bled only blackness
and rotting hands snatched at Jonno's feet. He looked for help, but
he was alone and could no longer scream. The hands were stronger
than his will and pulled him downwards, to the place he most
dreaded. He couldn't catch his breath and he fought to inhale gulps
of oxygen as the force dragged him down into the black river of
despair.

29 BLACK TIES

Jonno spat a mouthful of coffee onto the frosty concrete, startling a hungry robin that had been searching for bugs in his weed-ridden borders. It flew off into the icy air in search of new opportunities. His warm breath formed a cloud of crystallised fume that dissolved into the mid-winter atmosphere. A weak orange sun barely broke through the chalky grey sky as Magpies frantically cackled at each other and wrestled in the blue for air space. Jonno wanted to count them to see if it landed on a positive number but counting crows would be a waste of time. The way his life had panned out over the last year, it was a certainty that it would land on a bad number, so not worth the risk.

The fifteen days since he'd lost his brother had been his darkest, and today he was to be laid to rest. The mountains Jonno had climbed to get out of the dark waters he'd been drowning in now seemed like distant memories. He'd been pulling himself up off the canvas, knock-out after knock-out, but there are only so many punches you can take before there is no wind left in your sails. At some stage, you need to stay down and accept defeat. The hands that grapple at your torso and wrench you downwards are stronger than you, and less tired. It is only sheer will that keeps your boat afloat, and when that is gone, capsizing is inevitable. He hadn't done a great job at getting over Naz. He'd been back at work for a week, but his days were filled with a black emptiness of self-pity. He was annoyed that Naz had left him like this. He had to learn to live without him, but he couldn't really find a way how to do this. He found himself wandering around random areas in town or at work that brought back memories of when he was alive, fit and healthy. He was still a perfect version of himself and although Jonno knew that this musing wasn't going to help him, it was the only thing that brought him solace. He could still smell his Paco Rabanne aftershave in the air and clearly hear his voice calling him a *knobhead* or something as equally degrading. He was finding excuses to find reasons why he might still be alive. Like it was a dream, or a joke, or he'd made some amazing recovery and was back from the dead. He worried about the times ahead and how he'd get through things without him, like Christmas. It made him sick to the stomach that Emily wouldn't be getting a Christmas present from her dad. The shock of his death was one thing, but to continue on as normal because the world still turned seemed impossible. To Jonno, the world had stopped spinning that night in the ambulance, and the second he heard that repulsive gurgling noise he made as Naz's throat filled with blood. This emptiness was different than the depression he'd experienced before. He felt hollow inside, yet so heavy.

There's no textbook or training for grief; this was new to Jonno and he didn't have a clue how to deal with it. He'd spend his nights mumbling to a bottle of vodka but found himself too upset to cry. The tears would not come. Maybe anger was holding them back. If he could cry, he was sure it would release a load of tension and he'd suddenly feel better. People talk of time making it better, but for Jonno, that was for folk who had something to live for. Some light, or hope. He had nothing. Naz's death was the final nail in Jonno's coffin. He was the weak chick in the nest, getting shoved out by his fat siblings. *I might as well just let myself fall*, he lamented.

A silver jet cut through the ashen sky thousands of miles away and left a wispy vapour trail in its wake. Jonno guessed it was Naz jetting off to somewhere perfect and leaving a trail of memories behind him. He wished he was with him.

He swished the remaining coffee around the bottom of his

Flintstones mug, lashed it onto the frozen ground, and shut the back door. He stared deeply into the mirror and shocked himself at how old and weathered he looked. He felt he had a face beyond his years. He ran his fingers through his hair and adjusted the knot on his tie. It was important that he looked his best for Naz. Jonno would have expected the same of Naz.

Jonno hadn't planned on going to many funerals at the age of twenty-four, so he had nothing appropriate to wear. He'd borrowed a black tie from his dad and harmonised it with a pair of black pants and a white shirt. He had no black blazer, so he had to wear his coat. It was freezing anyway.

The walk to Naz's house where his body was resting was of a curt pace. It was too cold to be dragging his arse and he was in no mood for a leisurely stroll. As Jonno marched, he could hear a frantic mother screaming at her kids to get ready for school. A middle-aged, woollen hat-wearing man set off for work carting his lunch in an Asda carrier bag, slamming the front door behind him. An old guy was scraping a layer of ice off the windscreen of his twenty-year old Austin Allegro and a teenager stuffed copies of *The Birkenhead News* into letterboxes. A bus flew past Jonno with steamed-up windows, disguising school children and normal working folk going about their business.

The world was carrying on like nothing had happened.

It was just another normal Thursday morning in December. No one knew, or cared, that the only person that meant anything to Jonno had been dead for two weeks and was lying cold in his auntie's living room. Jonno seethed at the way life just ticked over without him, almost as though he'd never existed.

The front door was ajar, so Jonno walked in. The house was busy with people dressed in black, chatting away and sipping tea from Naz's dad's best china set. Sombre pan-pipe music played quietly in the background. *This is the type of thing Naz would hate,* Jonno thought; *he would probably prefer a bit of Paul van Dyk trance bursting the speakers.*

He shuffled past a few people before he spotted Steve and Birchy standing next to Naz in his casket. They were drinking whisky.

'Alright, boys, where did ya get the bevvies?'

'Off Naz's uncle. Naz wouldn't want us sippin' fuckin' tea, would he?' replied Birchy.
Jonno had seen Naz's uncle in work all last week and had already offered his condolences. He put a hand on his shoulder and gently squeezed it as he poured a large whisky into a chunky, crystal tumbler.

'Today isn't about us, lads. It's about Naz. We need to send him off right. That's what he would've wanted.'

As Jonno spoke to the lads, he felt a massive blow of guilt hit him. He was talking about Naz as though he wasn't there. He still hadn't let go of him and he was still alive to Jonno. Not in body. Not the cold, grey corpse that lay in the coffin with his hands crossed. A lifeless figure in a suit he'd never seen before, pumped with chemicals, and smelling of disinfectant. They'd even parted his hair wrong—he looked like a child from a Victorian boarding school. This wasn't his friend. It didn't resemble him at all. Maybe it would satisfy the morbid curiosity of one of his aunties who hadn't seen him for years, but not the lads. They saw him every day and they knew that wasn't him. Jonno spoke to the whisky that ebbed and flowed at the bottom of his raised glass.

'You will always be with us, mate. You will never walk alone. Until we meet again, brother.'
They clinked their glasses together and necked the whisky.

There was a small table next to where Naz lay, with photos of him. Jonno probably should have stayed away from it but he was drawn to it. He picked up a framed photo of the four of them at a party, from a couple of years earlier. They were all laughing hysterically on it, but Jonno couldn't remember why. It was just one of a million brilliant times they'd shared together. Naz had made a border around the photo with white card and written on it in felt pen,

'Brothers for Life.'
Little did he know when he was writing that, his life would be stolen from him way before his time by a vicious bully. The emotion was too much for Jonno to handle and he broke down. Two weeks of built-up tears exploded from his face and he shuddered uncontrollably. He felt like his knees were going to give way, but the boys grabbed hold of him and eased me into an armchair.

Steve cupped his hand and gently patted Jonno's cheek.

'C'mon, mate, we'll get through this. Us three need to stick together.'

'I fuckin' knew I should have done that 'orrible fucker,' claimed Birchy.

'What?' Steve asked.

'I should have killed that *Gargoyle* cunt when I had chance.'

'Well, we agreed we'd let the bizzies deal with it, Birch, didn't we?' Jonno mumbled through tears and sobbing.

'I still could have done him.'

'Well you can't now, coz he's in police custody, so let it run its course!' reasoned Steve.

Jonno thought the drive in the hearse to the church was upsetting, much worse was to come when they had to pick their friend up while he lay in peace in a wooded box. The three of them and Naz's uncle, Karim, stood by the side of the vehicle as the funeral directors slid the coffin out of the car and onto a stand. They spoke in a sincere and respectful fashion as they explained how they should lift Naz up to their shoulders. As Jonno lifted up the coffin onto his shoulder, he was shocked at how heavy it was. He inappropriately had a little pop at him under his breath, for eating too many pies. Steve and Karim, who were at the front, were much shorter than Birchy and Jonno, which made walking in a slow, military fashion extremely difficult. Jonno was relieved when they finally laid him down at the altar without dropping him.

The man who acted like the priest (but wasn't a priest because it was a civil ceremony) announced his name was Martin. *He looks like a Martin,* Jonno thought. He droned on about stories of Naz when he was a kid. The stories had obviously been fed to him by Naz's aunty because they were all squeaky clean. If the lads had been telling the stories, they'd have been about him *shagging barmaids from Grimsby* or *pissing his pants after being wiped out by tequila.* Naz would definitely have preferred those stories. Martin looked over at Jonno and nodded.

'Now, folks, Naseem's best friend, Danny, would like to say a few words.'

Jonno stood behind the lectern and looked down at the microphone, worrying about how badly his voice would sound in front of all these people. He looked up without moving his head to discover around eighty people sat and standing, waiting on his words. He coughed to clear his throat, which made it feel worse, so he had to cough again. He glanced at Steve and Birchy, who were nodding their heads to will him on. It was at that moment that Jonno felt he needed Naz more than ever. He was the one that gave him confidence. He'd be egging him on. He'd never have spoken to Becky for the first time if Naz hadn't had been by his side. He was his better half. Jonno leant down to speak into the microphone, which was unnecessary because it was way too loud when he did.

'I'm not very good with words,' he said, through the ear-piercing feedback.
He leant back and gave the microphone some distance.

'So, I've written a poem about Naz.'
He unfolded the scruffy piece of paper he had stashed in his pocket and cleared his throat one more time.

Naz would've loved to have been here
to see his friends and family, and sup a beer
to shake your hand, or kiss your cheek
he was the sunshine that could make your week

forever a smile upon his face
he did everything with class and the utmost grace
he loved his baby, his heart would burst
this hurt that remains, there is no worse
we should remember him alive, fit and well
stinking of aftershave and a head full of gel
he doesn't belong up there, he's still in his prime
stolen from us, it's not his time
he's not alone in this place we call heaven
the 96 just became the 97
you are the greatest human we've ever known
rest in peace mate, you'll never walk alone.

Jonno looked up slowly from his notes. People were weeping and hugging each other. The boys looked at him with pride and nodded with approval and recognition that he'd done a good job. Martin put a hand on Jonno's elbow and ushered him off the altar.

'Thank you, Danny. That was very special. Ladies and gents, we will now take Naseem to his final resting place, so please make your way outside. Thank you.'
As he finished talking, You'll Never Walk Alone started playing through the crematorium house speakers.

When you walk through a storm, hold your head up high.

They stood in a semi-circle around the hole that had been pre-dug to lay Naz in. He lay in a wooden box to the side of the hole. Martin went through his spiel.
'As we hold Naseem in our hearts and memories from this day
forward, we commit ourselves to carrying Naseem with us always.
We honour his memory by the following promises: to treat our
friends and family members the way that Naseem did, with a
caring heart and honest interaction; to move through life with a
quick wit, generous laugh, and brilliant smile; and the commitment
to holding our hearts open to allow others into our lives with the
intention of creating and honouring the family of God.
They gently lowered the coffin to the bottom of the grave using the straps wrapped around it. *This doesn't feel real*, thought Jonno. Martin held up a bowl of earth and then continued to talk.

'To signify this promise to Naseem, we will now each take up a handful of earth to place upon his grave. We begin with a portion of earth that comes from a very special place to Naseem- his family homestead here in Wirral where he grew up with his family. With the intention that laying this earth closest to him, his Spirit will be surrounded forevermore with all the love, happiness, and wonderment he felt there as a child.'

'I ask all who wish to, to now come forward and take this soil in your hand and bless Naseem's final resting place.'

The lads stood back and respectfully allowed Naz's family to go first. One after the other they threw a handful of soil upon his coffin and muttered some private words. People were sobbing and looking blankly into space, finding it difficult to comprehend how a young, perfectly fit man lay six feet below the ground. Jonno held the bowl of soil in his hand but couldn't find the strength to let it go. It felt like he was letting *him* go.

'C'mon, mate, let's get back the pub and have a drink to Naz,' Steve said.

'I'll follow you on, mate. I just need a bit of time on my own.'

People started to fritter away gradually, until Jonno was left alone. A gust of icy wind churned around his reddened face and made his watery eyes sting. He could smell the earth from the grave. It didn't feel like a nice place to rest. Jonno hoped he was alright down there. His chest hurt and his ravaged heart was in his mouth. He'd never felt pain like this before and the world right now seemed hopeless. He just wished Naz could talk to him one last time and tell me that it was okay. That it wasn't that bad, and he just needed to get on with his own life and stop worrying about him.

'I can't believe I'm doing this, mate. So, every time I want to talk to you, I have to talk to the grass. I don't know how I'm going to cope without you. I can't believe you've left me on my own.'

'You're not on your own, Danny.'

Jonno turned around to see Becky staring at him, with a sympathetic smile on her face.

30 HOSTIS HUMANI GENERIS

Jonno gently ran his hand over Becky's enlarged tummy and felt the little man kicking with the feistiness of a wild mustang.

'I think little Naz is ready to come out, ya know?'

'Behave, he's got another three weeks yet! And stop calling him Naz—I thought we'd agreed on Nat; Nathaniel' she said. 'Alright, Nat. But ya better feed him or whatever coz he's kickin' off about somethin'.'

'I just hope we get the right result today for Naz,' she whispered.

'We will. That arsehole is going down.'

It had been thirteen months since Naz had died, and although that monster had been held in police custody, it still felt to Jonno like justice hadn't been served. They'd waited a long time for their day in court and they all wanted to be there to witness this beast getting caged.

They arrived at Liverpool Crown Courts an hour early. It was a bold, red concrete panelled building with a coat of arms on the front façade and had been constructed in the seventies. It was said to have mimicked Liverpool castle, which had stood on the same spot. To Jonno, it now looked ugly and probably belonged back in the thirteenth century. They went through security and waited in a large reception area. There were a handful of people standing around waiting, but most folk looked busy as if they didn't have enough time in their lives. Jonno found a single seat for Becky and stood beside her while they waited for the lads.

Jonno was nervous. It felt like he was the one on trial. They all wanted *The Gargoyle* dead for what he'd done but had refrained from executing their vengeance. This was their retribution. This was how they would get their justice.

'Hiya, Danny.'
Jonno turned around to see Jodie standing there. If he'd have seen her coming, he would have avoided her but there was no warning.

'Oh, Hiya, Jodie. Didn't see you there.'

'You look well, Danny. Is this your girl?'

'Yeah, it is.' He didn't introduce them because he didn't want Becky to have anything to do with Jodie.

'What ya doin' 'ere? 'Ave ya come to support what's-his-face?'
Her expression changed from a narrow smile to a look of disgust.

'Ya wha'? Yer jokin', aren't ya? I'm here to see the rat go down.'

'So you're not together anymore then?'

'No chance. Listen, Dan, I'm so sorry for what happened to Naz. I loved him once and I know how much he adored Emily. That pig got me hooked on coke and I couldn't think straight. I was wasted all the time. I hate him. I'm so sorry, I know you loved Naz.'
Jonno wanted to be angry at her and vent his rage in her face, but he couldn't. She seemed genuine and sincere, maybe this monster just went through life destroying people he came into contact with. There was probably a lot of people waiting to see the animal hang.

'So how is little Emily?'

'Aw, she's great. She lives with my mum and I see her three times a week. I've got a suspended sentence for the coke I had in my house, so we're takin' it easy with Emily. She misses her dad.'

Jonno wanted to say something sarcastic and make her feel bad for treating Naz the way she had, especially around the baby, but he managed to hold his tongue. He saw in the corner of his eye that Steve and Birchy had arrived and were passing through security.

'Ah. here's the lads now.'

'I'll leave you to it, Danny. Take care of yourself.' She pecked him on the cheek and was then lost in the crowd.

The lads greeted Jonno and Becky, then they made their way to the public gallery in courtroom four. It was a large room with a crimson-coloured carpet and ash-style benches and cladding. It took twenty minutes for everyone to arrive and for Jonno to work out who was who.
The judge sat at the head of the room. He wasn't surprised to see that it was a red-cheeked, whisky-nosed old fella. He looked quite stern and serious, and even more condescending when he peered over his half-rimmed reading glasses. Jonno and the gang were situated on the flank with a handful of journalists. Opposite them sat the twelve members of the jury. They were a real mixed bunch of ages and races. To the right of the judge, there were a couple of ushers and an old girl taking notes. Directly in front of the judge were the prosecution and defence barristers with their aides, and at the back of the room sat *The Gargoyle* with a prison warden in close proximity.

Jonno looked at him, desperately trying to look respectable in a white shirt and floral tie, with his hair choirboy combed and parted. He looked over at them and threateningly sneered, as if he was coming for them. His face didn't show fear, worry or suffering. He didn't look upset in the slightest over the whole ordeal, or the fact that he had murdered their best friend in cold blood.

The defence barrister bleated on for over an hour how Julian had been mistreated as a child and had grown up with no father figure. He was raised on a deprived council estate and didn't have many positive things to look forward to in his life. *Weren't we all?* Jonno thought.

He'd fallen in with some undesirable people and had made some mistakes in his life. On the night in question, he had been in fear of his life and had attempted to defend himself. He did not mean to kill Mr Hasnawi, but merely scare him off. The actual striking of the knife into Mr Hasnawi's body was a complete accident, therefore, Julian Thorbinson, was not a murderer.

The jury looked and listened intently.

Surely, they weren't going to believe this bollocks? It was clear to see that this monster was capable of murder. You've been listening to how evil he is for the last three weeks. Please don't buckle now. Stand strong and send this animal to the dungeon, raged Jonno to himself.

The prosecution barrister approached the jury and rested his hand on the highly-varnished rail that boxed them in. He oozed intelligence and confidence. His index finger pushed up his delicate silver-framed glasses so that they rested just below his white, woollen wig. He exhaled slowly, then suddenly slammed the palm of his hand down onto the rail, and in a flash of genius, had all twelve members of the jury hanging on his every word.

"Members of the jury. You have been informed of the sequence of events on that fateful night that resulted in a young man losing his life. His baby daughter now has no father because of the reckless and malevolent actions of Julian Thorbinson. This was not a one-off event. You have heard how the accused had threatened the victim on several occasions before finally taking his life in cold blood. The accused has a string of offences and has already spent several years in prison. I put it to you that this man is a danger to the public and will almost certainly commit more crime in the future if he is not imprisoned for an exceedingly long time. It may be true that the accused did not have the most advantageous upbringing, but neither do most of the community from his area and they do not go out socialising with a nine-inch carving knife concealed upon their person. I would ask you to carefully consider the evidence and ensure that you do the right thing for the family and friends of Mr Naseem Hasnawi."

The judge ordered the jury to consider the evidence and return when they had made a decision. They went over the road to a pub called *The Crossed Keys* and had a bite to eat and a pint. They deliberated over how they thought the trial had gone and what the verdict would be.

Birchy was still banging on about administering justice if *The Gargoyle* somehow managed to get away with it. He was really annoying Jonno, chuntering on and increasing his stress level by the second.

'Shut the fuck up, Birch! Do you think that is what Naz would want? We haven't even got over losing him and then you'd be off to prison for GBH, or worse still, murder. How do you think me, and Steve would feel then? Just drop it, for fuck's sake.'

Jonno slammed his pint glass down on the table and Birchy slid his arse cheeks back six inches to distance himself from Jonno's blustery outburst. He cowered into the corner and nodded to indicate his submission.

They'd only been back in the waiting area for around thirty minutes when an usher bellowed across the hall,

"All return to courtroom number four, please. The jury have reached a decision."

This was it—judgement day. Jonno was nervous that the jury had made a decision within three hours. *Was that because it was blatantly obvious, or had they decided quickly that he was innocent?* As they gathered themselves, Jonno caught sight of Jodie. She smiled at him and lifted her crossed fingers up to her chest. Jonno hadn't really thought about how all this drama must have affected her. He guessed he thought it was partly her fault they were standing here, and he hadn't considered that this must have been awful for her too. This animal really needed to go down otherwise he'd make Jodie's life hell, and that would cause problems for Emily. Jonno couldn't let that happen. Him and Naz had never spoken of such a thing because they'd never imagined that this hell was possible, but he believed he had a sense of responsibility to make sure Emily was okay for the rest of her life. She needed to know who her dad was, and he was going to make sure that happened. He'd have her back, just like he had Naz's. If *The Gargoyle* got off with this, maybe Birchy's threat of blood-chilling retribution would be a feasible option. Jonno smiled and nodded back at Jodie as they made their way back to the public gallery of courtroom number four.

The jurors returned and sat down, followed by the barristers, and finally the judge. The court clerk stood in front of the jury and addressed the twelve people looking at her.

'Can the foreperson please stand?'
A middle-aged man stood up. He had short mousey hair and black framed glasses. He really didn't look as if he'd made an effort and was wearing jeans and a striped T-Shirt. Jonno surmised that he was probably desperate to get back to work and he hoped that they'd all made the right decision, and not rushed it.

'Have you reached a verdict upon which you are all agreed? Please answer yes or no.'

'Yes.'

'What is your verdict? Guilty or not guilty?'
The world stopped. Everything went into slow motion. Jonno looked around the room. He was moving perfectly normally but everyone else had frozen, paralysed by the deathly silence. It was almost as if Robbie Fowler was stepping up to take a last-minute penalty in the FA Cup Final. Jonno couldn't breathe the oxygen-free air that choked him. He felt weak and lightheaded with anxiousness. It was similar to the first time he spoke to Becky. The whole world got sucked into a vacuum, and he was left standing alone, shaking with fear. The one thing he truly wanted in life was to have Naz back, but that wasn't going to happen, and this was the next best thing.

'Guilty.'

They all rose simultaneously and punched the air, shouting,

'Yes!'

'Get in!' Birchy screamed.

They joyfully jumped up and down hugging each other. The last time they'd hugged like this was the night Naz had lost his life. It seemed fitting that they were doing it again in honour of his name. Jodie came over to join them and Jonno wrapped his arm around her. *The Gargoyle* slumped to his seat—he was broken. With his elbows propped on the handrail, his head fell into his hands and his greasy hair veiled his defeated eyes. The lines of anguish on his face were as abundant as contours on a mountain range map. He didn't look up at them. No smug sniggers or nonchalant smiles. He knew what was coming.

The judge cleared his throat then firmly tapped his varnished, hardwood gavel upon its wooden base. Jonno took a second or two to contemplate why judges were always old men. His face was well-worn, and his wispy grey hair perfectly complimented his woollen wig. His unkempt eyebrows looked like furry grey caterpillars jigging upon his forehead and his red, bulbous nose was the perfect fit to his sunken, baggy eyes. He spoke with confidence and authority and gave the impression that he'd been sending criminals to the dungeon since Sweeney *Todd*.

'Stand up, please.'
The Gargoyle reluctantly rose from his chair realising that every second he took delayed the judge from sealing his fate. He tried to stand proud and victorious, but it was plain to see that he was a fractured man and was but mere minutes from learning his fate. Jonno's mind drifted for a second and he almost felt sorry for him, before he regained his sanity and remembered that this monster was a cold-hearted killer.

'Julian Thorbinson, you have been convicted, on overwhelming evidence, of the barbaric murder of Naseem Hasnawi. He was just twenty-four years old. You have made it quite clear that you have no remorse for the murder. You took a large kitchen knife out on the night of the murder with the intention to harm or kill and the single stab wound that punctured Mr Hasnawi's pancreas was enough to take his life. You are a cruel, calculating, selfish and manipulative murderer, who has taken a son away from the family

of Mr Hasnawi. You, Julian Thorbinson, claim that you were under
the influence of alcohol and were acting in self-defence. You had
undoubtedly been drinking whisky from a bottle during the lead-up
to events that day but despite the expert's back-calculation of your
possible alcohol level, I reject entirely any suggestion that you
were so inebriated that you were unaware of what you were doing
and that you were disinhibited by the alcohol you had consumed.
The death and destruction for which you are responsible has
caused untold distress to the family and friends of Mr Hasnawi.
Many of those affected are in the court today. They are here in
court as a tribute to his memory and to see justice done. I have
considered very carefully all the submissions, both written and
oral, made so powerfully by your counsel, but despite those
submissions, I have no hesitation in reaching the conclusion that
there is a significant risk of serious harm to members of the public
from the commission by you of further offences. I must, however,
go on to consider my actual sentence.

In your case, Mr Thorbinson, there is no mitigation, and whilst to
state the obvious, this is not a case of mass or repeated murder, it is
nevertheless, one of those rare cases where not only is the
seriousness exceptionally high but the requirements of just
punishment and retribution make such an order the just penalty.
The sentence is one of life imprisonment. You will serve a
minimum of 33 years, less the 416 days you have spent on remand.
After that, it will be for the Parole Board to determine whether, and
if so when, you should be released. If and when you are released,
you will remain on license, liable to recall if you commit any
further offences or breach the terms of that license, for the rest of
your life.'

Shocked groans from the gallery filled the courtroom and *The
Gargoyle* slumped into his seat with a deflated sigh. There was no
cheering us celebrating from the lads, Jonno just gently shook a
victorious clenched fist in the air. There was nothing to celebrate
here. Many lives had been ruined by the decisions made yards
from *Maxine's* that night. They could have left the pub and stayed
in the taxi, rather than returning. Even then, it wasn't too late, they
could have ignored their goading and maybe Jonno could have
pulled Naz back from making a beeline for the person who would

become his murderer. Emily now had no dad, and Jodie had lost the support and income Naz would have indisputably offered for the rest of his life. Naz's dad had lost a son, and his uncle had lost a nephew and a loyal employee. For the lads, they had lost a key element that completed their shape. They were now a square with a corner missing that could never be replaced. Jonno doubted they'd ever be the same and he wondered what a night out in town would be like without Naz. He hoped that it would make the three of them stronger, but he also questioned himself— that it could break them.

Becky wrapped an arm around Jonno's waist and pulled him closer to her. He looked down at her magnificent bump and hoped that the little human inside it would help mend the deep scars that had been created by the loss of Naz. Two court security guards took *The Gargoyle* by the arms and ushered him from the stand and down the stairs. He trudged off with his head held low, like a beaten horse making its final journey to the slaughterhouse. Jonno looked up to the courtroom ceiling and muttered under his breath,

'It's over, mate. Rest in peace, brother.'

***

THE END
***

Printed in Great Britain
by Amazon

10971812R00154